# KILLING INFLUENCE

C. James Brown

ISBN: 978-1-7337498-3-1

cjamesbrown.com

© 2020 by C. James Brown

Cover design © 2020 by Sway

Cover photos © Guy Sagi and Pixattitude | Dreamstime.com

V 3

*for*

Alexander, Brownie, Sonny, Dad

*"The charm of fame is so great that we like every object to which it is attached, even death." – Blaise Pascal*

# 1

**W**henever I'm down and in need of a shot of confidence, I always seem to get a kick in the ass instead. This was running through my mind as the cold, black eyes of a mafia don assessed me. I was also debating whether the two thugs who'd advised me to climb into the back of their SUV, and brought me there, were going to blow the back of my head off.

His eyes shifted to a computer screen. "Look at that beautiful, innocent child." Giacomo 'Momo' Ragazzi, the don of mafia operations in New England, grinned adoringly at the video of his granddaughter, whom he'd previously announced is named Mona Lisa.

"Yeah, she's a sweet kid. Can't say I've ever seen her before," I said, choosing my words carefully.

"This is the first one she uploaded to the Internet," he waved a withered hand. "Six years ago, she was still wearing braces. Here's a more recent one." He pressed the mouse and sat back, trying to distance himself from the old-fashioned monitor. "It's a fuckin shame what this all turned into," he spat.

The video showed two young women, one of them the little girl in the previous clip now grown up, and out. Judging by posters in the background, they were in one's bedroom. Topics of conversation were the love life of Ariana Grande and the proper application of eye shadow. It would've been an innocent scene, except that they were both wearing string bikinis and were less than subtle about using what God hath given them to create a stir in viewership. I had no idea what to say to the don.

Momo's goons showed up outside my South Boston apartment thirty minutes prior and suggested I join them for a ride. Fortunately, it was a short trip to a warehouse a few miles away on Commercial Street in the North End, and even better, so far, they hadn't murdered me. Instead, they led me into the three-story brick warehouse, up a flight of stairs to a small office overlooking the main floor. Below us, a couple of sanitation trucks were being tuned up by mechanics in greasy coveralls. The sounds of soft rock seeping from dusty speakers suspended in the rafters did nothing to slow the beating of my heart as I wondered what this was all about. Judging by the bulge under each goon's cheap sport coat, both were carrying. I had been too, until they took it from me.

I was told to wait on the landing while the fat one, called Fat Tommy, went in to let the boss know I was ready for him. As I stood with the skinny one, whose nickname is Mikey—let's call him Skinny Mikey because I like to balance things out—a fight broke out between the greasers in the bay below. One of the men, whose body art would not be constrained by his oily jumpsuit, was being threatened by another guy gripping a lug wrench.

Skinny elbowed me in the ribs and said in all seriousness, "I'll bet you a C-note Bomber takes the wrench away and shoves it up his …" The door opened, and Fat Tommy waved us in.

The office was not exactly what one might conjure up for the leader of a multi-state criminal enterprise, but then again, given how decimated the organization's leadership had become over the past two decades, maybe it was fitting. Momo had survived the purge of federal racketeering, murder, and various other convictions that beset many of his rivals, but I'm not sure a trip to the big house wouldn't have been preferable.

The cramped space was sandwiched between a concrete floor stained with layers of God only knows what and the filthiest, most smoke-stained ceiling tiles I'd ever seen. The furniture was worn and grimy, and aside from the computer screen, all the light came from two tiles above us, each of which covered fluorescent tubes. Filtering this light was about a hundred generations of dead flies, spiders, and other insects that lined the yellowed panels. The only clean surfaces belonged to a gleaming chrome espresso machine that looked as though it had just been lifted from behind the bar at the Ritz, and a steel safe, spacious enough to hold me, if I'd been a practicing yogi. The room had no windows, and I felt sweat pooling above my temples.

"See the other girl." Momo removed a soggy cigar stub from between his wrinkled lips and used it to point at a skinny African American girl, barely past the training-bra stage. She was twerking to pop music as Mona Lisa laughed and posed next to her.

I nodded and took in the aging devil before me. Momo was well into what should have been his golden years, and my mind reeled back to an old German shepherd that my father had to put down when I was a boy. Every day for most of one summer, I woke up and my first thought was to wonder if that day would be his last. Unfortunately, Old Schultzy didn't make it to Labor Day, and I wasn't sure Momo would either.

"This girl here," he poked at the screen, "she's in the ICU at Mass General. Fentanyl overdose three nights ago. She's on life support, and they're going to pull the plug. A week and a half ago, another friend and fellow influencer was killed by her father in a murder-suicide. Both girls and my Mona Lisa work for the same company. They manage people like her and put them in pictures and videos." I must have looked confused. Momo barked, "What?"

"This isn't a high-production video; it's just a couple of kids in a bedroom."

"This is just one of the things they do. They're promoting makeup. They get paid for, uh ..." He looked over my shoulder. "Hey, what do they call those things Mona Lisa likes to get?"

"Clicks," growled Fat Tommy.

"Yeah, clicks," said Momo. "You'd be surprised what Mona Lisa earns with this shit. The production company connects them with advertisers, creates the ads, and puts them in music videos. It's this whole ..." He looked over my shoulder again and shouted, "What do they call it?"

Skinny Mikey beat Fat Tommy to the answer: "Social media."

"Yeah, *social media*," repeated Momo, as I watched a string of saliva stretch from his mouth to his soggy cigar. He clicked on an image, and a polished pop-music video replaced the bedroom scene. Now, his granddaughter and two girls were dancing behind a trio of heavily tattooed, squat-sized dudes singing in Spanish. They were on the lawn of a Newport mansion. The director used a drone-equipped, high-def camera to swoop down on the scene. It looked like a million bucks, and I thought to myself, damn, if I don't need to get a drone for surveillance work. I realized Momo was staring, waiting for me to say something.

"I'm following everything you've said, but what is it you need from me?"

The Godfather inhaled deeply through a beak that'd make Streisand feel inadequate, over which ran a thick network of aging capillaries, and let it out. "I don't believe in coincidence. Two girls out of a group of five in less than two weeks. No fuckin way!" His face flashed hot as though the timing of these events was a personal insult to him.

"I need someone with brains looking into this. My guys, their talents lie in other areas." He looked over my shoulder at the two henchmen sitting at opposite ends of a scuffed oak desk. Having them back there as I spoke with the don conjured images of ice picks, which was the point.

The godfather pointed a gnarled index finger and said, "So, you are going investigate, and if something is going on, you'll tell me, and my boys will take care of it. Easy peazy for a guy like you." He pressed the fingertips of his right hand together and waved it at me. "Capiche?"

He smiled, and I noticed the fillings in his bottom molars were made of gold. Probably come in handy in prison. I analyzed my options. I live in South Boston. At a minimum, Momo controlled my trash collection, but the old killer probably had his hands in a half-dozen other services too, all of which he could use to make my life hell. That is if I didn't get the message that his goons lurking behind me would deliver to my body if I refused. And, what was he asking for anyway? I just had to look into a couple unsuspicious deaths, determine nothing was amiss, and give him the good news.

I put as much frost on it as I could muster and answered, "Capiche."

"That's good," he said. "It's a good thing you're doing, helping an old man ensure the safety of his little baby granddaughter." It hurt to restrain my eyes from rolling.

"Have you talked to anyone else about your concerns?"

"What, go to the cops?" He smirked and motioned to the apes behind me, and they joined Momo in laughing for a good while before he went on. "Yeah, I don't have that kind of a relationship with the authorities. Look, I read about that thing down in Connecticut. Earl Town, a private eye from South Boston, takes on the snobs of Wall Street and kicks their asses. You're a smart guy, Town. You'll help me." He smiled as though we had become fast friends, and I felt my dinner setting rope lines and beginning the ascent back up into my throat.

Back in the fall, I solved a murder in Greenwich that made quite a splash in local and even national news. The press coverage was a Godsend to my business, allowing me to take fewer crappy insurance-fraud and cheating-spouse cases, which until then, I'd been living on. Now, the free media exposure had taken a turn for the macabre.

He snapped his fingers, and Skinny Mikey flicked on the espresso machine. The sound of grinding coffee beans filled the air, and I tried to use their scent to block out the smell of halitosis and immorality that saturated the cramped space.

"You said she's your granddaughter?"

"My daughter Ginerva's youngest kid. Last name is Angeloni." The goon handed him a small platter on which was perched a tiny cup of espresso. I wasn't offered one. "My only daughter, she marries a guy not in the family business. Eh, at least he was Italian, and a Sicilian no less. He's a commercial attorney in Waltham. They got divorced when Mona Lisa was still in diapers."

"And the production company?"

"Thomas will give you the details, and for Ginerva too. I told her to expect you." He let out a plume, set his sopping stub into a chipped ceramic ashtray, and threw daggers. "I don't need to tell you that this business stays between us."

"How about Mona Lisa's details? I'd like to speak to her soon."

"You'd better let her mother make an introduction. It'll go smoother that way."

"Okay, I'll start with Ginerva in the morning."

"*Ginny*. You call her Ginerva to her face, you better cover your balls with both hands."

"That's good to know," I told him, adding my rate, which is a grand a day with a three-day minimum, paid upfront, though I reimburse for unused time if three days aren't needed. I work fast, and I never drag my feet. Some people might be tempted to offer to work for free for a wise guy like Momo. They do so either out of fear or because they don't want his dirty money, but that kind of thinking can get a guy killed. All a working-class guy like me has going for him when dealing with a creature like Momo is respect. Without that, I'm nothing to him. I'm disposable.

He reached into his pocket, removed a roll of cash, and tossed it into my lap.

"There's five grand there. You do a good job, there'll be a bonus." He paused and inhaled through a pair of bushy nostrils. "You're really gonna want to earn that bonus. Cause if something happens to her because you didn't do your job ..." He then bared his yellow teeth. "Thomas and Mikey will take you home."

❊ ❊ ❊

Fat Tommy was truth in advertising. A good fifty pounds overweight and several inches short of six feet, Thomas Palermo, his grandparents were from the island, was a bear of a man. Mikey Colaposa was over six feet, but not as tall as me—I'm 6'3". At least I used to be before my aging feet began to flatten.

Fat Tommy held the door of their black Cadillac Escalade, and I climbed in the back. Skinny got behind the wheel, while Tommy rode shotgun. Tommy was the older of the two, and Mikey deferred to him. They had been quiet on the way over, but we were like old chums on the ride home.

Tommy said, "Gee, detective, I don't envy you. How are you gonna investigate a coupla deaths that the cops have determined are cut and dry? I mean, facts are facts, right?"

"I'm gonna look at the facts again, and when nothing seems amiss, I'm gonna tell your boss that everything's fine. And, then, I'm gonna sail off into the sunset."

"That's what I wanna hear," said Tommy. "The old man's not in good health. The sooner you come back with good news, the better. Right, Mikey?"

Mikey turned and grinned over his shoulder. "That's right."

"I'll keep that in mind," I said.

Fat Tommy said he liked my neighborhood as we rolled up in front of my building, though he said it wasn't nearly as nice as his place in Quincy. I pretended to care as he handed me my gun and a sheet of paper with contact information for the people Momo and I discussed. He got out and held the door while I extricated myself. Before they pulled away, I asked, "How do I get ahold of you guys?"

"You don't, but don't worry," said Fat Tommy, "*he*, or *we*, will be in touch with *you*." Apparently, this was really funny, because they both cut up.

It was nearly half past nine on a warm June evening. The goons had grabbed me as I returned from dinner with my big sister Emily and her son Edward Chase, whom I often put to work researching my cases. As we parted ways, I told Ed I didn't have any work for him, and now, just over an hour later, I planned to call him as soon as I walked through my door. Even with Ed's help, I was still looking at a late night of educating myself on the case and its constituents, and thus, I needed some supplies. I decided to grab an extra-large coffee and a six-pack at Santiago Market, a bodega two blocks from my second-floor bachelor pad and P.I. office.

Supplies in hand, I dialed Ed as soon I got settled in. Ed is an intelligent kid, savvy with computers, and always available because he is chronically under-employed and too spoiled to ever work a 9 to 5 job. Usually, he's a sarcastic SOB, too.

"I thought we were done with you an hour ago."

"I picked up a case after dinner and I need some research, stat."

"I may have some free time. What do you need?"

"Some free time? Mmm, is that what you call hanging out in sweats?" He didn't reply. "I need to know everything about a company in Norwood called Boom Productions. They manage a stable of, of … ah, shit. Hold on a moment." I looked around for my phone, where I'd made a couple of notes during my talk with Momo. "Here it is," I said, the phone to my ear again, "social media stars and music acts. I assume you know what a social media star is?"

Ed groaned.

"Okay then. Tell me about the people who run the company and the talent they manage. Now, here's the rub. One of their stars recently died in a murder-suicide."

"Harlowe Phillips?"

"Yeah, how'd you know?"

"Uh, I've seen her online."

"I'll bet you have. Another one, named Kenzie Knight, overdosed and is on life support."

"Yeah, I've seen her too."

"Good, so collect everything you can about her and Boom's other acts, especially a girl named Mona Lisa."

"What about Mona Lisa?"

"Oh, are you familiar with her?"

"Maybe, she's really lit."

"Uh-huh, well, don't just stare at her photos. Get me what you can on her background. And, do this in a couple of hours. I can't afford to pay you a ton." Actually, with Momo's roll, I could've afforded more, but Ed worked better under pressure.

"Okay."

"Okay? You're not going to ask me for more money?"

"Nope, I'm done doing that, Earl. Just know that one of these days I won't be here to help you, because I will be doing something that pays much better, and I'll have zero loyalty to you, the guy who took advantage of me for years."

I pretended to be hurt for a second. Then I said, "That's good stuff, Ed. Does my sister fall for that? God, I hope not. I'll come by tomorrow to compare notes."

"What time?"

"Why? You got a job to go to?" Silence. "Nighty-night, nephew."

# 2

Spring was in its final days. I admired the shot of fresh green leaves, as I popped a pill for the pollen chaser. Up at seven, out into the morning rush by eight, I crawled until I hit the highway, then slowed to a squirm. After an extended period of trying not to lose my temper at the stop and go, I reached the exit and a sense of glee as I caught sight of my destination—the home of the soon-to-be-deceased social media star Kenzie Knight.

The middle-class neighborhood sat only a stone's throw from a four-lane mini-freeway known as the Concord Turnpike. I could still hear the traffic as I exited my car, which I'd parked around the corner.

It was a modest split-level, with a large, open family room added to the west end and set back about 30 feet from the street and buffeted from the road by a fortuitous row of tightly packed fir trees. I scaled the front walkway, and its three concrete steps, and then rang the bell. I rang it again in two 30-second intervals. Oops, looks like no one's home.

I strolled around the nearest end and found a small yard backed by a tall concrete retaining wall. All the concealment made the place a thief's dream, so I decided I'd better look for an alarm system, because, if I lived here, I'd sure as hell have one. I stepped up on a small deck and knocked on the back slider, just in case. Still no signs of life. I peered inside, looking for a keypad.

Nothing. I moved to a window that overlooked the deck and examined each edge. I saw it. A simple Internet-connected sensor designed to alert someone, somewhere who'd call the local cops. This window was locked tight, but there was an open one on the second floor. I could tell by its smaller size that it was the upstairs bath.

I picked the lock on a side door and let myself into the garage. I'd gotten the picks and a few lessons on how to use them from an ex-con years before. As an ex-cop, I believe in the law, and I try not to break it, but as a private eye, I have to cross that line to get things done. As long as I'm doing it for a good cause, like the well-being of a young woman, I have no problem sleeping. I found a twelve-foot step ladder hanging on the wall, and, in no time, I scaled the rungs and swung my girth through the second-floor window into the house. I cracked the bathroom door and peered into the hallway. Judging by the color-scheme and wall art, my primary objective was through the last door on the left. It was the bedroom of Kenzie Knight.

The room was awash in soft tones. White trim, bed frame and side table, gray walls, teal and violet accents in the lamps, throws, and artwork, including the rainbow unicorn print hanging above the mid-century Scandinavian teak desk. It was neat and tidy and seemed more like a movie set than a real teenager's bedroom.

Kenzie had overdosed after leaving an event at Boom Productions' studios. She had taken a hit off a vape pen, passed out, and drove her car off the road. The accident was minor, and she barely got a scratch, thanks to her seatbelt. The overdose was massive. The cartridge in her pen was laced with high-grade fentanyl, but no one seemed to know where or when she got it.

I like to start with the areas where people spend most of their time. I lifted the mattress and looked between it and the box spring. I lifted the duvet and peeked under the bed. Spotless. I imagined what someone poking around under my bed would find and made a mental note to vacuum.

My phone buzzed, and I plucked it from a pocket. "Hey, Sheri.

What's up?"

I examined the sheets and pillows and looked behind the headboard. I once found a valuable clue taped to the headboard of a coffee shop barista who was terrorizing my married client with leaflets for progressive causes and indecent proposals.

"No, I'm on an investigation. Why are you at my place?" Next up was the side table. It sparkled, no dust, no rings. Single drawer, note pad, pen, compact, hand cream, headphones, a nail file, eye drops, contact lens case, lip balm and thick wool socks. No sign of a phone, tablet, or computer anywhere, which could unlock many secrets.

"Today? No, I did not say yes to that." The closet was over-flowing with colorful dresses and jackets with famous names on the labels. Several containers were piled on a high shelf. Inside, I found designer handbags, which proved to be empty.

On to the dresser. Arranged around the mirror frame were about a dozen photos of Kenzie, her friends, and her family. I said, "Hold that thought," and switched from phone to camera. I snapped away. One photo especially intrigued me. Two girls with their arms around a smiling boy. He had a baby's face and a man's grin under a shock of pink and blonde hair. He was looking at Kenzie, who smiled back at him, while Mona Lisa's eyes bore a hole through her. I heard Sheri shouting and put the phone back to my ear.

"Sorry, hon. What? I am not." The vanity in the attached bathroom yielded birth control pills, makeup, and an army's worth of hair accessories and costume jewelry, but still no elec-tronics.

"No. Look, why can't we just enjoy one another's company?" I moved downstairs and checked to see if it was quiet out front. It was.

"Okay, if that's how you feel. I'd like to keep ..." Click. I pocketed my phone as I left via the backdoor off the kitchen. On the counter by the door, I noticed a recent photo of the three Knights all smiling, a lush green lawn stretched out behind them. The perfect family.

My phone buzzed as I was pulling away from the house. I thought it was Sheri calling back to tell me I was still in love with my ex-wife again, which I've heard from just about everyone I've dated since the divorce—not that there's anything to it. It was an old friend instead.

"Hiney, thanks for getting back to me," I said to Ron Hines, my good friend and former sergeant when I was a small-town New Hampshire police chief before reluctantly entering the mostly boring world of private detection. He was now the chief of police in a toney Cape Cod community.

"Sure thing, Chief. What do you need?"

"That guy with half a pinky at your last New Year's party. He was a Quincy cop, no?"

"No, that's Bergie. He works for Falmouth. You want Quincy, you gotta talk to Pam. She's with Quincy P.D."

"Pam? The one who made the bean dip?"

"Yes, the one who had her tongue in your ear after the ball drop."

"I thought that was Samson," Hiney's aging basset hound.

"You never called her."

"Must have slipped my mind."

"What do you need in Quincy?"

"I'm looking into a recent murder-suicide. I'm on my way to the scene now, actually. Any chance you could ring her up, see if she'll give me the time of day?"

"I'll try, but don't expect a miracle."

"I gave up on those when I was in middle school."

"Late-bloomer, eh?"

*  *  *

The Quincy Quarries Reservation sits off I-93 just south of Boston proper. Once a life-extinguishing water hazard, it was filled in with the refuse of Boston's bloated Big Dig Tunnel Project. So, instead of a deadly swimming hole, it's now a set of granite outcroppings used by amateur climbers and graffiti artists. It was the place Ray Phillips drove his only child and murdered her with a single bullet from a 38-caliber Smith and Wesson handgun to the left temple. And only weeks before her eighteenth birthday. According to the news reports I'd fallen asleep to, Ray shot Harlowe Phillips while she sat in the passenger seat of his 2015 VW Passat sedan, which was parked on the street below. He then walked up the hill to the base of the nearest outcropping, sat down on a massive stone slab with the words "Fatal Mistake" sprayed across it in balloon-like gold letters, pressed the gun barrel against his right temple and blasted his brains into the ether.

I walked up a steep incline from the street to the outcropping. It took about two minutes, and I thought about the things that might have been running through Ray Phillips' mind as he made the same walk. Was he enraged at his ex-wife? Was he ashamed and disgusted with himself for what he had done? Or was he content in the knowledge that his actions would create massive pain and suffering for his ex-wife? Why did he decide to end it all not only for himself but his little girl too?

Of course, another possibility is that he was marched up there at the point of a gun and executed. As I was studying the scene for any signs of struggle, and coming up empty, I heard a distinctive female voice. One I had put out of my mind on January 1.

"Hey, idiot."

"Pam?"

"Good guess, Town."

"It can't have been more than fifteen minutes since I talked to Hiney."

"He called. I was in the neighborhood. Figured I'd come and get a look at you, see if you still think you're hot shit."

For a hard-ass city cop, Pamela Prentiss was maybe all of 5'5" and a hundred and twenty pounds. She made up for her small stature by crowding everyone's personnel space. I found it sexy after midnight and while full of cheap bubbly and scotch. Sober, and in the light of day, my tastes ran different.

She peered up from under a mean set of charcoal bangs and sneered, before poking me in the belly button. "You look good, Town. You gonna say something?"

"I didn't know you'd made plainclothes. Good for you, Pam. Congratulations." Her body was linear, and though I prefer curves, the athletic type works for me too. I believe in diversity and inclusivity.

"Gee, thanks, Town. You want to tell me why you're snooping around my case?" She poked me again.

"Ow, cut that out. Your case? As in you're lead on it?"

"Yeah, that's right. I'm the lead detective. Now, what do you want? You wanna make out again, Town? Is that why you're here? Cause I'm not feeling it right now."

I laughed, but she didn't join me. I sputtered, "I just wanted to see it for myself. You know, have a look at the place where Ray Phillips did himself in. I assume he did the daughter down there?" I pointed to the small patch of dirt and weeds where I'd parked the Caprice.

"Is that what it said in the news reports? You don't know shit, do you, Town?"

"I just took the case last night. Give me a couple of hours, and I'll have some questions for you. Right now, I'm just taking inventory, but I'd appreciate your help."

"Just because I let you feel me up on your friend's couch, doesn't mean I'm gonna answer all your questions. You haven't even offered me anything in return. I don't know if I should be happy that you're not treating me like a whore and offering me compensation, or angry that you think I'm so easy. No, that's not true. I do know, and I'm getting angry."

"Pam, come on. No one's suggesting either of those things. I've been hired to look into what happened in the Phillips' situation. That's all."

"By who?"

"I'm not at liberty to say."

She glared and folded her arms, weight resting on her back

foot, and stayed like this for a good while as I squirmed. Finally, she said, "Angry divorced dad says to his kid: *Hey, kid, let's go for a ride.* Drives to the base of the hill, parks, takes out a gun, and murders the kid to spite his ex-wife. He's a coward, like a lot of you men, and decides to off himself while taking in the view of the city. So, he scales the summit and sits his murderous ass down on that slab of granite. He enjoys the city lights for a bit, then fires a chunk of lead into his frontal lobe. What more do you need to know?"

"Are you sure it was a murder-suicide?"

Pam smirked, ignored my question, and asked, "You involved?"

"No, very recently dumped, actually."

She bit her bottom lip. "You want me to spill my guts, you're gonna have to buy me that dinner you owe me. Tomorrow, one o'clock, Les Zyg by South Station. Know it?"

"Yeah, who doesn't?"

"Good, bring your credit card and wear one of those nice jackets of yours. Not this one." She reached up and pinched the lapel. "You having money problems, Town? You're looking a little ragged."

"Ragged?" I smoothed my lapel. "No, my finances are great, thanks."

She began the walk down to the street. I called after her, "I'm sorry, I don't remember promising you a meal."

"You didn't. It's punishment for being a shit-heel." Pam was acting as judge and jury, and I hoped the third piece of that old trope would not also come to be.

# 3

I had an hour to kill until I was to meet Momo's daughter, so I decided to pay a visit to the Phillips' home in the Boston suburb of Concord. My hope was to have a look around, and if no one was home, let myself in as I had at the Knight's. In that instance, I was quite sure the Knight's would be at the hospital dealing with the final moments of their little girl's life. But, for all I knew, the widow Phillips was doing her mourning at home. I mentally prepared to ask her a few questions if she answered my knock.

I pulled up on the street in front of the red clapboard number with a sign in an old-timey font that read "1749." Before I was even out of the Caprice, a rotund, follicly challenged guy in shorts and knee-high socks waddled over from the farmer's porch across the street. "Can I help you?"

"You must be Sharon Phillips."

"Why, no, I'm Mrs. Phillips' neighbor, Ted. She's not at home, and you are?"

"I pull up in front of Sharon's house, and you run over here to greet me. Surely, you must be Sharon Phillips. Why else would you be asking me pointed questions and infringing on my rights?" Nosey neighbors are just above child murderers on my list.

"Well, I … wait. No one is infringing on your rights. We look out for our neighbors around here. Is there something you need?"

"I need you to leave me alone, Ted."

"She's not home."

"Well, since she obviously clears her schedule with you, when do you expect her back?"

Ted stepped back, sensing he had bitten off more than he could chew this time. "I can't say, but if you tell me your name, I'll let her know you came by."

"That your home there?"

"Sure is."

I reached into the Caprice and removed a notebook and pen. "I'm with Ace Termite Prevention Services, Ted. Why don't we go take a look at that siding. I see several potential problems from here." I stepped around his beachball belly and crossed the street toward his old farmhouse.

"Oh, ah, I don't have a termite problem!" he shouted after me.

"But you will, Ted. Take my word for it. Here, let me just point out some key problem areas." I picked up the pace and heard him wheezing behind me. "That's pine-board siding, isn't it?"

"Ah, yeah, it's pine board. Why? Is that bad?"

"It sure ain't good, Ted. Termites love this vertical stuff. They gobble it up like Cap'n Crunch." I was moving across his lawn at a quick pace, as he was struggling to keep up.

"You don't look like an exterminator."

"I'm the brains of the operation, Ted. I identify problems and send my expertly trained crew in to take care of them."

Ted shifted into a jog and tried to cut me off, so I broke into a little jog myself and raced up onto his porch, which ran the length of the house. "Ah, geez. I see signs of Reticulitermes flavipes. That's the most common type of termite around these parts, Ted. A good brood of the old flavipes can eat a pound of lumber a day. Oh no. This isn't pressure treated, is it, Ted?" I stomped lightly on the decking. "I see you've got security cameras on the exterior here. You're obviously a wise and concerned homeowner, but while these cameras are protecting you from criminals, your house is likely being eaten out from under you."

"I doubt that."

"Oh, jeez, *this is trouble*. You see this area over here?" I moved to where the house and deck came together, then squatted down. "You see this?" I pointed to a spot where moss had darkened the siding. "This is a danger sign. They love themselves some bryophyta."

"That's just a little moss." Ted wasn't as dumb as he looked.

I stared back at him and laughed like a crazy person. "Is it? It is, really, Ted? Is that what you think?"

His face flushed. He wasn't buying the termite story, but he was beginning to think that a potentially psychotic man was only inches from his front door. I turned to it and said. "Let's have a look inside for more signs." As I placed my hand on the knob, he jumped in front of me.

"No! Ah ... not right now. I have guests."

"Well, do you want your guests to stay in a termite-infested home, Ted? These flavipes are insatiable gluttons!"

I deeked to his left, then broke right and got an arm around him. I tugged on the door again, but he stepped back and pressed his considerable girth against it. Fear gripped his face. "I don't know what you want, but please leave me alone, or I'll call the police."

I stopped and looked contemplative. "I understand, Ted. I took you by surprise. Discovering one's beloved home is a ticking timebomb is no easy thing. I'll let you think it over and come back. Are you free later this afternoon, say two o'clock?"

"No, you don't understand. I don't want you to return, ever. Now please leave my property." He slipped inside and locked both the screen and exterior doors behind him.

It was difficult suppressing my laughter until I reached the Caprice, but I made it. It's a big car with a wide turning radius, and I may have *accidentally* run over a couple of Ted's pansies as I made the turn back toward the highway.

\* \* \*

While I was wrangling with the wannabe neighborhood watch commander, my friend Irv, a lawyer and occasional client, left a voicemail about a potential case. As his office was on the way to my next appointment, I decided to return the call in-person.

I pulled into Plaza 128, a small strip mall just off the freeway in Woburn, a blue-collar town about 10 miles north of Boston. The plaza was home to five businesses: Curves Fitness Center for Women, Liquor Junction, Yarn and Things, Mr. Li's Asian Take-out, and, at the far-end, Irving Wechsler, Attorney at Law.

Upon stepping foot into the disorganized, sparsely decorated office, Irv hit me with his sparkling wit. "You can't possibly still be driving that POS ex-police car? How is that thing still on the road, and how much of the body is duct tape and filler at this point?"

I sat down across from his desk in one of two severely cracked Naugahyde chairs. "It's a piece of precision American engineering, Irv, and it contains no duct tape and no Bondo, thank you," I said while waving through the window at my beat-to-hell 2002 Chevy Caprice, which was actually a former police car. "I see you're still wearing those $200 suits."

He looked genuinely hurt as he glanced down at his disco-era sports coat. "Hey, I told you my father was in textiles, and there's little difference in quality between this and the hand-me-down Brooks Brothers jackets you wear." I had grown fond of buying quality clothes in some of the consignment shops around my neighborhood. There was something to be said for putting on an expensive jacket in the morning, which was made even better by the knowledge that I hadn't paid full price for it.

"This is Armani," I said.

"Bullshit it is. Let me see the label."

I laughed. "Okay, so I was exaggerating. It's Italian, though." I flashed him the label.

I'd known Irv about fifteen years, ever since he got a perp that I'd busted acquitted of breaking and entering and assault charges. At the time, he was acting as a court-appointed lawyer in New Hampshire. He decided to move south a few years later. I followed his lead about five years ago, on the heels of the troubles that precipitated my departure from Princetown, New Hampshire, where I grew up and was the chief of police for close to a decade.

Irv's defense was genius. He got the kid off by claiming temporary insanity due to unintentional intoxication. The thief worked at an autobody shop and had painted a couple of cars that day. Of course, he was wearing a respirator when he did it and wasn't intoxicated, but Irv got a representative from a company that installed ventilation systems for dispersing chemical contagions to run some tests and testify that the autobody shop's system wasn't up to snuff. Therefore, the amount of particulate that the perp may have breathed in that day could have been enough to affect his cognitive abilities and cause even a citizen-of-the-year candidate to commit a couple of felonies. Yup, total bullshit, but smart lawyering.

The thief had been clear-headed enough to back up a box van to an Auto Center in the middle of the night and use it to access the roof, where he then entered the store via a skylight. However, the expert testimony and Irv's protestations that this kid was a model citizen were enough to convince a jury of rubes not to convict. Needless to say, I was impressed and befriended Irv soon after.

"So, you got a case for me or what?"

He sat back and peered over his big square glasses. "Unfortunately, I do. As I mentioned in the message, I'm concerned about this girl. I've been trying for a week to give her a check for a settlement I negotiated on her behalf. She's dropped out of sight."

"You practicing civil law now, Irv?"

"Not if I can help it. She's a friend."

"You talk to her family, friends, co-workers?"

"No. I don't know her family or friends, but I went by her place several times, and no one answers the door. I went to her workplace, and the manager said she'd be there that night. I went back and no sign of her. He told me she called in sick, but I didn't believe him. Something's up."

"What kind of work does she do?"

"She's a dancer."

"The Boston Ballet?"

"Ha, ha."

"An Alvin Ailey contemporary dance kind of thing?"

"Cut the shit, Town. The Man Cave on Route 1."

"Oh, she's a stripper?"

"Yes, she removes articles of clothing as she dances."

"A friend, huh?"

"Okay, an occasional screw, too, but what's wrong with that?" Irv liked 'em young and surgically enhanced.

"You did it again," I said.

"Did what?" Irv removed his vast black frames and began to polish the lenses with a Kleenex.

"You told me you paid for Lisa's implants, but then she cheated on you and dumped you. You never got to play with them, so you've been on a mission ever since to sleep with girls that have them."

"Bullshit, I have!"

"Marcia."

He sighed and waved me off.

"Kathy."

He sighed again and shook his head.

"Bonnie."

"Hers are real!"

"I introduced you two. Remember? I knew her before the enhancement. Hell, I know what she paid for them."

He stood up. "Okay, you moron. Enough!"

I stopped laughing long enough to convince him to sit back down and tried to make it up to him by playing nice. "You care about her. That's why you took the civil case, isn't it?"

He leaned back and studied the ceiling tiles. "We had some good nights. She's a really nice kid."

"What's her name?"

"Kenyatta Bell, but she goes by Unique." He opened a drawer and removed a black and white 8x12. What showbiz types call a headshot. "Take a look, she's incredible."

"Ah, a black girl too. She pressed all your buttons." She had sharp cheekbones, long shiny hair, and a beautiful smile. She looked young. "How old?"

"Old enough. I don't know 22, 23?"

"Eighteen?" I added. He ignored me. "Address?" He slipped a sheet of paper across the desk. "Okay, I picked up a case last night, but I'll move on this too."

"Thank you."

"Thank you for the business, Irv. Look, about our deal."

"Whoa, no! You trying to raise my price?" I billed Irv at half the rate of a typical client. We referred a good deal of business to one another, and he did the same when I needed his services, which was less often, and the scale had tipped in his favor.

"Irv, you gotta admit, I've been doing far more work for you than you have for me lately. The courtesy rate is starting to cost me money."

"Yeah, did you go to years of detective school? Becoming a lawyer costs time and money."

"I was a cop for fifteen."

"Yeah, and you got paid for it. I paid *them*."

"I know that, Irv. Say, how much do you pay for those spots on WRKO anyway?" For months, the local talk-radio station had been running ads for Irv during the morning and afternoon drive shows: *Got yourself in a bind? Get some peace of mind. Call 1-800-IRVINGW.*

"What does that mean, how much? Too much for the return I've been getting. You should see what's been walking through that door. Yesterday, I had a guy in here who got nabbed jerking his junk in front of a middle school."

"Are you representing him?"

"His money's green."

"So, you're not starving for money then?"

"That's not the point. I took the case because I need the money. He disgusts me."

"Alright, the usual rate it is, Irv, but one of these days, I'm really gonna need your help, and it's gonna cost you."

"Knowing you, I'm sure that day will come soon."

# 4

Ginny Angeloni lived in a five-bedroom Tuscan-style home with stucco exteriors and a well-groomed front yard. Where I grew up in New Hampshire, the house would be worth a half-million. In Weston, it probably cost two mill. I was fretting about running late as I pulled up because the address Fat Tommy had given me was incorrect. He sent me to Sunset Street and a far less ritzy enclave. After driving around wondering where the hell number 330 was, I looked up Ginny on my phone and found she was on Sunset *Avenue*. Thanks for the assist, Tommy.

I located 330 and parked behind a landscaper's van. I ran through a mental checklist of critical areas of inquiry as my eyes followed a shirtless young man maneuvering a lawn-mower. I threw him a friendly wave while scraping my loafers along a flagstone pathway that led to the front door.

I depressed the button, bells chimed, and a bronze 40ish woman topped by a mountain of dark hair appeared in the door-way. An apparition in snug jeans wearing a trowel's worth of mascara. She filtered her gaze through fake eyelashes. Her words emerged from a collagen-boosted maw. If I didn't know she was a woman, I might've thought she was imitating one.

"You Daddy's guy?"

"Daddy's guy? Ah, yup, I guess I am."

She waved me in and pointed beyond the living room to a

kitchen in the back-left corner.

"Grab a seat. You do a lot of work for him?" she asked as I pulled up a chair at a round table in a sunny breakfast nook.

"No. I only met him yesterday."

"Coffee? I still got half a pot here. Little cold, though."

"Cold's fine."

She handed me a ceramic mug with a basset hound encircled in a heart on the side. Her fingernails were long and hot pink. Somewhere buried under all of the makeup was an attractive middle-aged woman with a nice set of choppers and big brown eyes. Her hair was wavy and jet black, like the color on the box.

Over her shoulder, I watched another landscaper working in a back-yard flower bed. The flowers divided the back lawn from a brick patio and a kidney-shaped swimming pool. Beyond this were thick woods. It was a peaceful spot, and I wondered if it had been paid for with the proceeds of violence.

"So, what do you want to know, ah?" she fished the business card I'd handed her at the doorstep out of her pocket, and glanced down at it, "Earl." She said my name as though it was foreign to her.

"Mo …, er, your father has tasked me with looking into the death of Harlowe Phillips and the overdose of Kenzie Knight. He's concerned about Mona Lisa's safety."

"Yeah, well, so am I, but not because of what happened to those other girls. Oh, and I just heard, Kenzie Knight passed this morning."

"That's terrible."

"Yeah, so young. These kids and their drugs." *Yeah, and your old man probably facilitated the importation and distribution of them.*

"So, what concerns you about your daughter?"

She gave me a DUH look, then said, "It's that damn production company she's got managing her now. Those dumb kids don't know what they're doing. She and I built her social media presence together. We were approaching a quarter-a-million followers on Instagram when they stepped in and promised her the world."

"How many followers does she have now?"

"That's not important. It took a hell of an effort to establish her, then she takes off and leaves me behind. Well, I'm doing my own thing now. I got twenty-three thousand followers on Instagram, and it's growing every day." I began to feel great sympathy for Mona Lisa.

"That's impressive," I said while wondering just what she was putting out to attract all those eyeballs. "What does she think about the people from Boom?"

She pressed her lips together and sighed through flared nostrils. "She's twenty. She doesn't know much of anything."

I sipped the stale java. It had all the warmth and charm of its maker. "What do you think about these girls dying so suddenly? Is it all just a case of bad timing? Because Momo doesn't seem like a guy who jumps to wrong conclusions."

"No, he's not, and that worries me a little, but only a little. Look ..." She reached over and touched my forearm, and I noticed the sun catching a patch of white hair on her upper lip. "The deaths aren't connected. One is an overdose, which is commonplace these days, and the other is a murder-suicide by an angry father." She removed her hand and leaned back in the white lacquer dining chair. "Sorry, but that kind of shit happens all the time with you middle-aged men. You're ticking time bombs." She grinned, smug in her assuredness. I sipped caffeine from the basset-hound mug and did my best to pretend her logic was sound.

"So, there's no need to worry about your daughter?"

"Nope. No need."

"Well, I'm sure you're right, but Momo wants me to do some digging, so that's what I'm gonna do, and I could use your help."

"Sure, shoot."

"Tell me what you can about the Phillips and Knight families."

"The Knights I don't know well. The girl was only signed by Boom last fall. She seemed like a nice kid, though a little whorish and also snotty like her parents. But Mona Lisa liked her. She likes everyone. Connecting with people is her business. Mine too."

"Whorish?"

"She liked to attract viewers by posting in skimpy outfits." I recalled the bikini video Momo played for me. Ginny's daughter was dressed the same. I chewed on that.

"Did she ever use drugs around your daughter?"

"Probably."

"That doesn't upset you?"

"It depends. These days, pot's legal, everyone seems to be on something. You should see my medicine cabinet." She chuckled. "The opioids obviously are an issue, but I don't think she did those around Mona Lisa."

"Is Mona Lisa home? It'd be great to get her thoughts while I'm here."

"Probably, but she doesn't live here anymore. She moved in with Lake Gelson. She's a Boom girl too."

"A Boom girl?"

"That's what they call the girls who are signed with Boom Productions."

"I see. Do they live nearby?"

"No, they're in the city, on Columbus Avenue. The Phillips parents are a different story. That was a volcano everyone knew was gonna blow. All you had to do was watch the videos to see how crazy he was."

"The videos?"

"Yeah. What's his name, the father?"

"Ray."

"Yeah, Ray. He flipped out after the divorce last year and blamed all his problems on Boom and social media. He started posting these videos where he would rant and rave against the Boom kids. He was a real nut."

"Did he show up at events and things too?"

"Oh yeah, they had him taken into police custody more than once, and probably had a restraining order. I'm telling you, he was crazy. I considered telling Daddy about him. That woulda put a stop to it. Now, I kinda wish I had, but que sera, and all that."

"What about the kid, Harlowe?"

"Kind of a bitch. She wasn't very nice to Mona Lisa. She was a good little catholic girl, her schtick more innocent than the others. She talked about Jesus a lot in her videos."

"Seems like a bad fit for Boom, no?"

"That's what I told them, but all they care about is followers, and she had over a million when they signed her."

Just then, the guy who was mowing the front lawn burst into the kitchen. He looked past me and announced, "Another box van just pulled up, says he's got a load of Revlon."

"Goddammit!" she snarled. "Did you tell him off?"

"I tried."

Ginny sighed. "Excuse me, detective. I got to take care of this. Earl Town, meet Ron Shields, a guy who needs to grow a pair."

I turned to Ron, who shrugged and blushed. Ginny said, "Earl is here about the little bitch. It seems Daddy is concerned for her safety. At least he cares about one of us." She got up and headed for the front door.

I raised my mug to Ron and said, "A delivery from Revlon?"

"Yeah, we get trucks full of stuff all the time. Last weekend we went up to the White Mountains and found half a pallet of hair accessories and shampoo waiting for us when we got back. There's no more room in the garage. Ginny had to have her dad's guys come by and take it to a landfill."

"Really? The garage is full of this stuff?"

"Oh yeah, come, have a look." He led me into the short hallway that connected the garage to the house. He opened the door, and I could not believe my eyes. If anything, Ron had undersold Ginny's dilemma. Boxes of makeup, hair and jewelry accessories, clothing, and other assorted products were stacked from floor to ceiling in both bays.

"She tried calling the guys at Boom, but they don't care, so she called the companies directly, but they keep sending the stuff. I told her to have her old man take care of it, but she don't want to get him involved. Thinks he'll start roughing up Mona Lisa's future sponsors, which he definitely will, but that'll stop it anyway."

"If she's under contract with these companies for social media posts or whatever, why won't they stop sending her stuff?"

"That's the thing. These aren't from her current sponsors. These are from companies that want her to promote their products." I whistled long and low. Proof of Mona Lisa's influence was stacked from floor to ceiling.

I looked Ron over. "You know, I thought you were with the landscaper when I pulled up."

"No, he's working on the flower beds. I live here. Been seeing Ginny for a couple years off and on. Pretty much just on for the last six months."

We heard shouting. Ron pressed a button, and one of the garage doors began to rise. As it did, it revealed a picture of Ginny laying into the truck driver. The proud mama was spewing four-letter epithets with tremendous venom and efficiency. She was a Rembrandt in the medium of cursing.

"You're the same guys who left half a pallet of this shit here last week. I have no more room for it. I'm telling you, you are screwing with the wrong girl. If you value your life, you'll take this away and never come back."

The back-up beepers began to drown her out, and the truck soon drove off without making the delivery. She strolled our way, a sweet smile plastered on her face as though nothing out of the ordinary had occurred. She looked at me and declared, "I've got a yoga class in twenty minutes. Maybe we can talk more at the casino tonight."

"Casino?"

"Didn't you hear? Mona Lisa is a star of the grand opening of Finale Boston Harbor. It starts at five, so it'll be on the evening news, but she goes on after sunset with the big stars. All the local dignitaries will be there too. The mayor, congressmen, senators

—you know, all the guys that Daddy owns." She cracked herself up, then made a show of noticing I wasn't going along with the joke. "Well, Mr. Serious, I'm going to go and see what those Boom jerks screw up this time. Plus, I need to document the night for all of my Instafans. They insist that I do."

Mona Lisa didn't stand a chance.

# 5

It was time to regroup with my nephew, Ed. The Chase family—Ed and my sister Emily—lived in the right half of a two-story duplex north of Boston in Somerville. Like my lawyer Irving, Emily had moved south before me. She had worked in Boston hospitals for twenty plus years.

I rapped on the door and waited a full minute for Ed to answer.

"Hey," he said through the screen door with less enthusiasm than a coma patient.

"Glad to see you too," I said while brushing past him on my way into the living room. I dropped my keys on the coffee table and moved past the small sofa and half-wall that divided the living room from the kitchen and dining table. The two rooms made up the entire bottom floor. Upstairs was a master bedroom and bath, and a former guest room that I'd helped Emily convert into a walk-in closet. Ed was the troll that lived in the basement.

My sister filled the place with slightly worn second-hand furniture, mass-market wall hangings with syrupy musings on love and family, and loads of photographs of her, Ed, and Tim. Tim was Emily's first and only husband, who passed away when Ed was just eight. He was in the trades and working on an apartment building in Dorchester when five stories of scaffolding collapsed on him and a co-worker. Emily got enough money in the settlement to pay for this place and Ed's schooling, but that's about it.

I removed my jacket and hung it on a chairback as I passed the dining table on my way to the fridge. I announced, "I'm starving," as I slid the cold-cut drawer open and poked around.

Ed sat down at the dinner table while I loaded my arms with half a loaf of rye, some turkey, American cheese, and mayo. I sat across from him and began assembly. I decided to make nice and ask about his love life before getting down to business. "So, what's up with this girl of yours?"

I got eye roll and silence. "That's right, punk, your mother filled me in before you showed last night." My Diet Coke hissed as I cracked the seal.

"We're through, I'm not looking for any help, Earl."

"I'm not offering any, not for free anyway—I'd have to dock your wages."

"Yeah, well, she ghosted me, so let's move on." He opened his laptop and entered his password.

"Ghosted you?"

"Yeah, she's not returning my texts."

"So, go see her."

He smirked, "Okay, Gramps, I'll hook up the horse and buggy and go do that."

"What? So, actual in-person contact is out of the question with you Millennials? It's no wonder the birth rate is so low. Someday, you're gonna have to leave the basement, Ed."

"I just did, to answer the door, and look at what it got me."

\* \* \*

I finished foraging, so we moved outdoors into the warmth of bright midday sun and a couple of Adirondack chairs on a petite cedar deck. Ed said, "MonaLisa17 is her handle on social media, though she's now 20. She's pretty lit, well-built, olive skin, big caramel eyes."

"Ed, I've seen her videos. I don't need a physical description. Come on."

"Sorry. Any chance you can introduce me?"

"Oh, sure. I'll introduce you as my nephew, who lives in his mom's basement in Somerville. She'll be all over you."

"You're a dick."

"That may be, Ed, but this dick is paying you for your research skills, now shower me with facts."

"She got her first taste of fame via a reality show. You know the one about the burger chain launched by that goofy action-movie star and his brothers?"

"No, I must have missed it, but go on."

"It was about five years ago and filmed around Boston. Her dad was an investor and appeared in a couple of episodes with his pretty daughter Mona Lisa. It didn't take long for her YouTube channel to take off, and she parlayed that with an Instagram account. Today, she has a half-million followers on YouTube, and 2.1 million on Instagram."

"No, shit."

"Yup. Her YouTube videos have been watched more than 140 million times, and her Instagram account averages seven million views a day."

"What kind of income can a fanbase like this generate?"

"There's nothing published on her specifically, but I found articles about how much influencers, that's what they call people like her, can make based on the number of followers they have. Someone with that many fans usually gets paid between twenty-five hundred and ten-grand every time they promote a product through social media."

"Christ!" I said. "Why do I work so hard for a living?"

"Tell me about it," he replied, as I choked a little on my soda.

"I did some quick calculations based on how many sponsored posts Mona Lisa does each week and estimated her appearance fees. She does a lot of personal appearances, too. Someone like her gets about ten thousand per appearance."

Now, I did choke a little, and Ed paused as I wheezed. "You

okay?" I wasn't, but I waved him on.

"I figure she made between four- and five-hundred thousand last year."

"Fuck me!" I cursed at the sky and the God who had forsaken me to a life of labor while the mafia don's granddaughter lived the kind of life best described by the late Robin Leach.

Ed's used to my antics and ignored me. "Her main sponsors include Viva brand clothing, Maximum mascara, and Clear-Pores facial cleanser," he said, "but she does one-off promotions all the time too. Lately, she's been promoting the opening of the new casino."

"Those are some good, yet infuriating, facts, Ed. Thank you. What'd you find on the production company?"

"Boom Productions, Inc. was founded in 2015 by a pair of Harvard grads named Joshua Fagle and Kyan Sharpe. Fagle is 32 and Sharpe 34. The firm is privately held, with several venture-capital funds involved in the financing, but Fagle and Sharpe own a majority of the stock. They launched the company out of a warehouse in Brighton before moving into new digs in Norwood last year. The move coincided with the expansion of the company from just managing influencers like Mona Lisa, to also producing video content. In a recent interview with *Boston Magazine*, Fagle said they view Boom Productions as, and I quote, 'an arms dealer in the war being fought among platforms like YouTube, Netflix, Spotify, Apple Music, and Twitter.' He says all of those companies want fresh content to differentiate their services, and Boom is there to provide it through a combination of its state-of-the-art production capabilities and a stable of online media stars."

"Social media arms dealers. Right," I said.

"That's all I got on Boom. You want the background on the talent?"

"Yes, but I don't have a lot of time. Do you have anything I can take with me?"

"I'm printing out a few pages now."

"Cool, give me the main points on the dead girls and the

other two."

"According to her family and friends, Kenzie Knight, the girl who overdosed on fentanyl, had no history or signs of drug use, and they can't understand how this happened. She was planning to go to Hollywood after high school to make it as an actress."

"What a waste. What about the vape pen? I couldn't find any comments on that in the stories I read."

Ed scrolled through notes on his tablet and stopped on something. "Her parents told Channel 5 she did smoke a vape pen but had never taken hard drugs. The fentanyl overdose was a complete shock."

"Any theories on where she got it?"

"No, the press reports hint that it's reflective of her work in entertainment but leave it at that. Most of the coverage on her is from a 'look at what happens to these social media kids' angle. It's more opinion commentary than investigative journalism."

"Isn't all news now?" I editorialized. He nodded.

"Anything about where she was coming from when she crashed?"

"Yeah." He picked up his phone, tapped the screen a few times, and handed it to me. I said, "Send me the link but give me the gist. I can't see that thing in the sunshine."

"Uh-huh. Face it, your eyesight's going. I forget how old you are sometimes. It says Kenzie Knight was driving home following a record launch event for a band called Fatal Mistake."

"Timely name."

"Mmm, the party was at a club off Boylston called Karma. They said she wasn't drinking, was in good spirits, and left by herself about 10:30."

"What did she drive?"

"Judging by the picture, a newer model VW Beetle convertible. The crash was nothing, a little fender bender. The opioids killed her."

"I'm glad you don't do that shit," I said. "You don't, right?"

"Don't insult me."

"Sorry, I know you're a smart kid. Look, this party at the

Karma Club. These girls are always taking and posting photos and videos, right?"

"Ah, yeah," said Mr. Sarcasm.

"Collect as much of this stuff from that night as you can. In fact, save whatever these girls and anyone associated with Boom posted on their social media accounts that day and the next day."

"That's gonna take a couple of hours. I mean, it's one thing to scroll through the images, but another to save them. What are you looking for?"

"Moods, dispositions, menacing stares, the use of vape pens. In fact, see if you can get an image of the vape pen she used."

"Why?"

"If we can determine that the vape was fine earlier in that day, we can narrow the window of when and who might've switched in the killer cartridge."

"Come on, though. It was probably her. Her friend dies, she freaks out, kills herself."

"Doesn't fit, Ed."

"Why not?"

"Who kills themselves while driving down the street?"

He sighed. I said, "Keep 'em coming, though. I'm open to all ideas, but I just think that one's unlikely. Hey, how about the Phillips girl?"

"Let's see," he eyed his screen. "Her parents split up last year after the social media presence of their star daughter drove a wedge between them, the father pulled the girl out of school and ..."

"I got all that. How big a following did she have?"

He picked up a nearby iPad and began to read from it: "*Harlowe Phillips was only seventeen and a high school junior but had amassed more than a million followers on YouTube, where she made videos reviewing clothes, makeup, fashion accessories, and even movies and tv shows. She was a catholic and did not hide her religious beliefs. She possessed a biting wit and a pretty face.* I can attest to the latter, though I couldn't actually sit through any of the videos long enough to gauge the former. Can someone who says 'like' every five words really having a biting wit?" I shrugged.

"Oh, here's something." Ed tapped his screen and turned it to face me. He covered the top with a hand to block the sun.

A video played. A lean, balding middle-aged Ray Phillips in a polo shirt and jeans stood outside a three-story office building. He held the camera selfie-style.

"Ah, I heard about these," I said.

Ray's tone was angry. He looked into the camera and said, "What's the point of social media? You people were already slaves to your phones and your tablets and PCs, and now you're their slave too!" As he pointed over his shoulder at a Boom Productions sign, he continued his rant. "These horrible people are ruling you. They tell you what to buy, what to wear, and how to think. They convince you that you have no value without the products they're pushing. Wake up, people! It's all a big con, and you're the suckers. They're laughing at you, and me, and my daughter. They own every damn one of us!"

Ray began to shout louder over the rising screech of sirens. "They're using our kids to sell lies, and we can't get enough of it! We're in a race with our friends, neighbors, and people we've never even met!" Car doors slammed in the distance, and voices loomed. "It's a race to have the latest fashion or coolest selfie, and for what? For what!"

Shadows converged behind Ray. The camera jerked about as he fought with first responders. He fired off a "take your hands off me" at his assailants and twisted around. The camera fell to the ground and settled onto a blue sky, as a man's voice said, "Sir, you are leaving," followed by Ray shouting, "You'll have to me put me in chains!"

The clip ended, and Ed said, "That was recorded two days before the murder-suicide."

"Holy cow, good work."

"Thanks," he said. "Now, on to the others. Madison Pontiforno, 19, blonde hair, azure eyes, from Hyde Park. She graduated high school last year and is pursuing acting and modeling careers. She has 800,000 Instagram followers and small roles in a couple movies, including the one on the marathon bombing. Here's the weird thing, though, she started out as a gamer."

"A what?"

"Sorry, T. Rex, I forgot to speak dinosaur. She played video games on Twitch ..."

"On what?"

"Do you know what a video game is?"

"Of course, I've played video games. I'm not that old, Ed. I like the ones where I get to shoot people."

"Twitch is a platform for video gamers, and people who like to watch them play."

"People watch other people play video games?"

"You watch grown men play football."

"In addition to being about the acquisition of territory via force, which makes it great, football requires strength and skills that extend beyond the wrist."

"Again, I must remind you that you were born in the middle of the last century, Earl."

"Right. When people associated athletics with perspiration. Thanks for the reminder."

He groaned. "As I was saying, Madison still has a massive following on Twitch and recently signed a deal with Rankhouse Games to promote their new titles."

"Rankhouse, got it. And the last girl?"

"Lake Gelson. The oldest of the bunch. She's 22, and from Ithaca. She moved here to attend Boston University. She has long dark hair, great bone structure, and a set of breasts that could've kept the Nazi infantry alive through the Russian winter. What I'm saying is her breasts could've changed the outcome of world conflict. And, before you tell me to calm down, if she didn't want me to talk about them, she wouldn't make them the focus of every Instagram post. To date, the pair has attracted over 600,000 Instagram followers, and another quarter-million YouTube subscribers, where she does try-on videos."

"Try-on videos?"

He shook his head in disgust. "She tries on clothes that designers send her, including swimwear and lingerie." He smiled.

"*You* should be paying *me* for this research."

"Yeah, well, I may have had a head start on this one."

"Mental images! Please, say no more! Either of these girls make any news recently, or have family members in organized crime like Mona Lisa?"

"No," he said. "They're boring aside from their looks, which are exceptional."

# 6

S andwiched between mattress stores, car dealerships, and chain restaurants lay The Man Cave, a single-story, all-nude dive bar constructed of cinder blocks on the edge of a dirt lot set back from Route 1, a busy four-lane roadway that had been the main coastal drag in the days before the interstate.

It was after the lunch rush, and there were only a handful of cars in the lot. Despite the lack of clientele, the mountain of a man guarding the entrance informed me it cost twenty bucks to enter. When I complained, he laughed and told me I was getting off easy. The two-drink minimum didn't start until four. Thus, I wasn't obligated to buy the watered-down, over-priced drinks.

The room was dark and bathed in red and blue neon. The product was not as fresh and inflated as it would be later when business picked up. Instead of a silicon smorgasbord, my eyes were treated to a buffet breakfast—aging fried eggs on center stage, drooping flapjacks in the side alcove. Given Irv's predilections, I doubted Unique ever worked the day shift.

A couple of guys in dungarees and work boots were getting private dances in a small alcove to my left. Beyond them was the bar. I turned left and caught the eye of the barkeep. Though dressed like a youngster, the lines above her eyes and pouches under them let slip the truth. I leaned against the brass rail and laid down a twenty-dollar bill and a photo of Unique.

"I knew you were a PI the moment you walked in." Her words

came via a gravelly two-pack-a-day drawl, which was difficult to hear above the screaming heavy metal to which the girls were grinding.

"Really? I usually get cop. Why you'd go with private eye?"

"The jacket and shoes. Too nice for a cop. Nope, you ain't one of them, though I'll you bet were."

"Jesus, you ever do any detective work?"

"Doesn't pay enough."

"My rate's a grand a day, plus expenses."

"I make that on weekends and do very well during the week. How many days did you work last month?"

"You hiring?"

She feigned a laugh. "You got a card, Sherlock?"

"Name's Earl, what's yours?" I handed over my card. She eyed it before tucking it into her infant-size t-shirt.

"Missy. You should talk to Rajeev. He runs the place." She motioned to a door in the back with STAFF ONLY splashed across it.

"Okay. I like talking to you, though. You see Unique lately?"

"We got a couple girls that look like her. One of them was here last night, but I couldn't tell you which one. After a while, they all look the same."

"These ladies don't look like her."

"Come back tonight."

"Maybe I will. Do you want to alert the boss for me, or should I just stumble in there and get my ass shot off?"

"I already did. Here comes your escort."

"You're an impressive woman."

"Eh, they all say that Earl, but thank you." She winked, took my twenty, and snuggled it up to my business card.

I followed another huge bouncer into a short hallway with a dressing room on one side and an office on the other. He pointed to the closest of two seats by an aluminum desk, behind which reclined a young man in a tracksuit. His features told me his ancestors were from Southeast Asia, though I doubt he'd spent much time there, given his American style and local accent. He held a cell phone to his ear, raised his eyebrows at me, and held up his index finger. I sat back, crossed one leg over the over, and rubbed my arthritic ankle. The bouncer loomed over me.

Rajeev said, "Look, babe, I told you I gotta go. No, I gotta take care of business, not that kind of business. I told you, you're my one and only. Alright, alright, see you tonight." He laughed. "Yeah, that's right. You do that." He put the phone down and examined the card and photo I'd laid on his desk.

"Her? What'd she do?"

"You thought I was here about someone else?"

"No, but she's a good girl. Some of the others, they have ah, bad habits. Unique is a nice girl."

"When did you last see her?"

He leaned back and studied the ceiling like he was really giving it some thought. "Musta been two days ago. Did the night shift per usual." Irv had given me the impression he was there looking for her that night.

"You got a schedule you can check just to be sure?"

"No."

"When is she coming in next?"

"She's not. I told her we're through at the end of her shift."

"You said she was a good girl."

"She is. She's also a pain in the ass. Some of the girls they do private gigs on the side. You know, bachelor parties and shit. Those pay pretty well, so they start blowing off the club to make the easy money. I got a business to run. I need them here. So, they get three strikes. Unique struck out."

I weighed my options, which were severely limited by the Coke machine standing over me. "You got an address for her? My client has a check with her name on it, and I'd like to see that she gets it."

"No."

I took out my phone and pulled up a picture of Irving and me during a night of revelry a few months prior. "You recognize this guy?"

"Nope, never seen him."

"Weird, he was in here two nights ago looking for Unique. He said you told him she wasn't here."

Rajeev smirked. "Look, I got better things to do."

"You don't recall speaking with this man two nights ago?"

He sighed. "Do I look like some punk bitch to you?"

"I'm just trying to find a young woman who may be in danger."

"And I answered your questions."

"Okay, if that's your story. It's not gonna end well for you." I felt a big paw clamp down on my shoulder.

"What does that mean?"

"I don't think you're telling me the truth, and when I prove it, I'm coming back to settle up with you. That's all."

The bouncer tightened his grip, which hurt like hell, though I did my best not to show it.

"Get out of my club, cop."

I was lifted up out of my chair, shoved through the door and down the hallway. The big man pushed me into the bar area and growled, "You got five seconds to reach the exit. Run, white boy."

I didn't run, but I didn't exactly walk either.

* * *

Kenyatta "Unique" Bell lived in a Dorchester triple-decker, in what had once been a nice neighborhood, but is now the kind of place that gets more than its share of local news media coverage. The killing of young black men and other poor souls caught in the crossfire were common here, and I wondered why a girl making good money would still live there.

Her place was an attic apartment. On the bottom floor lived someone named Rocky Quina. I knocked, and Rocky cracked the door and peered out at me through suspicious eyes.

I held up a card. "My name's Earl Town. I'm looking for Kenyatta Bell." His gaze narrowed.

"She ain't home."

"I figured. Can you tell me when you last saw her? Friends of hers are concerned for her well-being."

He opened the door a little wider and ran a gnarled hand over a silver-spackled chin. "Well, she was supposed to pay me her damned rent a week ago, and I haven't seen hide nor hair of her. Can I see that card?"

I handed it over. He said, "Wait here."

He returned a couple minutes later, holding a cellphone. "Okay, I looked you up. You're for real. What else to do you want to know?"

"I'd like to take a look around her place. You the owner?"

"I don't know about that," he stepped back from the door.

I said, "Wait, if you want your rent, let me take a look around. The faster I find her, the faster you get paid."

He told me to wait again and closed the door. He returned with a set of keys and instructed me to lead the way up to No. 3.

The air inside the studio apartment was stale and stifling. I removed my jacket. Rocky eyed my Glock, which I keep in a shoulder holster.

"Sorry about the piece, not everyone I meet is as hospitable as you."

"Shit, you don't think I'm carrying?" He turned and lifted his baggy t-shirt. The butt of a snub nose protruded from his briefs. No wonder he had me go up the stairs first.

He opened a window over the sink, then headed for a tiny sitting room in front and cracked two more. I scanned surfaces and focused on the refrigerator, on which were several slips of paper and photos held on by magnets. Unique was tastefully dressed in each of the pics. One image jumped out, Unique and a group of women all in pink t-shirts with "Proud" written across the front.

Rocky saw me eyeing it, and said, "I remember that t-shirt. It fit her well. That was at the last Gay Pride parade. She went with the girls from the clinic."

"The clinic?"

"Yeah, you know, a women's clinic. She volunteered there."

Below the photo was a brochure for just such a clinic in Jamaica Plain. "You know if she has a boyfriend or steady mate? Someone I can track down who may know where she is." He shook his head.

"Any family?" More shaking.

"You know her to take off for a while without telling you? You know, take a vacation, or go on a business trip."

"Not really. She told me when she was going to Mexico a few months back. And that was only for a long weekend."

I found nothing but a couple of bottles of water in the fridge. Rocky announced, "Girl never ate a meal at home. Couldn't boil water." He watched for the next twenty minutes as I went through the place. It was fruitless. I found no purse, no cell phone or computer, no notes to suggest where she might have gone. She'd left behind a lot of clothes, luggage, a few pieces of furniture, and about seven hundred in cash stashed behind a radiator in an Altoids canister. I read it all as an indication that she'd been prevented from returning. Otherwise, she'd would've taken her luggage and probably notified Rocky she'd be gone for a while.

"Who lives on 2?"

"Myra Holden."

"Is Myra an older woman?" I asked.

"Yeah, probably close to my age." Rocky looked about sixty.

"She work nearby?"

"Downtown. One of them big financial houses."

I wrote *Please call me about your neighbor in Apt. 3* on the back of a business card, which I slipped under the door of No. 2 on my way out.

Before I left, I said, "You should call the cops and tell them she's missing."

"Why the hell would I do that? They only come around here to take away the bodies and rinse the blood from the street."

"It wouldn't hurt to try. The girl could be in trouble."

"Then you better get to finding her."

# 7

I could see Finale Boston Harbor from my position on the upper deck of I-93. The name sounds better than Finale Everett, which is accurate. Finale Everett Mystic River is even more accurate because it isn't on the harbor either. It's an odd thing to first see a building on one side of the country then to have it pop up in your backyard. I'd been on a couple of costly trips to Las Vegas shortly after my marriage imploded, and now it seemed like a little piece of Vegas had stuck to my shoe and come home with me. It was the spitting image of the casino in the desert.

The colossal new hotel, casino, and events center are spread across 33 acres of formerly acid- and arsenic-saturated soil left-over from a chemical plant. All the bigshots from Las Vegas had to do to get permission to build on it was to pony up tens of millions to clean up a Superfund site. That, and kiss ass and grease the palms of too many politicians and hacks to count. If I had to choose which of those two jobs I had to undertake, I'd take the one with the higher risk of cancer, though Boston politicians have been known to cause that too.

The grand opening festivities were being held in a waterfront park and boardwalk that they'd built to welcome the water taxis full of suckers coming from Logan Airport and actual Boston Harbor. I suppose it also kept the revelers out of the way of the gaming tables and slots, which were already humming as the casino's investors were eager to finally reverse the flow of capital. Places that cater to vice invariably do get back to black, and usually quickly, but Finale Boston Harbor seems like a bigger gamble than most. Maybe the house won't win this hand.

The event was partially open to the public—suckers, and their money and all that—but the night was really about the VIPs who were being shown what a swell place this was. It was a high-profile boondoggle for government hacks, local celebrities, and a select group of national names that were paid well and flown in for the event to show everyone that, yes, stars really do want to hang out at a former Superfund site a stone's throw away from a Home Depot.

I took in the scene from level six of a concrete parking garage. A temporary stage had been erected by the water, where a band with a Miami Sound Machine vibe was jamming in front of a crowd of waving arms. I made my way down and watched for a bit. An MC came on, fumbled her line, giggled, then started over: "We're pleased to have with us this evening a group of acts and individuals I know you all want to see." A loud roiling chorus of squeals, shrieks, and screams arose. I leaned into the space of a guy and his wife and said, "This next band must be something else."

He swallowed a mouthful of brats, licked mustard from the flesh between thumb and index finger, and said, "It's for the Boom Girls. They're on soon."

"The cheers are for them?"

"Yeah, our 15-year-old and her cousin are in the crowd there. They're members of MonaNation."

"As in Mona Lisa Angeloni?"

"I don't know her last name. Do you, Hon?" He turned to his wife, who shrugged.

These girls were like rock stars, but as far as I could tell, their talent was product promotion. It was akin to attending a demonstration of the Pocket Fisherman by Ron Popeil, screaming in ecstasy and rushing the stage. The kids shouting and waving were convinced the key to popularity was to emulate their heroes by purchasing the products they promoted. Buy it, show it off, and collect your rightful spot in the cool clique. It was a commercial circle-jerk, and I hated everything about it.

I spotted my means of access and weaved through the teen mob to the side of the stage and Ginny Angeloni. If I hadn't seen her, I could've just followed my ears. She was engaged in the epic bitching out of a young man in a headset with CREW written across his t-shirt. I walked up alongside her lawn boy, Ron Shields, who was looking on emotionless, as though it was just another day at the office. We exchanged glances, and I asked him, "What's she so hot about?"

"This guy thinks he can stop her from going backstage."

We stood and watched as Ginny gave the business to one, then two security staff. Then she caught the attention of a young, dark woman with an air of superiority. The new girl was a boss, and she gave the two security dudes the old heave-ho via some serious side-eye and waved Ginny backstage. Daddy's girl turned to Ron, fired a look that said *told you so*, saw me, squinted then smiled, and waved us both over.

I poked Ron and pointed to the dark angel.

"Divya Singh, head of talent at Boom. She's the real brains, handles the day-to-day. The two owners have *the vision*," he rolled his eyes and directed me toward a pair of bearded hipsters standing by a backstage bar.

"Fagle and Sharpe?"

Shields nodded and said, "The carrot-top is Fagle." Sharpe had darker features and looked to be a mix of Asian and Caucasian.

They were making time with a group of VIPs, most of whom were local politicos. We had entered the party within the party, where everyone is rich and everything free—the VIPs wouldn't have it any other way. I spotted the goofy local kid turned action-movie star Ed had mentioned earlier. He'd said Mona Lisa got her first break on his tv show, and I wondered if he recognized the little girl he once knew in the young woman of today.

He was speaking with Rory Quinn, Boston's marble-mouthed mayor, and a congressman and pretend tough guy from my district named Sweeney.

I glanced at Shields. He wasn't as young as I thought when I saw him at Ginny's. He had long, shoulder length dirty blonde hair, a scruffy face, and a tattoo on the left side of his neck, but he was closer to forty than thirty and was beginning to show the signs of a life of hard living. He wore a nice tan blazer over a designer t-shirt, and I assumed Ginny bought his clothes, and he was a kept man.

While Ginny's arm candy and I took in the scene, she moved past the riff-raff at the bar and over to a group of young women wearing tight-fitting dresses and spiked heels, one of whom was Mona Lisa. Judging by the hair and builds of the others, they included Madison and Lake—the other surviving Boom Girls.

I stepped toward them, and Shields grabbed my arm. He said, "It's not a good idea to talk to her before she goes on stage. She'll destroy you if you mess with her chi. Trust me."

I weighed this and was about to go talk to her anyway when she spotted me and waved. I looked at Shields, who shrugged. Ginny had a grip on her arm and was clearly talking about me.

I made my way over, introduced myself, and held out my hand. Mona Lisa ignored it, and said, "My grandfather says I have to be nice to you."

"Most grandfathers suggest that for everyone, but it's nice being an exception, I guess."

"Come," she said as though talking to a poodle, before slinking off toward a set of trailers parked behind the stage.

Ginny looked at me and said, "Move it, I got you an audience, you gotta make it fast. She goes on in fifteen."

Soon I sat across from Mona Lisa at a small table inside a backstage trailer while Ginny leaned against the counter with arms folded, ears open. I asked, "How well did you know Harlowe and Kenzie?"

Mona Lisa rolled her eyes and threw shade at Ginny, who said, "Please, baby, for your grandfather."

The princess sighed and said, "Harlowe was my friend. Kenzie, not so much."

I started to ask my follow up when she leaned over, cracked open a window, and shouted, "Get me some $H_2O$, bitch!"

I started again, only to be interrupted by a scrawny boy who came running in with a bottle of designer brand water. He cracked it open, set it down in front of Mona Lisa, and awaited further instruction. She said, "Get lost," so he did, in a hurry.

"Who is that?" I asked.

"That's Tard, my assistant. He's awfully annoying, but who isn't?" She stared straight at me.

"Tard?"

Ginny cut in, "His name's Todd. He's pre-med at Tufts University, and he's Mona Lisa's biggest fan."

"What's wrong with him?" I asked.

"What?" asked Mona Lisa.

"Nothing. Tell me about the days leading up to the deaths of Harlowe and Kenzie? How were they? Did anything seem odd about them or others around them?"

"Harlowe's psycho father killed her, and Kenzie was a dumbass who smoked heroin. I don't understand the question."

Ginny corrected her, "Fentanyl, honey."

"Yeah, whatever," said Grampy's angel.

"Did Harlowe ever complain about her dad, or say things that suggested he was harming her?"

"No. She was all wrapped up with some guy she'd been seeing. She wasn't saying much to anyone, just keeping secrets as usual."

"Who was her boyfriend?"

"I don't know, that was one of her secrets."

Ginny said, "I heard through the grapevine that it was one of the boys in the band."

"It better not have been Trey. He's mine," said Mona Lisa.

"He's the cutest," said Ginny.

"How would you know? You're older than his grandmother."

"I am not!"

Ginny's phone buzzed, and she eyed the screen. She said, "Nine thousand!"

I turned back to Mona Lisa and looked at her until she pulled her eyes from her phone screen as well. "Did you know that Kenzie had a drug problem?"

She had dark, Mediterranean features, like a young Sophia Loren. When not staring at her phone, she studied herself in a mirror set on the tabletop. She looked up and said, "No, but we never talked. She was a bitch who was never gonna make it in this business anyway. Half her followers were fake, I'm sure of it."

"Are fake followers a concern of yours?" I asked.

"I'm sure I have a few, everyone does, but not like her. She was a phony. I could tell."

"In what way?"

Ginny said, "Bingo! Eight minutes, fifteen seconds."

Mona Lisa held her smartphone to her thick crimson lips and spoke into the receiver, "Eight fifteen, bitch. Beat that."

I turned to Ginny and stared until I got an explanation. "We keep time for fun. We see how long it takes her posts to get 10,000 likes. Her record is two minutes forty-three. That was an amazing night!"

I looked at Mona Lisa, who was staring accusatorially at Ginny. She said, "Was it really eight-fifteen, or did you shave some time off?"

"No, I would never. It was eight-fifteen."

"Good!" said Mona Lisa as she turned to the mirror. Ginny winked at me.

I asked Mona Lisa, "What did you say to get ten thousand likes in under three minutes?"

Ginny answered for her. "My baby was among the first five influencers to send her wishes to poor Ariana Grande after those terrorists blew her fans to smithereens. I'm so proud of you," she said to her little girl, who smiled at the memory.

I said, "Oh yeah, poor *Ariana*."

There was a knock on the door, and Divya Singh stuck her

head in. "Five minutes," she said with a curious glance at me before closing the door.

"I gotta get ready to go on," said Mona Lisa as she stood. She was tall, probably close to six feet in heels, and statuesque.

"Thank you for your time," I said. "If you think of anything …" I held out my card until she plucked it from my fingers.

"Sure, I'll text you."

Ginny walked me to an area on stage right where Ron Shields and a group of Boom executives and local celebrities were gathered. She said, "Sorry she wasn't much help, but there's not much to tell. I mean, Daddy is blowing things out of proportion."

"Yeah, to smithereens."

"What?"

"I'm confused about something. How is it that her friend Harlowe was murdered not two weeks ago, and one of her co-workers passed away this morning, and she seems completely unfazed?"

"Well, we were all made aware of the plans for Kenzie and have had a few days to process what happened to both girls. And, sad to say, the show must go on. This is an important night for Mona Lisa. There are a lot of movers and shakers here."

We met up with Ron, and Ginny left us for the bar. Several of the dignitaries were double-fisting cocktails. I leaned into the boyfriend and asked, "What exactly is Mona Lisa going to do when she hits the stage?"

"Aw, she'll probably wave to the crowd, say a few words, hand out free samples from the sponsors, then do a Q & A."

"What kind of questions?"

"The products she likes, her favorite apps, tips on hair and skin care. Nothing of substance, that's for damn sure."

"Does she sing or dance or anything?"

"Nope," he shook his head. "Before I met Ginny, I had no idea about this social media thing. It's crazy, right?"

"That's a nice word for it. I can think of a few others."

I watched as Divya Singh ushered the three Boom girls to

stage right, where they then engaged in a pre-show prayer/ psych circle. You would've thought it was a stadium concert the way they carried on, and it all seemed ridiculous until they hit center stage, and a roar erupted from the five hundred or so teens who were there just for them.

I caught up with Divya on her way back from the stage.

"Ms. Singh!" She stopped and looked me over.

"You the private eye?"

"Word gets around fast."

"Mmm, it does at that. Look, we don't need anyone stirring up trouble. We're devastated about what's happened, but there's nothing sinister about it."

"I'm sure you're correct," I said. "That's why you should let me ask you a few questions. The sooner I do, the sooner I can report back to my client all is well."

She sighed and looked at her watch, which was a porcelain number from Chanel. I knew this because my ex-wife had one. I didn't buy it for her. My replacement did. His bank statements come with more zeros.

"See the courtesy area?" She pointed a black fingernail at the entrance to a long white tent set up on the boardwalk. "Give me five minutes."

# 8

The courtesy tent was a little oasis of peace and quiet away from the noise and crowds of the opening festivities. They'd rolled green Astroturf over the boardwalk and divided it into an array of intimate spaces via an arrangement of rattan and wicker sofas and glass-topped tables. At the back was a table of snacks waiting for hungry VIPs under a row of sterling silver serving dishes. Next to this was an assortment of water, soda, wine, and beer on ice, and alongside this was a full bar, behind which stood a young woman with indigo-tipped locks, a round face, and a stressed smile that said *please ask me for a drink, so I've something to do.* Aside from Divya Singh and me, the place was nearly empty. The hacks had already been through, and I wondered if they'd left any shrimp. My stomach growled, and I longed to grab a plate, but this was business, so the next move belonged to the pretty young executive sitting across from me.

She sat crossed legged, her capri pants short enough to reveal a tattoo of a tiger wrapped around her left calf and ankle. Its canvas was a flawless mocha flesh, and the combination of her South-Asian ancestry and the tiger made me think of the Hindu goddess Durga, who liked to ride the big cats and who also slew the devious buffalo demon known as Mahishasura. I wondered how many men the alluring Divya Singh had treated to a similar fate.

As she smiled and seductively tilted her head, she said, "The girls will only be on stage for a short while. Fire away, detective."

"Harlowe Phillips was murdered not even two weeks ago. This morning Kenzie Knight took her last breath. Why on earth does it seem as though no one around here gives a shit?"

She exhaled, raised an eyebrow, and replied, "So, it's going to be like that, is it? Good for you. I like it head-on."

"I'm glad you do, but please answer the question."

She signaled the barkeep. "A lot of us are distraught. I spent time this afternoon with the Knights, who are devastated. Let me assure you that myself, and all of us at Boom, are deeply saddened, but ..." The barkeep appeared beside our table. Divya ordered a gin and tonic with lime. I asked the barkeep if she wouldn't mind grabbing me a plate of shrimp.

Divya said, "Look, this is a great night for Boom. It's not every day a billion-dollar casino opens in Boston and Boom talent takes part."

"I've wondered about that. This audience is too young to gamble. None of this makes any sense to me."

"The girls in this crowd are young, yes, but their parents are affluent. The average Boom superfan comes from a family with an income in the top quintile of U.S. households. Many of their parents are in the casino tonight. But that's not the main reason we're here. A majority of our social media audience is actually affluent young adults, women mainly, in their twenties and thirties. Many of whom have substantial disposable income and can afford to gamble, as well as purchase the higher-end items that we are looking to align our brand with."

"So, women like you."

She smiled, and it was a doozy. She said, "Like me," and added a wink. I caught myself looking at her hands. It was instinctual, even though I easily had more than a decade on her. No rock, no band.

"So, this is about social media promotion? The stage show is a red herring."

"The appearance is an important lure for our younger fan base, and their wealthy friends and parents. It is also being filmed to create content for social media. However, the real benefit of hiring Boom Productions is all of the promotion we're doing for the casino across social media platforms."

"Were Harlowe and Kenzie promoting the casino too?"

"All Boom talent is."

"I still can't get over the girls not seeming particularly upset, despite their colleague passing away this very morning. This is not normal behavior."

"Which girls?"

"Well, I just spoke with Mona Lisa."

"Oh, well, I know she's hurting, as we all are, but she's a professional."

"She's got an interesting family?" I'd baited the hook and cast, now I waited.

She shrugged, smiled, and said, "Yeah, well, she's a great producer."

"What do you mean by producer?"

"Revenue. She produces substantial revenue. With our management behind her, she's going to be a household name in less than two years. Mark my words, detective."

"But she has no discernible talent."

"Ah, you are wrong. You heard those cheers. They were mainly for Mona Lisa. She is a star." She raised her hands above her head and looked up at the pink dusk sky. "People don't care about her talent. They care about her opinions. She has something special—charisma, charm, appeal, allure—call it what you want, it's a star quality that draws people's attention and admiration. Her influence is palpable. When she promotes a product, it flies off shelves."

"So, why aren't you more concerned about her safety? Two of your stars died in the last week and a half."

"But, surely, you don't think the deaths are related?"

"That's what I was hired to find out, Ms. Singh. I'm just getting started, but the timing of these events is odd, and when things are odd, there's usually a reason."

"So, one of our employees committed three homicides, including Ray Phillips? That's what you're suggesting?"

"No, I'm not suggesting that. I'm just not ruling anything out. I'm also interested in why you would jump to that conclusion. Is there something, or someone, I should be aware of?"

Divya's eyes focused on someone behind me. A Boom staffer was waving to her. She stood and said, "I've got to get back to my responsibilities, detective. Please don't go putting crazy notions in the minds of our people. The deaths are tragic, and we are hurting."

I watched her glide away while I noshed. The shrimp was good, the view even better.

✻ ✻ ✻

I managed to catch the tail end of Mona Lisa's act. She wore a little black dress and tasteful jewelry and makeup. She was playing the role of brand spokeswoman and handing out advice on everything a girl needed to buy to increase her popularity. The don's grandkid owned center stage as she perched crossed-legged on a stool, red-soled stiletto bouncing as she smiled, laughed, and gave the crowd "awe shucks." The MC, a local tv magazine show host, asked Mona Lisa a battery of softball questions, each designed to elicit a product promotion, and I wondered how much the sponsors were paying her.

Mona Lisa was nothing like the girl I had just met in the trailer. She was confident, but humble, funny, but not mean. Like a seasoned vet, she looked straight into the eyes of each questioner, asked them something about themselves, smiled, laughed, answered the question with a product pitch, and even cracked a couple of self-deprecating jokes. She reminded me more of a politician than a product pitchman, and I found myself thinking about Ginny and Momo and how traits sometimes skip a generation. It takes a charismatic and ruthless figure to lead a crime family. Mona Lisa clearly possessed the first half of that equation. Did she have the other half as well? My spine tingled as I pondered the possibility.

A girl in the crowd called out a question, and Mona Lisa repeated it before answering. "What do I think of virtual influencers like Lil Miquela? Wow, that's a great question? I think they're cool. I follow Lil Miquela too. But they're not nearly as cool as real people. Those people who program Miquela will never love you like I do." I watched tween girls and their mothers swoon as she said this.

Madison Pontiforno and Lake Gelson sat on either side of Mona Lisa, like Betty and Veronica surrounding Archie Andrews, and they took questions too, but the don's grandkid was the star. Someone asked Mona Lisa about skincare, and what do you know? Not only did she have a terrific answer that centered on a rather expensive skin cream with a French name, but as she answered, Boom staff emerged with baskets full of free samples. The crowd reacted by elevating the decibel level and practically climbing over one another to get a small silver packet containing what probably amounted to a couple bucks' worth of hand cream. At first, I watched in amusement, then in growing horror as a pack of girls at the back, where the samples weren't being distributed, began to violently shove their way toward the stage.

Then I watched with a drooping jaw as a girl no more than fourteen and all of a hundred pounds pulled a larger girl to the ground by the hair, gave her three swift kicks, and stepped over her to get some free swag. I heard laughter and turned to see Boom's owners, Kyan Sharpe and Josh Fagle, and a couple of state politicians, including Congressman Sweeney, chuckling at the scene.

I nudged Ginny, who was busy complaining to her house boy about how Mona Lisa's microphone wasn't loud enough, and asked if the violence was normal.

"Normal? No, they're on better behavior tonight. If this were a store opening, it'd be *much* worse. A girl from Framingham lost an eye in a scrum at the Faneuil Hall Sephora last year."

"You're kidding?" I said. Her expression told me she wasn't.

Mona Lisa started to speak but was quickly drowned out by a series of high-pitched screams and had to wait for things to calm down. When the noise subsided, the social media princess spoke with all of the earnestness and gravitas of a modern pop star. "I know, I'm sorry we have to go now, but you know who is up next? Fatal Mistake is just itching to play for you." A fresh round of squeals and screams rose from the pubescent mosh pit.

"On behalf of myself and my ladies," Madison and Lake moved in and put an arm around Mona Lisa, "I just want to thank all of you for coming out tonight to support us. I, er we, have the best fans in the world!" Cue the shrieks. "Before we go, we would like to thank you for not asking questions about our dear departed friends tonight, as our wounds are still very fresh. In the near future, we will pay tribute to them in a fashion worthy of their great talent. Now, let's all engage in a moment of silence for our fallen sisters—Harlowe Phillips and Kenzie Knight." I watched as the three surviving Boom Girls held hands and bowed heads while most of the crowd managed to calm down and be respectful for a few seconds.

They left the stage to cheers, though for what I still did not know. I loafed for a while and watched some of Fatal Mistake's set. They were dressed like punk rockers, with safety pins, strategically torn t-shirts with lame slogans like "Pretty Girls Kill," and hair colored like a box of Crayola. They had baby faces, except for the drummer. All four possessed tattoos and attitude, but none appeared to have any discernable talent, except for the drummer. Their four-song set was badly lip-synced, and they kept forgetting to pretend to play their guitars. The crowd went wild for it anyway. Then I recognized the singer as the kid in Kenzie's photo. The one Mona Lisa was staring daggers at.

After their set, I watched as the band and a couple of fangirls went into one of the backstage trailers. I gave it three minutes and let myself in. The tiny space reeked of cannabis, and no one noticed the stranger over the laughter and early stages of foreplay.

I cleared my throat and asked, "Where's the drummer?"

They stopped jabbering and turned to me. The bass and guitar players looked at the lead singer who was trying to hold in a hit. Through a cloud and a cough, he said, "Who the hell are you?"

"I'm Earl, and I've been sent to get some answers, whatever it takes." I opened my jacket enough for them to see my weapon and said, "I think you girls better leave." I opened the door and shooed them and most of the smoke away." The ladies gave me the evil eye but moved out in a hurry.

"What do you think you're doing?" said the waif with the pink troll hairdo.

"You guys suck. You know that, right?" I said. "Who are you to appropriate the clothes of Vivian Westwood and the attitude of Johnny Rotten?" I loved using politically correct buzzwords with Millennials, as it never failed to put them on defense.

"Who?" asked the bass player.

"We're not appropriating anything!" said the singer with the pink hair.

I shook my head. "You idiots don't even know who you're stealing from. No one would accuse you of stealing their music, though. Some of those early punks could barely play their instruments, but they were still better than you fakers. Hell, Marcel Marceau is rolling over in his grave. That was the worst damn guitar-miming I've ever seen."

"What's your problem, man?" asked the eye-shadowed guitar player.

"My problem is you jerk-offs are making barrels of money for that steaming pile you just laid out there."

The singer said, "Our last single has fifteen million views on YouTube and a 170,000 likes. You don't know shit, Boomer."

This old man wasn't going to win a pissing contest, nor did I care to. I had knocked them off balance, so it was time to knock them on their asses. "I'm not a Boomer, I'm Gen X, and I have the chip on my shoulder to prove it. Now, which one of you pukes put the fentanyl in Kenzie's vape pen?"

Two of the three stood. The bassist slammed the back of his head on the underside of a cabinet and cursed. The singer said, "Whoa! You are out of your mind, man. Who are you?" I handed him my card. It took a while for him to focus on it, then read it one syllable at a time. Then he passed it to the guitar player.

I said, "If it wasn't one of you, then it was the drummer. Maybe I need to bust his ass." I looked at the singer. "What's your name?"

"Trey."

"Trey, huh? You're dating Mona Lisa."

"No." He looked at his comrades and added, "Well, yes, but it's not public."

"But, you were also intimate with Kenzie Knight?"

"No! Well, yes, but come on, you're gonna mess things up for me, cut it out."

"What about Harlowe? Which one of you was tagging her?"

They eyed one another, dubious. The guitar player spoke up. "You've come to the wrong place. You should look higher up in the organization."

"What do you mean?"

The bass player said, "Some girls like rock stars," as if one of those was present, "others prefer management."

"Harlowe was dating Boom brass? Is that what you're telling me?"

"That's what I heard," said Trey. "Me too," chimed dumb and dumber.

"Which one?"

Trey leaned back and smiled. "Why should we tell you?"

"Because I know that you were feeding Kenzie your little baby gherkin, and you don't want Mona Lisa to find out."

Trey said, "Josh Fagle."

I smiled, and he added, "Now if you'll kindly leave and send the girls back in on your way out." He held a lighter to an enormous joint.

I reached out and plucked the joint from his fingers and

crumpled it.

"Hey!" he said. "Give me that. How'd you do that?"

"Well, for one thing, I'm not *high*, Trey. Though, if I don't leave soon, I may be."

The three amigos looked at one another as though they saw an extraterrestrial. I said, "Before I go, you guys are gonna tell me about Kenzie's last night. The party at Club Karma, where you were and what you saw."

Trey said, "Nothin!" The bass player said, "We were drinking. The girls were dancing."

"Where was Kenzie?"

"She was dancing," said the guitar player.

"What's your name?" I asked.

"Felix."

I looked at the bass player who was twirling a guitar pick on the laminate table, "Is he lying to me?" He shook his head.

"Who was she with?"

Trey answered. "She was with Madison mostly. She didn't get along with Mona Lisa or Lake. She danced for a bit, said bye to us and the boss, then left."

"The boss?"

"Divya," said Felix.

"Then what?"

"That's it," said Felix. "She left."

Trey said, "Why do you think we gave her the drugs? Maybe she killed herself."

"Who wanted her dead?"

The bass player looked at Trey. Felix looked at Trey. With considerable reluctance, Trey said, "Mona Lisa, if she found out about Kenzie and me."

"Did she find out?"

"I don't know, and I'm not asking," said the pink-haired waif.

"Well, that's the smartest thing you said all night, Trey. Gentlemen, I thank you for your candor, and I expect that we will speak again. Goodnight."

I ran into the groupies as I exited the trailer and felt obligated to mention that something wasn't right with Trey's dinner and that he had stuff coming out of both ends. I added that they should hold their noses when going back in. They discussed the situation among themselves and followed me out.

It was going to be a lonely night for the pseudo rock stars. Oh well, groupies are for real musicians.

# 9

It was time to meet Boom ownership, who I had been watching from the shadows of the courtesy tent while sampling the stuffed mushrooms and crab rangoon. Josh Fagle and Kyan Sharpe were making time with some casino bigwigs and the owner of one of Boston's big four sports teams. The diminutive mogul had a model on his arm about fifty years his junior and six inches his senior. I wanted to walk over there and play bull in the China shop, but I knew it wouldn't go over well with that crowd. I was waiting for a break in the conversation when I felt a tremor move through the boardwalk underneath my loafers and thought that a boat had run into the pier. That was until I heard the screams.

I turned around to see the last of the line of backstage trailers engulfed in flame. It began on the undercarriage and climbed up one side and over the top. The only door in and out of the little metal box was behind a wall of fire, and I hoped to God it was empty. Then I heard another scream: "GET ME OUT!" It was a young woman.

I sprinted to it, the heat so intense I was forced to give it a wide berth, and ran around an end, hoping to find a window on the other side that was large enough to pull someone out. But the only access points were the door and two rectangular windows already engulfed in flame.

A security guard ran up, shouting about fire extinguishers. I turned to see four men in staff attire, looking at one another. No one seemed to know where to find one. Then a man in a BFD hat sprinted up with an ax in each hand. I yelled, "Let me help!" and reached out. He handed me one, moved in close to the trailer's rear wall, swung the ax back over his shoulder, brought it forward, and slammed it into the siding. I lurched forward as he recoiled and sliced my ax into the tear he'd made. We went back and forth, and I said, "How in hell is this metal box on fire?"

"It's gotta be an accelerant," he shouted back as the siding finally gave way. We quickly smashed through a layer of insulation, then the inside paneling as Ginny Angeloni screamed from somewhere behind us, "Oh my God. My baby's in there!"

Smoke began to seep from the wound. We dropped the hardware, and with the help of a group that had formed around us, we tore a gash wide enough to birth a pony. Mona Lisa's tear-streaked face soon emerged, and the fireman scooped her up. Seconds later, a fireboat appeared along the dock and began to soak everything down with foam, and I stumbled away from the smoldering mess. I was having trouble catching my breath and decided to sit down.

✳ ✳ ✳

The sound of voices and people moving around me blasted out from the tunnel in which they'd been restrained, and I came to as an urgent firefly flew in front of my eyes—back and forth, back and forth. Controlling it was an Asian man in an EMT's jacket. I was flat on my back, hands gripping the cold steel of a gurney. I spoke and wondered why I couldn't understand what I was saying. I felt my heart race, then mellow as I solved the puzzle and realized there was an oxygen mask encasing my mouth and nose.

The young technician and I were a good distance from the foam-soaked rubble of the trailer. He had applied moist compresses to my forehead. I ripped off the mask, stood on wobbly knees until I felt safe to move, then stepped toward the pathway that led back to the casino.

The EMT grabbed hold of my shoulder. I took hold of his wrist and pinched. "Ow, let me go. That hurts!"

I lessened the pressure, but retained my grip, leaned in close, and said, "Where's the girl?" before I released him.

He rubbed his sore joint and glared. "She inhaled a lot of smoke, even more than you. They took her to Mass General."

I moved past him, and he shouted after me, "You should keep breathing in that oxygen for a while. Your lungs are not working at full capacity. You'll be sorry!"

I dismissed him with a wave and walked on.

A half-hour later, as I was leaning against the hospital reception desk trying to catch my breath, I heard a gruff voice from the hallway to my right say, "Hey, detective, down here." It was Skinny Mikey. His voluminous partner was standing a few feet away, holding a cellphone to his ear. I didn't need to be a private eye to figure out who he was talking to.

Skinny looked me up and down. "Jesus, you look like shit."

The skin on my forehead was tightening and radiating heat like I'd been in the sun all day, but I didn't want to know how bad it looked. I shrugged and listened in on Fat Tommy's end of the conversation. "He just got here. He don't look too good, kinda like a sausage just off the grill." Then he handed the phone to me.

I covered the mouthpiece and asked the thugs, "How is she?"

Tommy held up a plump thumb, and I breathed a sigh of relief, before realizing how much it hurt my lungs to do so. I put the phone to my ear and said, "Town here."

"Ginny says you pulled my granddaughter from that inferno. I'm furious that she was in it to begin with, but since she's gonna be okay, I guess I owe you some gratitude. It's a good thing for you she's gonna make it." I didn't respond. I wasn't in the mood for threats.

"What the hell happened, detective?"

"I don't know. Everything was fine one minute, and the next

thing her trailer was a ball of flame, which makes no sense as it's sided in aluminum. One of the firemen told me there had to be an accelerant."

"And you didn't see anything?"

"No, but there are cameras mounted on the light posts. They've gotta have the perp on tape."

"Yeah? That's good to know. So, what have you got on the two dead girls?"

"Well, it's a little early in the game, but I learned one of them may have been sleeping with a Boom Productions executive."

"Which one?"

"The girl or the executive?"

"Do not waste my time."

"Harlowe Phillips and Josh Fagle."

"Huh, Josh Fagle. Does he walk with a limp?"

"No."

"Not yet," he growled. "What about the fresh one?"

She had died that morning, so I guess he thought of her as the day's catch. I thought about the photo of Mona Lisa, Trey, and Kenzie, and Trey's comment. His granddaughter was my only suspect. "I got nothing so far, but tomorrow is another day."

"Give the phone back to Thomas." I did and then asked Skinny where Mona Lisa was. He pointed to the elevator and said, "318."

Ginny Angeloni's voice penetrated the metal box before the doors opened. She was holding her phone in her left hand, the camera trained on her face. "I'm here, at the hospital, everyone. My baby is going to be okay. Thank you all for your prayers and kind words as I struggle to maintain a brave face. Mona Lisa is using a respirator right now, so she can't be on camera. Her little lungs are hurting, but she'll be okay. In the meantime, if you haven't already, please click on the nearby links to follow me on Facebook, Instagram, everywhere!"

I stopped in my tracks, amazed at the gall. She saw me, made a beeline, and threw her arms around me, all the while keeping the camera fixed on her. "Thank you, thank you for saving my baby!" I instinctively pulled away. She stared at the screen and said, "I'm going to go so I can properly thank this hero, but I'll be back with an update soon. Please send prayers, and don't forget to follow me!" She smiled, forgetting that she was supposed to be in concerned mama bear pose.

Camera off, she dropped the act and turned to face me. "She's being treated for smoke inhalation and has to stay overnight, but she'll be fine. Who the hell did this?"

"I don't know, but I'm going to find out. Did you see anything suspicious?"

"No, I was at the bar speaking with a businessman about opportunities to advertise via my Instagram. I'd be a perfect pitchwoman for his industrial air compressors."

A doctor passed by in the corridor, and Ginny grabbed hold of her sleeve. "Hey, Doc! This hero needs some attention. You can see, he's burned and is having a hard time breathing. How about a little service?" I would've blushed if my face wasn't scorched.

The doctor acquiesced and took me into an examination room. She told me my skin wasn't as bad as it looked and would be fine in a couple of days, as she applied a salve to my face, hands, and neck, before handing me an oxygen mask and telling me to relax for a bit. Wiped out, I closed my eyes and napped for about an hour. Upon waking, I paroled myself. I found Ron Shields waiting outside. He said, "Ginny insists on speaking with you tonight. She'll kill me if I don't bring you to her."

"What's up?" I asked.

He shrugged. "She don't tell me nothin."

We made our way back to the princess's private room, which was rapidly filling with flowers. There were roses and carnations, tulips and hydrangeas, pansies and peonies, it was like taking a stroll through the backyard at Versailles. "How the hell did all these get here so fast?" I asked.

Ginny swelled with pride, "My daughter's corporate suitors. They all want to get on her good side." Just then, another delivery arrived, and Ginny said, "Those look worse for wear. Put them in the corner over there."

Mona Lisa was dozing beneath an oxygen mask. She looked good, all things considered. Ginny turned to me. "You missed the Boom team. They came to see her, but I sent them home. She needs her rest. She told me something the other day that seems important in light of tonight."

"Something you forgot to mention to me earlier?"

"Sure, I forgot."

"Okay, what is it?"

"Kenzie sought out Mona Lisa the day after Harlowe died and told her something."

"Yes?"

"Harlowe called her rather franticly the night she died."

"Harlowe called Kenzie?"

"Yes."

"About?"

"Mona Lisa doesn't know. She told Kenzie to get lost, and she did. They were fighting over a boy."

"But you think this call had something to do with the deaths?"

"I didn't before, but now... I don't know. Death often comes in threes, and my little girl was almost number three."

"You think someone tried to kill Mona Lisa tonight?"

She rolled her eyes. "Obviously."

"After Mona Lisa told her to get lost, might Kenzie have talked to someone else?"

"I don't know."

"Lake or Madison, maybe?"

She shrugged.

"Who would want to kill your daughter?"

"No one."

* * *

I lowered the windows as I cruised home to let the night

air cool my skin. I contemplated the phone call from Harlowe to Kenzie, which suggested a link between the deaths, though a weak one. I mulled over the possible affair between Harlowe and Josh Fagle, and the fire that had nearly killed Mona Lisa. I turned up the radio and listened to Elton John singing "Someone Saved My Life Tonight" and tried to sing along, but I began to cough instead, and I realized that the fire had killed any hope that I would be done with the don in short order. There would be no easy resolution, no quick five grand. I consoled myself by considering the case of Kenyatta Bell. At least that one should be straightforward. I'd pay a visit to the clinic where she volunteered and see what clues her colleagues could provide. Surely, they would be of more help than Rajeev and the gang at The Man Cave.

I parked on the street around the corner from my place and flirted with stopping by Smitty's for last-call, but a quick peek at my reflection in the rearview window changed that, and I was pretty sure I had a few beers leftover from the weekend anyway. I was on the stoop turning the key when someone said, "Good evening." Before I could turn around, I was propelled face-first into my door by a hard kick to the spine. Then my attacker and his partner lifted me up and threw me down the stone steps onto the sidewalk, where they proceeded to kick the crap out of me. They relented after about a dozen shots to my legs and stomach. At one point I tried to lift my head and was told in clear terms that if I looked at their faces, they'd kill me.

One of them toed the back of my skull with a leather boot and said in a throaty whisper, "Listen up. You're off the stripper case. You keep poking around, and we'll come back and finish you. You hear me?"

I didn't respond immediately, which earned me another shot to the gut. I said, "I hear you, asshole."

That's when the second one said, "Asshole? Get out of my way, I'm gonna shoot him."

I started to reach under my body for my Glock, when the first one stepped down hard on my hand, and said, "Don't you dare move another inch, scumbag." Then he spoke to his partner. "We were told to deliver a message, and we did. Now let's go."

"Screw that. Let's solve the problem now."

"Ah, I don't know." I heard the click of a gun safety, followed by, "Wait, don't miss and hit me."

"Well, step aside then, and you won't have to worry."

"Okay, I will. No, wait! What if you hit a rib and it ricochets like the time last year? Don't shoot him. Let's get out of here."

"Aw, come on. It's been a while. I'll make sure to hit only vital organs."

That's when I heard the sound of a car turning the corner, and the pair decided to go without killing me first. They gave me one more kick for the insult, then another for the road, and left me curled in a ball trying to squeeze the pain from my guts.

I passed out for a bit until Maeve, a retired postal worker and neighborhood barfly, found me and rousted Smitty and a few others from the pub. I refused to let them call an ambulance, so the gang helped me into my place, cleaned me up a bit and lay me down on my bed where I spent the night, my thoughts boomeranging between wondering if it was a mistake not to let them call the EMTs, and what I was going to do with these cases, the first of which was still unclear, the second of which was now life-threatening.

Before finally falling asleep for a couple of hours, I called Irv and left a voicemail: "You scumbag. I don't know what you got me into, but if I need a doctor, you're sure as hell paying the bill. And, if I die, well, thanks a lot."

# 10

My body was bruised, and my spirit breaking, when I awoke not long after daybreak the next morning. I downed some pain relievers, examined my bruises in the bathroom mirror, then dressed in slow motion to minimize the pain. I needed to clear my head and think things through, so I threw Charlie Mingus on my old turntable, set the volume low to keep from waking my neighbors, and moved into the kitchen.

I started the coffee maker, then removed all the items I'd need from the fridge in one fell swoop. I arranged them on the old Formica countertop and turned on the nearest gas burner.

I laid three strips of bacon onto the surface of a Teflon-coated frying pan and watched them, grooving to Charlie's bass line. The doorbell rang as I was pouring the grease into an empty can, so I switched off the burner and padded downstairs, slippers sliding along the old floorboards. Standing on the stoop was a pair of cop buddies, who I liked to call B.S.

B.S. was short for Bull and Stan, which was shorter still for Bullpett and Stanowicz. DeShawn Bullpett and his partner Carl Stanowicz were plain-clothes cops from a nearby Boston PD precinct. I'd met them at Smitty's. Being an ex-cop, and also a Celtics fan from the glory days of Bird and company, we'd shared stories and reminisced over suds on a number of occasions. I stepped back and waved them in and said, "You guys have breakfast? I got plenty of eggs and bacon." They looked at one another, then Bull spoke: "I could use a couple over medium and a little swine. If that's alright?"

"Sure, no problem."

"Same for me?" asked Stan.

"You got it. Follow your nose," I said, and we moved into the kitchen. I set the coffee pot and a couple of mugs in front of them and got to work on a second batch of thick, smokey bacon, the good stuff I get from a neighborhood butcher.

Bull was average height and big-boned, to put it nicely, and was also the bigger talker. They were obviously here for a reason. Bull got down to it. "We got a friend in a certain federal organization. We got to talking, and your name came up. Long story short, we offered to come by and talk to you about something."

I eyed him as I placed the first batch of bacon down between them. "The eggs and more pig will be ready in a minute. If you want toast, there's more bread in the box. Here's the butter." I handed the dish to Bull. Stan was fishing the last pieces of pumpernickel out of a plastic bag. He was as tall as me, and I realized it'd been a while since I'd dusted above the cabinets.

With a wave of the spatula, I directed Bull to continue his thought. "We heard you paid a visit to The Man Cave yesterday and spoke with a fella named Rajeev."

"Yeah, I did. That little prick needs an attitude adjustment."

Bull stopped gnawing on a thick strip of sweet, smokey swine and said, "See, now that's the kind of thing we're here to prevent."

"Really? Does this mean that puke might be going to jail sometime soon? I guess I can play nice if that's the case."

"Yes. You change the tile in the backsplash? It looks good."

"You got a good memory," I said, cracking an egg and dropping its payload into the bubbling fat. "It's been a couple of years since we played poker here."

"We should do that again," Stan piped up. "Where are the forks?"

I pointed to a drawer and then set a plate with two perfectly fried eggs in front of each of them. Soon after, I took my plate and sat down across from them at my small dining table. We all dug in, and it was quiet for a bit before I broke the silence.

"So, nice job of changing the subject earlier. What exactly is Rajeev into?"

Bull pushed his chair back and stood to feed more seeded rye into the toaster. He leaned against the edge of the counter and folded his arms. "We don't know that, Earl. And we wouldn't tell you if we did."

"Is that true, Stan? You'd hold out on me?"

He laughed and said, "You know I would. It's business, Earl."

Bull said, "Maybe we can play nice and help one another. Why did you go to see Rajeev?"

"I'm looking for a girl. A dancer of his." I pointed to a manila folder on the counter behind Stan, and he handed it over. I extracted her headshot and placed it on the table. "Name's Kenyatta Bell, but when she dances she goes by Unique. According to her landlord, she hasn't been around for at least a week, but Rajeev told me she worked at the club two nights ago. He lied."

"Can I take a snap?" asked Stan, who was now holding the photo. He set it on the table next to his plate and snapped it with his phone. Bull said, "We'll show it to our friends and see if they know anything."

"I don't know how long they've been watching him, but I'd love to know when they last saw her at the club."

"Duly noted," said Bull. "What happened to you? You just winced picking up your mug, and I've seen you do it a dozen other times."

"It's this case. A couple of guys jumped me out on my stoop last night. Told me to stay away."

"Really?" Bull raised an eyebrow, while Stan stopped chewing and leaned in close. "Fascinating. My contact may want to speak with you," said Bull while eyeing Stan.

I looked from one to the other. "Okay. I'm willing to compare notes. There's another case I could use a little help on."

Bull groaned. "The breakfast hit the spot. I mean, that's some fine bacon, but you may be pushing your luck, Earl."

"I know, just hear me out. I'd like to speak with the lead officer on the Kenzie Knight case. She's a young girl that overdosed after leaving a club on Boylston four nights ago. I'm trying to determine where she got the fentanyl, make sure it was accidental."

"This is an open investigation?"

"I believe so. There's been little in the press since it happened."

"You got information that would help the investigation?"

*Not really, I've got a motive for Mona Lisa to kill her, though.* I said, "Absolutely."

❊ ❊ ❊

My phone rang seconds after I saw Bull and Stan out.

"Earl's House of Pain."

"What the hell happened?" asked Irv.

"A couple of guys jumped me in front of my place last night, played kickball with my guts, and discussed murdering me until a car came along. You should've been there."

"Holy crap. Why?"

"Let's see, as I recall, they said something like 'You're off the stripper case. You keep poking around, and we'll come back and finish you.'"

"You sure he meant Unique?"

"Yes, I'm sure," I said through gritted teeth.

"Sorry. Are you alright?"

"I think so. I just ate breakfast and didn't spring any leaks. What aren't you telling me about this girl, Irv?"

"Nothing. I told you what I know."

"Who'd she sue?"

"That's not pertinent, Earl."

"Who'd she sue?"

"A plastic surgeon in New Jersey, where she used to dance. He botched a procedure and nearly killed her, then offered to fix it. When she said no, he denied culpability and told her to screw."

"It's good she was smart enough not to let him try to fix it."

"Yeah, fortunately. Guy's a total hack. Myriad complaints. We sued for a million. Once he saw the case I'd built, including signed affidavits from a collection of his victims, he came around."

"That's when he wrote the check."

"That's right."

"Is it enough for him to pay someone to kill her and threaten me?"

"Nope. I tried to get her to push for more, but she settled for about three hundred thousand. He made close to two million last year, so there's no way he'd kill for three-hundred grand."

"Then who kicked the crap out of me?"

"I have no idea."

"Rajeev?"

"The club manager?"

"That's the one," I said.

"Why?"

"Doesn't like white guys? I don't know, but I didn't get a good vibe from him yesterday."

\* \* \*

A half-hour later, I found myself in the office of Candace Steinhauer, chief administrator of the clinic where Kenyatta Bell volunteered her time. Candace, who clearly spent considerable time in the gym for a woman her age, ran her eyes over me and gnawed on a pencil. We sat on opposite sides of a wide oak desk, but the way she was looking at me, I could've crawled under it and emerged in her lap, and she wouldn't have resisted. After a while, she said, "Rose, who manages the office on Saturday, told me Kenyatta hadn't come in or called last weekend. We were counting on her help too."

"When was she last in?" She turned to her monitor, and a few mouse clicks later, said, "The prior Saturday. She helped us get a new fundraising campaign out, then did some data entry." She ran the tip of her tongue over her bottom lip while she looked at the screen and added, "She worked exclusively on Saturdays, except for special events during the week. That is if they were on Monday or Tuesday. She had commitments on other nights. She's a lovely girl. Is something wrong?"

"I hope not. No one I've spoken to has seen her since the Sunday before last. Well, there was one guy, but he was lying."

"Have you checked her home and with her other employer?"

"I have. You know, I'd been told Kenyatta worked on fundraising campaigns, but you mentioned data entry too."

"Yes. Sometimes we get backed up on paperwork here. I mean, there are so many forms to be filled out for every procedure. Even when there is no procedure, the government, insurance forms, forms for medical equipment providers, and drug companies. It never ends."

"So, Kenyatta would help fill out these forms via the computer network?"

"That's right."

"Could she have been privy to patient information?"

"Oh, I don't know, Mr. Town. What's the relevancy of that?"

"I don't know, I'm just trying to understand why she might have disappeared on her own or been made to disappear. Personal information of the type you have here is one possible angle."

"Well, I think that's far-fetched."

"So do I, Ms. Steinhauer, but I have to ask these questions. I suspect it had something to do with a man. It usually does. Did she ever mention a boyfriend to you, or bring one to an event?"

"No, not that I'm aware of. Let me go and collect a couple of girls who regularly work on Saturday and have had more interaction with Kenyatta than I."

"Thank you," I said, as I eagerly watched her wiggle past me. I know, I'm a pig, but as the great Gaga says, 'Baby I was born this way.' Besides, it'd been too long since Little Earl had seen any action, and he was getting restless.

Curvy Candace came back with a couple of young women who stood in the doorway waiting for me to fire away, so I did.

"What can you tell me about Kenyatta? Did she talk about family, friends, men, places she'd like to visit on short notice?"

"Family?" said Locke, a pale young woman.

"She said her momma died of ovarian cancer," said Penny, a white-haired senior.

"Men?" I said.

"She said she had met someone a few months back. I think it was at her other job, but she didn't say much about him."

"He had money, though," chimed Penny.

"That's right. He flew her to one of those all-inclusive beach-side resorts. Cancun, I think it was. Remember that weekend she took off?" Locke said to Penny.

"When was that?" I asked.

"Back in, I want to say, April." She tugged at her ponytail as she searched her brain for the date.

Candace clicked a few keys, "She was out on April fourth. That was the last Saturday she wasn't in, until last week.

"You said he had money? Did he give gifts?"

"Not that I remember, do you?" Penny asked Locke, who shook her head.

"He had a nice new SUV," said Locke.

"You saw it?" asked Penny

"Yeah. Remember when that congressman hit on her at the Woman's Solidarity event?"

"Oh, that jerk," said Candace.

"Sweeney?" I asked.

"Yes, that's right," said Candace, as she stroked my arm.

Locke said, "I was outside when she was waiting for her ride. She was telling me her boyfriend would kick the living hell out of him if she told him what happened. She said she was so mad that she might tell. I guess she didn't, though."

"Did you see him?" Candace beat me to it.

"No," said Penny. "The windows were tinted."

"Did she ever mention his name?" I asked.

They shook their heads in unison.

"That's okay," I said. "This has been helpful."

"I think they broke up," said Penny.

Locke said, "Did they? I know she was worried about him."

"Worried about what?" I asked.

"She thought he was two-timing her."

I thought about The Man Cave and all of the girls that worked there. Girls over whom little Rajeev had power. There had been an SUV parked in front of the club that likely belonged to Rajeev, as it was parked in a manner that only an *asshole* would park it. The vehicle was long and black, with tinted windows. I started to salivate a little at the thought of meeting up with Rajeev again—FBI be damned.

# 11

I called Boom Productions and inquired if either Josh Fagle or Kyan Sharpe was in and was told both were. I was heading south toward them when my phone rang. It was a private number.

"Earl Town."

"Good morning, detective. I'd like to see you now."

"We can't talk over the phone?"

"No." He'd paid the extra two grand, but I should've known enough to hand it back.

"Okay, where?" He handed the phone to Fat Tommy, who told me to go to North Somerville High School. I did a double-take and asked why the high school. He thought that was funny and told Mikey, who thought it was a riot. I hung up. Nearly a half-hour later, I pulled up next to Skinny Mikey. He was leaning against an Escalade alongside the auditorium.

Mikey said, "The boss is inside." He motioned to a gray steel door that read STAGE. I stepped toward it, and he grabbed my arm. I stared at his hand until he removed it.

"What?"

"You know the routine. Hands up, legs apart." He began to pat me down.

"I left it in the car."

"Yeah, well, no one sees the boss without getting checked first."

"I think you're just doing it to cop a feel." I winked at him, and he jumped back like I was St. Damien of Molokai.

"You're not my type, Mikey." I moved past him.

Momo's voice reached out from the shadows as soon I stepped inside, and it wasn't long before I came upon the godfather. He was seated next to a young woman in a pair of canvas director's chairs. Momo wore a gray cardigan, while his companion had on a long denim skirt and a boutique's worth of bracelets. Her body language read flustered, and I was about to speak when I realized things were heated.

Momo shook his head and said, "Fine, let's go with quim then."

"No," said the 40ish woman.

"Okay then, twat."

"No, Mr. Ragazzi, we cannot say that word in a high school drama club production.

"What's the problem here, Shirley? You got one. Half of those kids got one. It's just a body part."

"Please refrain from referencing my and the student's genitalia, Mr. Ragazzi."

"I don't understand, you let me use balls in the title."

Shirley covered her face, and I watched as a little tremor started at her tailbone and made its way to her hips, then along her spine and up through her shoulders, to her neck, and right on through the hairs on the top of her head. "That word is only mildly offensive, and I told you it has not been approved by the school board as of yet."

"And I told you, I own four outta five of those jamokes. Why don't you ask them about cunt? Trust me, they'll be fine with it."

She sighed heavily, her shoulders sagged. In a hushed voice, she said, "I will not ask the school board to approve the words cunt, quim, or twat in the first verse of the opening number, Mr. Ragazzi."

He grunted his disapproval, and I cleared my throat. Momo swung his sagging mug around. "Hey, it's the local hero! You save any lives today, hero?"

"No, but it's not even noontime."

"That's good. Funny guy now, eh? Shirley Munson, meet Earl Town. He's legit."

Shirley waved a polite hello as she watched a group of kids acting out a scene on stage right. An older boy appeared to be directing. One of them was kneeling with a cord around his neck, while another stood close behind. They seemed to be trying out different ways for the one on the floor to die of strangulation. Should he stick out his tongue and fall forward, or maybe convulse and slump to his side? I'd have combined the two. Why play it safe?

Ms. Munson reminded me of the teachers of my youth, many of whom had been flower children, and had a sexy Earth Mother appeal. She was lean and angular with long brown hair, and I'll be damned if Momo didn't give her backside a quick slap as she stood up. I saw her stiffen as it landed. She gave a slight shake of her head and walked across the stage.

"Have a seat, detective." Momo motioned for me to take Shirley's place.

He said, "You like these chairs? First day of rehearsal, I show up to supervise, and they give me one of those folding aluminum pieces of shit. I said what the fuck is this? Are we putting on a show or not?" He bobbed his head, and I nodded along as though I cared. "So, the second rehearsal comes, and I bring one of these for me and one for Shirley. She's a terrific drama teacher." *And a saint.*

"What's it called?" I asked Momo.

"*Brains, Brawn, and Balls: A Life in Three Acts.*" He'd been scanning the small auditorium as he spoke and finally found what he was looking for, "Hey! Richie! Get over here and meet this guy already."

Richie was tall, dark, and cocksure. Well-dressed and tightly quaffed, he possessed a salesman's smile. My loathing for him was instantaneous.

He had been sitting in the third row with an attractive young woman in a taut sweater and was now ascending a set of steps that led to the stage. He reached out his hand as he arrived and said: "Hey, good to know ya."

I shook it and waited for the bomb to drop. This was obviously the reason for the meeting, and I had a bad feeling about where this was going.

Momo motioned for Richie to lean in close to him, and said in a hushed tone, "I told you to be nice with these young girls."

Richie, for whom no clue was obvious enough, failed to lower his voice and announced, "It's okay. She's not a student, she's a guidance counselor."

Shirley Munson, who was speaking pointedly to the girl, heard this and spun on her heel. "Is that what she told you?"

"Yeah," he said, hands out.

"She is a *sophomore*," said Shirley, disgust dripping from each syllable, before spinning back around. "Aurora Jones, I am disappointed in you."

Richie shrugged and looked at Momo.

Momo turned to me and said, "Richie is my son Vincente's boy and Mona Lisa's cousin." From bad to worse.

"Richie goes to Brown University. He's on scholarship for the fencing team."

"Really?" I said. "You fence?"

"Huh? Oh, yeah. All the time. Like one of the three musketeers." He feigned stabbing the air with his trusty sword.

"Yeah, which one?"

"Huh?"

Momo glared at me, and I decided to chew on my lip for a bit.

The don sunk his fragile shoulders into the canvas chair onto which the word "Playwright" was stenciled across the back. There was a little bit of breakfast residue on his sweater and in the lap of his pants, which were about two inches too short. To top it off, he had on corrective footwear. I wanted to feel bad for him, but it was all a disguise. The old man façade hid the face of a cold-blooded killer. I was sure he still had it in him.

He went back to watching Ms. Munson and the kids. "How

did all of this come to be?" I asked him.

"The school made some improvements to the gymnasium."

"You paid for the improvements?"

He reeled back and snorted, then looked at Richie, who began to chuckle. I felt my face redden even more.

"I made sure the refuse got taken away. A project like that creates a lot of garbage."

"Isn't that extortion?" My mood had taken a dive, and I wanted to poke him back. It only made things worse. Now he laughed out loud and elbowed his grandbrat in the belly. The punk doubled over in an exaggerated laugh, and both of them enjoyed a good rollicking hoot at my expense. Some of the students looked over. Their stares were a mix of curiosity and fear.

Finally, Momo said to Richie, "Guess what this guy used to do before he was a PI."

"Aw, that's easy," said Richie looking me over with a goofy grin. "He was a cop."

"You got it," said a cheery Momo.

I interrupted their good time. "You were saying, about your grandson?"

"Yeah, let's get down to it, so I can get back to my magnum opus. My granddaughter, God bless her, was nearly killed last night. She's lying in a bed in Mass General right now. This is taking too long, and my baby is in danger. I need you focused on this case and producing results. Richie is going to help you pick up the pace."

"Help me?"

"Yeah, he's gonna keep you focused on the case."

"Just because you're paying me, doesn't mean you get to tell me how to run my business, Mr. Ragazzi."

He smiled and retrieved a gold lighter from a pocket in his cardigan. He looked around. Ms. Munson and the kids were taking a break, and most were off stage. He lit up the soggy cigar he'd been chewing and wagging at me, inhaled a big mouthful, and blew it slowly into the back of the theater away from the teacher and her students. Finally, he said, "I'm not gonna threaten you because you're smart enough to know what's gonna happen. And, I don't like doing that kind of thing in front of family." I glanced at Richie and watched as he nodded like an obedient Pekingese.

"I'm gonna make it easy for you. This case needs to be solved yesterday. If anyone hurts her again ..." He stopped and let the words hang in the air for a bit.

"Understood," I said. "What else?"

"You spent the morning entertaining cops and then at a health clinic in Jamaica Plain."

"You're watching me?"

"I keep an eye on my investments." I shook my head and kicked myself in the ass for accepting the five grand.

"Like I said, Richie will keep you focused and report back to me, which will keep me off your ass. Take my word for it, you don't want the alternative."

He had a script binder under his arm as we spoke, and now he took a manila folder from inside and handed it to me.

I flipped open the cover and found an array of stills from the video cameras at Finale Boston Harbor. There was a timestamp in the lower-left corner of each snap. They were taken in the seconds before the fire. The pics showed a man spraying something onto the trailer and igniting it. However, the view was from above, and all I could tell about the perp is that he had dark hair and no signs of male pattern baldness.

"How did you ...? Forget it. It doesn't matter." I was dumbstruck by the efficiency with which he obtained the material and the nonchalance with which he offered it.

I turned to Richie and said, "You really want to spend a boring-ass day with me?" He shrugged like he had nothing better to do, which I didn't doubt was the case, so I turned back to Momo and said something I wish I could take back: "Okay."

# 12

"You're kidding me, right?" Richie was staring at the Caprice with a mix of horror and disgust.

"Do I look like a comedian? Let's see. Mic stand? Nope. Brick wall and baby grand? Nope. Clever one-liners? Okay, I got some of those. Look, kid, it's a great car, but if it's not to your taste, maybe you don't want to work with me. That's cool. Go hang with granddad."

"No, you ain't getting rid of me that easy. I just don't wanna be seen in a cop car, let alone one this shitty."

"Shitty? The distressed look is by design to keep idiots from messing with it. What's underneath the hood is all that matters, and this is a good, reliable car. What do you drive?"

"A hybrid SUV."

"You drive a hybrid? I thought you'd be a Cadillac man, like your grandfather, and every mobster in every movie."

"I am, and I will be after I graduate, but getting laid by Ivy league coeds is a lot easier in a German hybrid. They think they're saving the world just driving in it. You know what really turns them on?"

"I can only dream of possessing such knowledge."

"Getting it on in the back of a hybrid SUV."

I turned the key, and the engine roared to life. The lanky Italian looked over at me wide-eyed and with a goofy grin, and said, "Sounds alright." I put on my sunglasses and pulled out into traffic.

I'd wanted to arrive at Boom an hour ago and was eager to get on the highway, but Richie wanted to stop at a convenience store to pick up some "supplies." I said, "Hold onto your dick," and roared onto I-93. Once in the fast lane, I checked my phone and found I had a voicemail from Unique's second-floor neighbor. She left a number and told me to call back, so I did, despite the mole sitting to my right.

"Myra Holden."

"Hi, it's Earl Town. Is this a convenient time?"

"Yeah, it'll do. What do you need?"

"Your upstairs neighbor, Kenyatta Bell. When did you last see her or hear her moving about?"

"Oh, right. You're the detective. Uh, I guess it was the Sunday before last, so, what's that, ten days? Is something wrong?"

"You haven't seen or heard her since?"

"No, it's been quiet up there. I did notice her mailbox was filling up. Is she okay?"

"I don't know. Did you ever meet any of her friends or family or a boyfriend?"

"I hardly ever saw her. Our schedules are quite different. I hear her come home late at night sometimes, like 2 or 3 in the morning. There is a man. They're rather noisy when they …. anyway, I never met him."

"Have you ever seen him?"

"No, I'm sorry. There was that guy lurking around here last weekend. He was an odd one. I don't think he was her boyfriend, though."

"What did he look like?"

"Ah, average height, lean, big mop of curly brown hair and these thick square glasses like that old Hollywood agent."

"Swifty Lazar?"

"Yeah, that's it. How did you know?"

"He's my friend?"

"Swifty Lazar?"

"No, the guy lurking around your apartment. He's a friend of

Kenyatta's too. He's worried about her."

"Oh, sorry."

"No problem," I said. "You said you didn't think my friend was her boyfriend, why not?"

"Her boyfriend had a big black SUV. I saw it parked in front a few mornings when I left for work. He liked to park in front of the hydrant. Real considerate."

"Tinted windows?"

"Yes, that's right."

I asked Myra to call if she remembered anything else or heard anything stirring in Unique's apartment, and we hung up.

"What was that about?" asked Richie.

"None of your business."

"I thought the old man made it clear that you're not to spend time on anything but this case."

"It's not a case. She's dating a friend of mine. It's personal, and it took no time away from what we're doing. We're still driving to Boom Productions, so keep your opinions to yourself."

For the first time in a long time, I felt like I had a boss, and a twenty-something product of nepotism, no less. This case couldn't get much worse. Could it?

❄ ❄ ❄

I listened to the rumble of the Caprice's 5.7-liter 350 V8 engine as we rolled into a lot beside Boom Productions. The company resided on the bottom floor of a four-story glass and steel cube on the edge of a commercial office park. The building was nearly identical to others we'd passed on the way in, except for the posters of Boom's social media stars hanging from the lamp posts in visitor parking.

Richie tugged on the visor then primped in its mirror, while I thought through the approach I would take, such as the progression of questions, and how it might differ if my targets were alone or together. My goal was to surprise Josh Fagle and Kyan

Sharpe, the two wunderkinds behind Boom. I snapped out of it and said, "You look fine, you mook, let's go."

Richie climbed out of the coupe and said, "You can't call me that."

"No, why not?"

"Cause you can't. Don't make me angry, E."

"E?" I said. "Are you kidding me? Earl is one syllable—there's no reason to shorten it."

He said, "Nope, it's got two, maybe three beats. E, that's one beat. Eaarrrlll, that's two or three."

I shook my head.

"Fine, I'll call you Town, then."

"So, Town, but not T?"

"Why would I call you T?"

"No reason," I said while stifling a chuckle.

"You making fun of me?"

"If you're as smart as you think you are, then you already know the answer."

He thought about this as we strolled up a winding concrete pathway, through a couple sets of doors, and into the self-described "arms dealer in the platform wars."

The dandy young fella behind the counter in the sunny, modern reception area told us to have a seat after we showed ID. We sat in a pair of Barcelona chairs, which I've found are virtually impossible to get comfortable in, given that they raise one's knees above the navel. I think that's the primary reason rich little shits like Boom's owners put them in reception areas, to create a sense of unease. I watched as the exquisitely quaffed, baby-faced boy in a floral-patterned shirt picked up the phone and told someone our names. Then he said, in a surly tone, "No, I'm not mistaken. They're staring at me as I speak. Yes, I'll do that." There was a long pause, then, "Okay!"

"Problem?" I gazed at the kid over the day's *Wall Street Journal*, which I was using a fan. It was a scorcher. He tossed me a half-smile and headshake, but words escaped him. I noticed he was wearing pearl earrings. One in each lobe. Interesting choice.

We waited for a while, then a while more. The receptionist was doing his best to ignore us. Every so often, I'd stare at him until he couldn't stand it anymore, and he would be forced to look up and acknowledge me. I'd smile and cock an eyebrow, and he'd quickly turn his gaze back to his monitor.

We did this a half-dozen times, and I started to get angry. Richie was on his phone, oblivious. Every so often, he'd giggle, and I'd try to look over at his screen, but he'd see me and pull it out of my sight.

At some point, I'd had enough. The reception area was pleasant but seemed to be undergoing an overhaul. There were a couple of prints on the walls, but also several gaps, where it appeared something had been hanging until recently. Next to one of these gaps was a pair of glass shelves with a display of awards won by the company for various video productions and promotional campaigns. I didn't recognize any of the acronyms, but it all looked professional.

I picked up a particularly intricate award from the top shelf and examined it. It was constructed of delicate strands of glass in emerald shades wound in three successively larger knots. I admired it for a while, then let it slip from my hands only to catch it just before it hit the terrazzo floor. I heard the receptionist gasp and pick up the phone. Within a minute, Josh Fagle emerged from his office and shook my hand.

I introduced Richie as my associate, then said, "Is Kyan Sharpe here? It'd be great to speak with both of you, so we can wrap this up and get out of your way."

"Hey, thank you for what you did last night. Please come in, have a seat, both of you," he said, motioning us into his sunny office.

Richie chilled in one of two red leather club chairs opposite Fagle's desk. I took a spin around the room, looking over the bland abstract art and mid-century furniture. Like the reception area, Josh's office was open and airy and full of natural sunlight that entered via a floor-to-ceiling window in the wall behind Fagle's desk. On the other side of it was a collection of shrubs and small trees in a bed of cedar mulch.

I pointed to another gap in the art and asked, "You guys waiting for the next batch of prints or something?"

He did a double-take and said, "No. We're doing some repairs and had to move a few things."

"You didn't say if Kyan Sharpe is here or not."

"I didn't? Oh, sorry. No, he had to go to Essex. There's a new Sandler movie filming there, and a couple of the girls have small parts. Kyan went along with them to do a little networking. You know, use the local crews that we know to make introductions to the Hollywood people."

"Which girls?" I asked.

"Madison and Lake."

"That's too bad, I had hoped to speak with them too. Will they be gone all day?"

"Probably. Hollywood productions move slow."

"How convenient. What happened to your face?" I asked Fagle. He had a burgeoning shiner around his left eye, which had been obscured by the Clark Kent glasses when we'd shaken hands, but I could see in the brightly lit office. Then I added, "Ah, they caught up with you."

This startled him. "You know who did this?"

"I think so. Look familiar to you, Richie?"

"Yup."

Fagle picked up his cellphone. "Maybe I should call the police."

As I sat down next to Richie, I said, "Excellent. We can discuss you dipping your wick into the underage talent."

Richie let out, "Oooh, that stings."

Fagle went red. "I've never touched anything underage."

"So, you do admit to sleeping with the talent? That seems like bad business, Josh." I leaned back and assumed alpha status. "What would the folks from *Forbes* think about that, Mr. 40 Under 40?"

"Isn't kicking my ass this morning enough? Now you're here to rub it in?"

"We're here because two of your girls died recently, at least one of whom you were intimate with, and we want some answers. You're gonna give us some. Let's start with this, who have you hired to investigate?"

He stammered, "Wha, what do you mean?"

"Two of your biggest talents died in the past two weeks, and someone tried to kill Mona Lisa last night. Who have you hired?"

"Hired? We haven't hired anyone."

I leaped to my feet, and he nearly tipped his chair over backwards. "That is a big problem, Fagle. Your talent is dropping like flies, and you don't care. I don't buy it. Maybe you're the one making them drop."

"You are making some big accusations."

"Which one of you killed Ray and Harlowe Phillips?"

"Get out of my office!"

"Get out? Richie, tell Josh about yourself and remind him why we're here. I thought he understood all of this, but he clearly needs a refresher."

Richie spoke with a cool demeanor. "Right, well, I'm Mona Lisa's first cousin. My father and her mother are the children of Giacomo Ragazzi. You know him, right?"

Josh croaked, "Yeah."

"That's good," said Richie. "The don is really concerned about Mona Lisa. I mean so concerned, I don't even want to think about what he might do, or ask me to do, to anyone who fails to cooperate in Mr. Town's investigation."

"Okay. But, look, I've been instrumental in Mona Lisa's career development. Let's not put that in jeopardy. Ray Phillips was a lunatic. I can show you videos to prove it."

I said, "I've seen them. When did you start fucking his daughter?"

He looked away. "I can assure you she was past the age of consent. It's sixteen in Mass."

I looked at Richie, thinking of his sophomore friend. He replied with a knowing grin. I shook my head and turned back to

Josh. "I asked you when."

"Ah, let's see. It was right around the time we brought Kenzie on last fall. We held an event at that new steakhouse on the waterfront to celebrate her signing. It was close to Halloween, I recall the decorations."

"How long did it last?"

"Until Ray did what he did. I really cared for her. Very much."

"She was a high school senior, and you're 32 years old, Josh. If you cared for her, you'd have let her grow up first."

"She was a special girl."

"She was murdered 10 days ago, and you don't seem to be in mourning." He started to plead his case, but I talked over him. "Tell us about Kenzie Knight."

"What do you want to know?"

"Who gave her the tainted cartridge?"

"I don't know."

"Tell me about that night at Club Karma."

He brightened up, "I wasn't there! I had an early flight to New York the next day to meet with our investors. Ask anyone! I wasn't there." He was all prideful, like he'd accomplished something.

I turned to Richie. "I guess he wasn't there," then back to Fagle, "Did you see her use drugs?"

"Yes. She had a problem. Kyan and I, we spoke to her about it, weeks ago. We asked her to get help. She did it to herself."

"She spent most of her time working for you. Who around here is selling fentanyl?"

"No one."

"Do you believe that, Richie?"

"No."

"Where does your talent get its drugs? Those idiots who did the lip-sync routine last night had about a quarter pound of weed in their trailer." He shrugged.

"Come on, Josh. You and your talent are too rich and too young to not be getting high. Where do you get *your* drugs?"

"I don't use."

Richie started to get out of his seat, and Josh jumped out of his and stood behind it. It was a tall black leather number.

I grabbed Richie's arm to signal hold on. "Where were you the night Ray Phillips killed Harlowe?"

"I was with Kyan, at his house. There were other guests. We spent most of the night in his firing range." I turned to Richie and raised an eyebrow. He returned my look with a double-raise.

"Are you armed now?" I asked Fagle.

"What do you think?"

"I think it doesn't matter because I am." I opened my jacket and showed the butt of my Glock. "And I'm a swift draw. I've also killed before, shot a man in half last year."

Richie shouted, "No shit?"

I glared at him, then turned back to Fagle. "I don't think you have the stones to try anything."

"That's where you're wrong," he said.

Richie announced, "I want to punch the smug off his face."

I said, "I'm done with the questions, given his crap answers." That was a mistake. I lost control of the room.

Richie stood and stepped toward Josh, but the businessman was ready. He shot up and stepped behind his chair. Then, out of nowhere, he produced a Japanese Katana. Fagle kicked the chair away, and I saw a sheath attached to the chair back. Most guys keep a gun in the desk drawer, Josh had more flair. Too bad, I had a gun.

I put one hand on the butt of the Glock but left it holstered. I put my other in the air and said, "Whoa now, let's not be rash, and let's not forget who has a gun. That's a nice sword, but my Glock is nicer."

"I also have a gun, but I don't think he has it in him," announced Richie. The dumb ox took another step, one that brought him to the edge of the desk. Two more and they'd be face-to-face.

Josh brought the sword above his head and whipped it around so fast it whistled like a bottle-rocket taking flight. The tip nearly grazed the top of Richie's head. I said, "Richie, step back. Josh, let's not do anything crazy. You hurt him, you die. You know that, right?"

Richie wasn't listening to me. I said, "Richie, why don't you come back over to this side of the desk? We got what we came for. You can pound the smug off Josh at another time."

Richie stood frozen, eyeing his prey, then, instead of retreating, the young dummy squatted down and latched onto one of the club chairs. As he stood, he flipped the chair up over his head. He held it there, smiling like a kid about to spike the punch at the school dance.

I said, "Relax, Richie, put that down. Put that *down*." Fagle flicked the blade ... I shouted, "No!"

I reached for Richie's arm but caught only air as he rocked back and heaved the chair at the head of Josh Fagle, who surprised me again with his quick reflexes. He ducked just in time, and the base of a chair leg connected full force with the center of the giant window. There was a loud crash, then a chorus of thousands of tiny chimes as the nearly microscopic glass crystals rained down on Fagle, covering his desk like fresh snow before tumbling across the terrazzo floor and pooling around our shoes.

Though momentarily stunned as glass cascaded down around him, Josh did what any savvy entrepreneur does when opportunity knocks—he pounced on it. With only arborvitae now standing between him and freedom, Fagle stepped through the opening, ducked between the small trees, and sprinted across the pavement to a beautiful forest green Porsche 911. He hopped in, fired up the finely crafted German engine, and wasted no time peeling out of there.

I looked at Richie and said. "You dick! You stupid dick!"

He held out his hands. "What?"

# 13

"You are such an asshole, Town. I'm leaving. I only stayed to tell you what an asshole you are."

"I'm sorry! I was in Norwood this morning and left plenty of time, but you know how it is. I hit two road crews on the way, and I just got a new phone last week. I still haven't migrated all the information over, so I didn't have your number."

"You could have called the restaurant."

"Ah, yeah, you're right, but I was busy doing everything I could to get around the traffic. Look, I was at Boom Productions. You know, where Harlowe Phillips worked. There's some weird shit going on there that you need to know about. Let's go back to the table before they give it to someone else. *Please.*"

"That case is closed," said a visibly angry Pam Prentiss. She was in another well-tailored pantsuit. Her black bangs were severe and sexy, and it wasn't even after midnight. We were standing by the zinc bar at Les Zygomates. She saw me coming and met me half-way. It was nearly 1:30 pm.

I said, "What if I told you Josh Fagle was playing hide the sausage with Harlowe Phillips?"

"Well, that would explain why she was ten weeks pregnant when her father murdered her."

"What? Are you serious?"

"Yeah. So, you think you can tell *me* something. I don't think so."

"She called Kenzie Knight in the hours before she was killed. It might be a link between the two deaths."

She stood, arms folded, eyeing the door, then me, then the door, then me. Finally, she said, "I will *fucking* regret this. Let's go." She led me over to our table.

We sat, and I looked around for Richie. He exited the men's room and headed for a barstool. It took some effort to get him to leave me alone with Pam. We'd argued on the way into Les Zyg.

"She's the lead investigator on the Phillips case. I'm not slacking off. She won't share anything with *us*. I have to do this alone."

"Yeah, that sounds good, but Momo told me to stick to your side like glue. So, I'm gonna stick to your side. Capiche?"

"Capiche this." I gave him the finger.

"Whatever. I'm doing as I was told."

"No, you are not."

It went on like this until we entered the restaurant. Then he saw Pam coming straight at me with fire in her eyes and said, "On second thought, I'll leave you to it," and broke for the rest-room. I didn't blame him.

Pam and I ordered salads and asked the waiter to speed it up, as Pam only had thirty minutes left. She waited for the kid to depart and said, "So one teenage girl calls another teenage girl, and you think that means they were murdered? What are you, an idiot?"

"I'm told Kenzie Knight was troubled the day she OD'd. What if she had some knowledge about the Phillips case? Knowledge about the real killer."

"Yeah, that's quite a stretch. I'm doing well, by the way. Thanks for asking."

"Ah, yeah, sorry, we started talking about the case by the bar, and you brought it up again at the table, but you're right. How have you been?"

"Eat me. I'm fucking with you, Town. You're a little slow on the upkeep, huh?"

I almost replied with something nasty but took a few breaths. I flashed my pearly whites and said, "I remember you being pretty assertive on New Year's Eve, but this seems excessive, Pam. Something got your goat?"

"I'm shocked you can remember anything about New Year's, you were a real lush."

"Are you admitting to sexually assaulting a man who was too drunk to give consent?"

"You were the one with roving hands, not me."

"Me thinks you would've put me in a chokehold if you hadn't liked how I was using them."

She gnawed on her lower lip, then started to say something, changed her mind and said, "Where are the fucking salads?"

"So, back to the case?" She nodded.

I leaned back and felt a sharp pain on my right side. She noticed me wince and asked what happened.

"I took a case for my lawyer yesterday. Trying to find a girl who dropped off the face of the earth last week."

"Your lawyer? You mean that jerk with the big frames?"

"Irving Wechsler."

"Yeah, that idiot is repping a guy that a friend of mine caught tugging his little dinkus in front of Wellesley Middle School. Your lawyer will do anything for a buck."

"My lawyer, and dear friend, believes that everyone, no matter how despicable, has a right to good counsel. Irv is a good man."

Pam eyed the ceiling tiles. "So, you were saying, about the girl?"

"Yeah, so I ask around yesterday. Go the club and talk to the boss, who's a complete prick, then I convince the landlord to let me into her apartment. She didn't plan on not coming home."

"Why are you wincing in pain?"

"Two guys jumped me outside my place last night. They warned me to drop the case. Kicked the hell out of my guts."

"Thank you for the heads up on your soft spots. Who do you think is behind it?"

"Her boss at the club. A little guy named Rajeev. Likes to surround himself with huge bouncers, but I'm gonna get him alone."

She shushed me. "Don't incriminate yourself. Do you think he's harmed her?"

"Yeah, I do."

"Is BPD looking into it?"

"I hope so. I told the landlord to call them. I'm gonna check back later. If he doesn't call them, he becomes a suspect too."

"What's his name?" I told her, and she told me she'd run a check on him and check to see that he'd called the cops. It was a nice gesture, and also gave her an excuse to call me again.

She said, "Well, at least one of your cases is legit. You're wasting your time with the Phillips case."

Our niçoise salads arrived, and we dove in, talking between mouthfuls.

"Tell me about the crime scene," I said.

"What's there to tell?"

"Anything out of place or inconsistent with the murder-suicide angle?"

"Nope. We found her in the passenger seat, a single bullet in the left temple. We found the father up on the hill. He sat on a rock, put the barrel to his head, and blammo."

"What about the gun?" She squinted as though she didn't understand.

"Where did he get the weapon? Was it his?"

"We don't know. It's a street special, no number, no history."

"Really? Why would a straight-laced, middle-aged white guy have one of those? Why not buy one over the counter or at a gun show?"

"Maybe he only decided to get one recently, and he figured those crazy rant videos would come up during the background check."

"It stinks, Pam, and you know it," I said. "What about tracks?"

"Impossible. More than a hundred people visit the place

daily. Tell me something, Dick Tracy, what do you think happened up there?"

"Somebody could've driven them there, or met them there, killed her in the car, and marched him up the hill to his death. Why is that so impossible?"

"Who has a motive?"

"That's what I'm working on. What if Fagle wanted to terminate the pregnancy, and she didn't?"

She smirked.

"What if she told the father she was pregnant, and he threatened to go public?"

"Go public with what? The girl was legal."

"Knocking up the young talent can't be good for business."

"So, the threat of losing a few clients, and he murders the mother of his kid and her old man? Do you hear yourself, Town?"

"Look, I'm not saying I believe this stuff. I just have to eliminate the possibility. Do you have anything to disprove it? If you do, I'm all ears. I want the case closed and this client off my back."

"Who is the client, anyway?"

"I'm not comfortable discussing that. Tell me something, was Ray Phillips on anti-depressants?"

Pam dabbed the edges of her mouth. "No, he wasn't on anything other than a statin for cholesterol. Not a drinker either. His ex-wife said he didn't seem off, other than the rant videos. You haven't harassed her, have you?"

"No, absolutely not. I've never met the woman." I'd planned to soon, though.

"Somehow, despite your lack of intellectual ability, you've stumbled across the one glaring inconsistency. He showed no signs of being violent toward himself or his kid. The videos were directed at the company. Why not go in there and shoot the place up instead of killing his kid? That troubles me."

"Wow, refreshing honesty. You're alright, Prentiss."

"Oh, gee, your approval means a lot, Town."

"So, you admit there's a glaring inconsistency, but you've closed the case, correct?"

"Of course, it's an obvious murder-suicide. You find some actual facts that say otherwise; you let me know. Now, I gotta be someplace else. Thanks for lunch, and fuck you for making me wait."

She stood, and I followed. I said, "Hey, don't go away angry. I enjoyed the lunch."

She shook her head and started to move past me. I said, "Wait. You heard about the fire last night?"

"Yes."

"That would have been the third dead Boom Girl. Are you telling me this is all just coincidence?"

"Jeez, catch up, man. They know who did it. Some college intern for one of the girls must be a firebug. They're looking for him now. If you find a motive for him to murder the others, call me. In the meantime, enjoy beating your head against a wall. Some private dick you are."

With that, she headed for the exit. I sat back down to finish my salad. Shortly after, Richie slid into Pam's chair.

"Man, what did you do to her? She started off pissed and left even more pissed."

"I can't remember, or maybe it's because I didn't call her one time. I'm not sure."

"What'd she say about the case?"

"That it's an obvious murder-suicide, and I'm wasting my time."

"Anything new?"

I signaled for the check and answered, "She told me Harlowe was pregnant."

"Jesus, that's awful," he offered. "On a positive note, I had a great steak and fries." He pointed at Pam's half-eaten salad. "What the hell is this anyway?"

"Salad Niçoise, it's delicious."

"What is it?"

"You got a phone, look it up. Oh, she said the fire-starter is an intern who worked for one of the girls. The cops are looking for him now."

Richie raised an eyebrow and said, "I'd better tell Momo. Mona Lisa has an intern." I recalled seeing the kid, and her treating him terribly. A motive for murder, though?

"Call him on the way to the car. I need to take another look at those photos he gave me."

I went back over the pics. The subject appeared to be of average height, male and Caucasian, with a flair for exciting footwear, which I had not noticed earlier. It sure looked like the kid Mona Lisa called Tard. I hadn't recognized him before, but with more information, it was obvious now. I recalled feeling sorry for him but hadn't really paid attention to him.

I had started driving when Richie nudged my arm and said, "Hey, look at this." He held up his phone. On the screen was a photo of a young man seated at a café table sipping a glass of white wine.

"Yeah?"

"It's Todd, the intern. Aunt Ginny just sent it to Momo and me. He posted this on Instagram only ten minutes ago. It's the North End, we can be there in minutes."

I hit the gas, and Richie's head hit the seat. "Ow, geez!"

"Sorry about that, but the cops may have seen it too. We need to get there first."

"That's what Momo said."

# 14

F rail and nervous by nature, Todd looked like a before ad for anti-anxiety medication, as Richie and I took seats at his table. He and his companion, a clean-cut, similar-size boy with dark features had been holding hands when we sat down. Now both were staring down at the grain in the marble tabletop, trying not to look either Richie or me in the eye. I started the questioning.

"You are Todd Farnham. I am Earl Town, a private investigator, and this is my associate Richie Ragazzi. Richie is also the cousin of your friend, Mona Lisa Angeloni. Isn't that right, Richie?"

"Mmm, hmm," said Richie. The couple was sitting side by side at an outdoor table off of a little square in Boston's touristy North End. They had knocked back a dozen oysters along with half a bottle of Prosecco and were starting in on some calamari when we sat down.

"What do you want?" asked Todd in a childlike voice.

"We want to know where you were when the fire broke out."

Todd looked into his friend's eyes for reassurance before answering. "I was in another trailer getting Mona Lisa's things ready. She said she wanted to get right out of there after leaving the stage. She left her purse and clothes in Lake's trailer. They like to get ready together."

"Okay, let me rephrase the question. Where were you thirty

seconds before the fire broke out?"

He stammered, and his friend squeezed his hand. I didn't want him giving Todd any help, so I started in on the friend. "What's your name."

"Uh, Skyler."

"Skyler, I think it would be great if you'd give us a few minutes alone with your friend Todd."

"No," said Todd. "Don't leave."

Skyler was a good friend and said, "I'm not going anywhere. Anything you want to say to Todd, you can say in front of me."

Richie was sitting on Skyler's left. He calmly asked, "So, do you like them?"

Skyler's head spun around, and he looked curiously at Richie. "Do I like what?"

"Your balls," said Richie motioning down to Skyler's crotch.

Skyler's gaze fell to his lap. Skyler then peeked under the table and turned white. Todd and I followed suit and found that Richie had a snub-nose 38 revolver pointed at Skyler's boys. I hoped the kid wasn't going to piss himself.

He eyed Todd and said, "Ah, I think I better go."

"No!" cried Todd.

I agreed. "No, it's too late for that. You sit right where you are and keep your hands on the table. You too, Todd."

I watched Todd's Adam's apple bouncing as he fidgeted in his chair.

"You two make a nice couple," I said, laying eyes on Todd. "I hope it works out for you. Now answer my fucking question."

"I was backstage getting Mona Lisa a water. She asked for a cold one."

"Let me see your feet," I said as Richie licked calamari grease from his fingertips.

"What? Why?"

"Push your chair back and put one of your feet on the table here." I moved his plate out of the way.

He looked for a savior but found none and did as he was told. He was wearing an odd-looking pair of tennis shoes. The heel and toe were covered in gray wool, but the middle and the area around the laces was a tan leather. It was a wingtip design on a sneaker. I reached into my jacket and removed one of the pictures of the fire starter.

I said, "Strange coincidence, don't you think, that you and this guy, who started the fire last night, have the same incredibly distinctive footwear? I mean, what are you thinking? You gotta get rid of the shoes, pal." I leaned back and snapped a photo of Todd and his sneaker before he could put his foot back on the ground.

"Richie, what was that cop's name again. I suspect he'll want to speak to Todd about his shoes."

Richie said, "I don't know no cops." I glared at him.

Todd said, "I'm sorry. Thank God Mona Lisa is okay. I only did it because she told me to."

"What?" said Richie in a threatening manner. Todd recoiled.

"Let the witness speak, Richie. Please go on, Todd. Ignore him."

"After what happened to Harlowe and Kenzie, she thought if she was nearly killed, it'd get a ton of publicity, and that would elevate her status. That's all she wants, to be seen as the breakout star."

"Bullshit," said Richie.

I turned to him. "Look, partner, if you don't like what he has to say, go get an espresso, and leave me to it. This is my job, you're here to help."

"He's lying about my cousin."

"If he is, I'll get to the bottom of it. Now leave or shut up." Todd's eyes were bouncing back and forth like he was at Flushing Meadows for the Open. He had begun to sweat. Skyler looked catatonic.

"Fine," said Richie.

"What did you use to start the fire?"

"Cheveux Parfaite hairspray. They're one of Mona Lisa's sponsors. She uses it to kill bugs. It makes a great flamethrower."

"What did she offer you?"

"This is bullshit!" said Richie. I told him to shut up again, and then reassured Todd that I would make sure nothing bad happened if he kept telling the truth.

"Nothing. I'm her intern, and she made it seem like it wasn't a big deal. It would just be a small fire, she'd be rescued, and the media would link it to Harlowe and Kenzie and start talking about the curse of Boom Productions. The story would blow up and she'd get a ton of press. And, she'd hire me to be her full-time personal assistant."

"You could go to jail for arson and attempted murder, and she's not even paying you?" I said, amazed at the casualness with which the kid approached multiple felonies—Millennials. "What are you gonna do?"

"Do?"

"Yeah, the cops are looking for you. When were you last at your home?"

"This morning."

"They have someone watching your place now. You need to turn yourself in, kid."

Richie stood. "No fucking way! He does that, he incriminates Mona Lisa."

I stood toe to toe with him. He had about a half-inch on me and twenty fewer years, and, like me, he was packing heat.

I said, "Richie, the kid sprayed accelerant all around the door and windows. The cops aren't going to believe him. Use your head."

I turned back to Todd. "Your story is bullshit."

Todd threw his chair back, vaulted over the wrought-iron barrier between the restaurant and the street, and tore off like Usain Bolt. Richie and I jumped the railing and gave chase.

Todd was making the most of his wingtipped tennis shoes. He took off up an old cobblestone alleyway that I knew forked to the right and onto Hanover Street, one of the North End's main drags.

I yelled to Richie, "You follow, I'll cut him off at Hanover!" Then I turned onto another side street that would get me to a spot where I knew I could catch up to him. Just as I reached Hanover, Todd flew out of the alley, turned toward me, and nearly leaped out of his briefs at the sight of me. He spun and nearly ran into Richie's arms, but managed to duck the big meatball's grasp and run into a restaurant called Carmella's. It was almost 3 pm, and the crowd was thin. Todd dodged the maître d', an older heavyset woman with a carnation above her ear, and raced up a set of stairs to a second-floor dining room. I was right behind him, while Richie lagged.

To my amazement, all I found on the second floor was an open room and no intern. A frazzled waitress pointed to a set of restroom doors. I turned the men's room knob, but it was locked, and I was about to throw my shoulder into it when the waitress shouted, "The ladies!" It, too, was locked, so I laid into it.

Inside were a toilet, sink, and open window, which led to a fire escape. Rust fell from the steel treads above and got into my hair as I peeked out. I climbed through the window and carefully made my way up the rickety steps, wondering when it had last been inspected. I reached the four-story roof just in time to see Todd coming at me, and I steadied myself to take him down. But he was just trying to make a little runway. He stopped, pivoted, and ran as fast as he could to the building's edge, where he launched into the air, flew across an alley, and landed in stride on the next rooftop.

I stopped and studied my options and immediately ruled out going after him. I mean, only a moron would risk his life. I scanned the neighboring rooftops to see if he'd try it again, figuring I'd run back down and meet him in the street. Just then, Richie emerged from a nearby transom and spotted Todd. Without even thinking about it, the dumb lummox ran straight past me toward the brink. I had a vision of telling Momo his grandson was dead and shouted, "Don't do it!" But the kid kept going, and amazingly, he stuck the landing, but only on the very edge, where he awkwardly wavered back and forth before regaining his balance and running at Todd, who was preparing to jump to the next building.

The intern narrowly escaped Richie's grasp and bolted for the roof's edge and a jump over an even wider gap. I didn't think he'd make it, but I'll never know. This roof was different from the first one. The tarpaper needed replacing and was in the process of disintegrating. This created a layer of loose gravel in a few areas, most notably in the space leading up to the roof's edge. Todd spent the last seconds of his life skidding into oblivion and doing everything he could to stop his momentum before he disappeared with a shout of "Nooooo!"

Richie jogged over to the edge and gawked. He turned to me as I heard a scream from the street. "He didn't make it!" He squatted and picked something up. "A couple of his fingernails did, though!"

"You'll make a fine detective someday!"

He flipped me the bird and tugged on a door that would get him into the building. It was locked. "Dammit!"

I called out. "I suggest you find the fire escape or take the express like Todd! I'll collect the car and meet you at Mike's Pastry!"

# 15

"If you'd listened to me, that kid would still be alive. Christ, you're lucky you didn't get killed jumping over that alley."

"Yeah, that was ballsy shit, right there. You were just gonna let him get away."

"No, I was going to catch him when he came down. What? You think he was going to leap his way to Charlestown?"

"Whatever. I had the balls to do it, and you didn't. Live with it."

"You're an ass. You could have died for nothing. You would've fucked me over too. Momo would've blamed me, and I would've had to go on the lam."

"Good luck with that. He's got ears everywhere. He'd find you in no time."

"That makes me feel better. You really screwed the pooch back there. You're supposed to be along for the ride, not interjecting and fucking with my witnesses."

"You wanted him to incriminate Mona Lisa? You think Momo is gonna like that? I saved your ass, man. If that kid talks to the cops, Mona Lisa gets involved, and you take a long, hard fall."

"Nope. You need to stop and think things through before opening your big trap. It would've been her word versus his. He's the one on video, and like I said, he sprayed accelerant all over the place. It was attempted murder. The cops had nothing on Mona Lisa. Nothing!" Richie's phone rang.

I was driving toward the center of Boston, trying to figure out where to go next and putting as much distance as I could between the two of us and Mona Lisa's late intern, all while wondering what his friend Skyler would tell the cops and when they'd show up at my door asking questions.

Richie was smart enough not to say too much on the phone. There were some uh huh's and yeah's before he hung up. His eyes told the story. In a demonstration of his omnipotence in the North End of Boston, Momo had already gotten word of what had happened and had summoned his charges to explain.

Richie said, "You know the old tannery at Fort Point Channel?"

"On A Street."

"That's the one. He's in the dance studio on the second floor and wants to see us, *now*."

Ten minutes later, I trudged up a flight of stairs and turned the corner to find the old man barking orders at a pair of frazzled women in yoga pants. Standing behind them along a wall looking apprehensive were a half-dozen high school kids, most I recognized from earlier in the day, and Shirley Munson. She was speaking with the kids in hushed tones while Momo shouted at the two young women.

Skinny Mikey came jogging over, and I turned and spread my feet, palms on the wall in an exaggerated fashion. I did it to annoy, but I think it scared some of the kids too. I made a couple of cooing sounds as Mikey ran his mitts over me. He said, "Not funny, Town. Tommy says you're not a homo, you're just messin' with me. You know what I think?"

"You think I really am a homo, don't you?" I said, beating him to his punchline.

He looked confused as to what to say next and mumbled something like, "Yeah, that's right, faggot," while Momo bared his fangs at the poor women who stood in front of him.

"I'm not gonna say this again. I need something snappy. It's an upbeat number, and all you girls want to give me is "The Rich Man's Frug." I don't want them shimmying around the stage like Bob Goddamn Fosse! I want something like Manning and Miller, and the swinging Lindy Hoppers! You know, boys and girls holding hands and jitterbugging. Like they used to before all this woman's movement bullshit. If you can't give me that, I'll find someone who can."

The taller of the two women muttered, "Sure you will."

Momo glared, "What did you say?"

"Isn't the show in like *a week*? How are the kids going to learn an entirely new routine?"

"You just give me what I want, and I'll make sure they learn it." Momo called out, "Take fifteen, everyone!" Then he looked at the women and growled, "Come back with something worth a shit or go home."

To my surprise, the pair seemed unphased, as though choreographing a musical for an angry mafia don was a minor nuisance.

Now he shouted at Shirley, "Make that ten for you, Ms. Munson, I want to go back over the first number. There's something off in the first verse." She gritted her teeth and turned away. I noticed she was keeping out of his reach.

Momo waved us over. He sat atop his canvas chair along an exterior wall backed by century-old windows from when this place was one of a thousand New England textile factories. Tommy and Mikey went back to playing gin rummy at a nearby folding table. Tommy was focused on his cards, while Mikey was sizing me up. Momo pointed to a pair of folding chairs and said, "Just what I needed, more problems from my private eye. I paid you to *solve* problems. First, my granddaughter is nearly broiled, and now you run the little finocchio off a building."

I saw Mikey's ears perk up and caught him eyeing me over his cards. I said, "The interview was going fine until your grandson spooked the witness."

Richie chimed in, "Town was encouraging the kid to talk to the cops, and after he said Mona Lisa told him to start the fire. He would've incriminated her." Momo arched an eyebrow at me.

"The cops were going to catch up to him soon anyway, and they had zero proof of anything having to do with Mona Lisa. It was his word versus hers, and they had him on video spraying accelerant all over the place. With her brains and your lawyers, she would've been fine. The only question is why he tried to kill her."

Momo turned back to Richie. Richie said, "What?"

"He makes a good argument Riccardo. What did I tell you about stopping to think things through?" Richie became fascinated by something on the floor.

I said, "What do you hear about the witnesses and police investigation?"

Momo said, "Maybe you should be paying me." I winced. "You're lucky, people in the neighborhood are loyal and will keep their mouths shut. So, unless a tourist recognized you, I think we'll be okay."

"What about the kid's date?"

"He's been spoken to."

"What does that mean?" I was wishing I hadn't asked before the words even finished leaving my mouth, but he ignored me and put a hand on his grandson's slumped shoulder.

"He gets a little ahead of himself sometimes. His father was the same way. Richie will learn."

I noticed Shirley and several of the kids looking on from across the room, watching and waiting to see if this would be the moment when their crazy benefactor would kill someone before their very eyes. The choreographers had two kids spinning one another around, testing them to see what moves they could handle. I said, "Seems like there's still a lot to be done for a play that's only days away."

"Yeah, well, they gave me Shirley, the kids, and the auditorium, but not much time to rehearse. Some of these kids are graduating, so the show must go on. Shirley's had the script for a while, so the troop knows their lines and the songs. We just gotta work out the blocking and tackling."

"Songs?"

"Yeah, there are three numbers in each act, or maybe only two in act one if Shirley and I can't come to some agreement about the lyrics."

"Did you write the words and music?"

"I did."

"Gramps is a great musical talent," said Richie.

Momo shouted across the room, "Shirley, have Hunter sing a few bars of the opener for our guests."

Ms. Munson spoke to an acne bomb with knobby knees, and the mop-top sat down at an upright piano and began to play a dour ballad. Then Hunter took a deep breath and began to sing:

*A boy from far away across the sea.*
*Forced to leave his home in Sicily.*
*To a new world where he must fight.*
*Where hardship lies and hunger bites.*
*He adapts, spreads his wings and flies.*
*His enemies they run, hide, repent, and die.*
*Transmogrified, the man now knows how to hunt.*
*His enemies vanquished like weak little jerks.*

"Goddamn it, Shirley!" shouted an incensed Momo. "Jerks? That's the best you can do? I told you, if you wanna replace it, then you gotta come up with something that rhymes. Jerks does not rhyme with hunt. You know what does, however?"

Shirley's shoulders sagged. "Yes, please don't say it again." Then she told the boy to go take a seat with the others along the wall. "Why can't we change *hunt* to *work*?" She asked while still keeping her distance.

"I like *hunt!*" Momo said, before turning back to me.

I said, "It's really great. Strong melody, expressive lyrics. I mean—transmogrified! Andy Webber's got nothing on you." He shrugged as though my critique meant nothing to him, even though I knew it did. His ego needed constant stroking. I'll bet that was one of Fat Tommy's chief jobs. I noticed he and Skinny Mikey were hanging on my every word.

Momo said, "Richie filled me in on your talk with that Fagle fuck. What'd the cop broad have to say over lunch?"

I looked at Richie, who shrugged like it wasn't his fault he was reporting on my every move. "She said Ray Phillips didn't drink or take drugs. The ex-wife didn't see it coming, and the cops don't understand why he didn't just shoot up Boom Productions if that's who he was mad at. Oh, and the gun was a 38 special with a filed number. Your instincts are good, the pieces don't seem to fit."

"My instincts are good?" He chuckled. "I woulda been killed six times over by now if they weren't. Remember Paul Castellano?"

"Yeah, he was gunned down outside a Midtown steakhouse."

"Yeah, I told him he had bad instincts about Gotti. Two weeks later ... So how are you gonna prove it was murder?"

"Pffft, I'm open to suggestions."

"Well, the cop must know more than she told you, and Richie says she's got eyes for you. Feed her your salami and engage in a little pillow talk."

"I'll see what I can do," I said.

"You ain't married, and Richie said she's alright. You like the boys or something?" I noticed Mikey's ears perk.

"No, I do not like *the boys*. I know this woman. She's more than a little crazy, and she carries a gun. I gotta go easy, or I might be the next one getting *suicided*."

He laughed. "Now, that's funny." Then he turned and shouted, "Alright, time's up!" He pointed to the choreographers and directed them to the middle of the floor. When they'd arrived, and he also had the attention of Ms. Munson and the actors, Momo shouted, "Okay, ladies, shake some ass and show us what you got!"

# 16

Richie was hungry again, I needed a drink, and we were near my apartment, so I parked in my usual spot, and we headed over to Smitty's. Richie noticed the sign in my window, which reads *Gumshoe for Hire,* and said, "What the hell's a gumshoe?" I shook my head.

I said hello to Smitty and the regulars and ordered a Sam Adams while Richie got the fish and chips, though I told him to have the Reuben, which is excellent. Not too much butter on the bread, which is the downfall of many a soggy excuse for one. I finally checked my voicemail, as the icon had been flashing for a while.

"Mr. Town. This is Sharon Phillips. I understand you're investigating the deaths of my daughter and ex-husband. It's important that we speak, please call me." Her voice was smooth and even, her tone serious. I took my beer over to a quiet corner and called her back. We dispensed with the introductions, and she got down to it.

"How did you hear about me, Mrs. Phillips?"

"Ginny Angeloni called and told me I absolutely *had* to talk to you. Don't get me wrong, I was glad to hear you're on the case. I just didn't appreciate her tone."

"Her tone?"

"Yes, it was threatening. She said if I valued my trash pickup, I better call you. What does that even mean?"

I appreciated Ginny's effort, so I decided not to tell her it was literal. "I've no idea, but that Ginny sure is a hoot, isn't she?"

"Uh, yeah, a hoot."

"You said you were glad to hear I was on the case. Do you have some doubts about the official version of events?"

"Official version? Yes, I do. I got the distinct sense that the police weren't as concerned about the truth as they were about closing the case."

"What makes you say that?"

"Raymond was a deeply religious man, Mr. Town. He didn't believe in suicide and would certainly never have committed homicide."

"And certainly not of his own flesh and blood," I added.

She corrected me. "That has nothing to do with it, Mr. Town. We are all God's creatures. He made us in his image and loves us all equally."

"I understand your daughter talked openly of her faith, Mrs. Phillips."

"Yes, she did, with pride."

"The other girls with whom she worked take a different approach."

"Yes. And yes, neither her father nor I was pleased about it. But she told us it was God's calling to engage with those charlatans because they would amplify her message. She wanted to do good for mankind."

"I was led to understand that your daughter's career was a point of difference between you and Raymond." I watched with concern as Richie grew bored waiting for his food, left the bar and approached the pool sharks in the back.

Sharon said, "At first, we were of the same mind on that. Then Raymond began to see things differently."

"In what way, Mrs. Phillips?" I watched Richie put a bill on the table and Pollack Joe, a 70ish soldier who'd survived the Tet Offensive and had half a leg blown off by a North Vietnamese booby trap, racked the balls. I sipped my beer.

"He began to believe social media and Boom Productions, in

particular, are the work of Satan himself."

"What caused that shift in his thinking?"

"Those Boom people are a pack of vipers. Mr. Fagle is a particularly vile creature." She left it at that.

"Why do you say that, Mrs. Phillips?"

"I'd rather not say."

"Your daughter was pregnant with his child."

"That's a rather disgusting remark, Mr. Town."

"And it's the truth. You need to come down from Mt. Pious and level with me, Mrs. Phillips. Or would you rather your family's killer remain free?" There was a long pause, and I watched Richie losing to Sal, another Vietnam vet and a star at running the table. Sal was also the kind of guy who wouldn't hesitate to kneecap anyone who tried to welch on a bet.

Mrs. Phillips said, almost in a whisper, "That evil Mr. Fagle wanted my girl to kill her baby. Imagine that, Mr. Town. Killing my grandchild. Well, my daughter had the sense to say no."

"That's very good, Mrs. Phillips. Your daughter told you this."

"No, not about Mr. Fagle's evil desires. She told me about the baby, of course. And, coming on the heels of the death of her grandmother, I thought it was a gift from God himself, but look at what's happened."

"I'm sorry for your losses."

"Thank you, Mr. Town. Where was I?"

"Your daughter didn't tell you about Mr. Fagle's desire to terminate."

"Ah, yes, and the proper term for what Mr. Fagle had in mind is murder, Mr. Town. I was saddened by her behavior and encouraged her to marry the man. I suspect she never told me about his desire to destroy the child because she didn't want me to think even less of him. After all, he was to be the father of my grandchild."

"Then how did you know he asked her to abort?"

"Kenzie Knight told me." I choked on my Heineken a little.

"Are you alright, Mr. Town?"

"Ah, yes. Kenzie Knight, tell me everything she said."

"It was after Harlowe's afternoon service."

"Her wake?"

"Yes. She said she had something to tell me while in the receiving line. She stayed until most of the others had left, and we spoke."

I heard raised voices and looked up to see Richie shove Sal in the chest, followed by Sal and his wheelchair rolling into the jukebox, which skipped a beat.

Sharon Phillips said, "She told me that she knew about the child and was praying for its soul. I greatly appreciated the gesture."

I watched as Rob, a former Navy helicopter pilot, swung a pool cue into Richie's back, and he and Joe pinned Richie's to the table. I jogged toward the fracas, phone still to my ear.

Sharon said, "I told her how thoughtful it was and asked how she knew, and she told me ..." I muted the phone and shouted. "Guys! GUYS! Come on! He's with me. Richie cut the shit!"

I unmuted the phone and said, "Mrs. Phillips, could you say that again? A loud vehicle just went by my window."

She sighed. "She told me ..."

"Kenzie Knight told you?"

"Yes, detective. She said Harlowe had confided in her, and her only. She then asked if she could tell me something else, something that had been troubling her."

I had turned my back as they were untangling from one another, but when I turned back, Richie was being overpowered again, and I needed to intervene. I said to Sharon, "Please excuse me for 30 seconds. I have an urgent matter to attend to, but it will only take seconds." I muted her again without listening to her response.

I pulled Joe off of Richie as Joe was saying, "You gonna play with the big boys, you gotta learn to pay up, son."

Richie said, "I just want one more game to make it back."

"That's what you said the first time. Now, you pay up."

I said, "Please let him go, Joe, and I'll make you whole. I just gotta finish this call." I turned my back to them and unmuted. "I'm back, Mrs. Phillips. I'm sorry about that. You were saying Kenzie Knight had something else to tell you."

"Yes. Is this a good time, Mr. Town?"

"Absolutely, Mrs. Phillips."

"Well then, Kenzie told me there was another girl before Harlowe. A Boom girl who went through with the evil deeds prescribed by Joshua Fagle and murdered her child." She paused.

"An *unborn* child?"

"Yes, they are God's children too, Mr. Town."

"Well, who was it?" I demanded.

"I don't know. She didn't say, and it is not my nature to pry."

I noticed Smitty looking over my shoulder and turned to see Richie on Sal's lap. Sal had Richie's arms pinned back while Rob reeled back, ready to lash Richie with the fat end of a cue stick.

I covered the phone and said, "Richie! What is your problem? Guys, come on, let him go." Sal released him. Richie stood and leered at the group as he smoothed his sleeves. Then he made a motion like he was going for his gun. The old-timers took a step back and Richie grinned at them, like he had proven a point.

"Richie, come over here." I pointed to a nearby chair.

I turned away again, "Have you told anyone else what you've just told me?"

"No."

"Why not tell the police?"

"That woman was rude to me. I don't see any reason to call her."

"Detective Prentiss?"

"Yes. She closed the case up so fast it made my head spin. That one's not looking for the truth."

"I don't know about that, Mrs. Phillips. I think she's a good egg."

"She's a sinner," said the obviously angelic Sharon Phillips. My mind flashed on New Year's Eve.

Eager to get Richie out of there before the embers ignited again and someone got shot, I said, "Thank you for your help,

Mrs. Phillips. Please keep safe."

"I'll be safe in the arms of Jesus Christ, my lord and savior. In whose arms do you seek salvation, Mr. Town?"

"I usually seek trouble, not salvation, Mrs. Phillips. But I'd sure appreciate it if you could put in a good word with your guy for me?"

"Mmm, hmm," said the good widow.

*  *  *

"You owe me a hundred and twenty bucks."

"To hell, I do. They cheated me. I should've shot the lot of them."

"They played you for a fool. I could've told you they would."

"Yeah, why didn't you?"

"I was talking to the mother of the first dead girl. Hey, those guys put their asses on the line for this country. You should show them some respect."

"What'd she say?" He took out his phone, getting ready to make some notes to report back to Momo.

"You owe me a hundred and twenty bucks."

"Good luck getting it out of me. What did Mrs. Phillips say?"

I reeled back. "Mrs. Phillips, you say? So, Riccardo has been paying attention."

"Don't call me that."

I turned south toward Marina Bay in Quincy. I was thinking about how someone may have killed Kenzie for knowing too much.

"Mrs. Phillips said nothing of value. She's a religious woman, says it's all in God's hands now. She told me I should drop the case."

"Really?"

"Yup."

"Don't hold out on me, Town."

"I'm not, Ragazzi."

"Where are we going?"

"To stake out Josh Fagle's place."

"Stakeout, like, you mean all night?"

"Yeah, as long as it takes. That's the job, man. You want to be my shadow, you gotta come along for the sucky work too."

"But I got a couple of dates lined up this evening. You're gonna have to manage without me."

I cocked my head and grinned at him. I couldn't have stopped myself from doing it if I'd wanted to. I said, "How will I ever do that, Richie?"

"Funny. Hey, take the next exit and bring me back to town."

"You're here to observe, not dictate. We're going to Marina Bay. You can arrange an Uber to pick you up."

Twenty minutes later, we were parked within sight of Josh Fagle's condo. Richie waited for his ride while I observed the scene through a pair of high-powered binoculars, looking for signs that Josh was home. I doubted he was. I didn't see the Porsche, but sometimes you have to wait until nightfall when the lights go on to really know.

I sucked on a breath mint, and said: "So, who'll be following me tonight, Richie?"

He stopped swiping and looked over at me. "What's that supposed to mean?"

"The old man as much as admitted to having me watched when we spoke this morning. You don't think I'm dumb enough to believe he won't do it tonight too? Do yah?"

He actually clicked off his phone screen. It was the first time I'd seen him do it. He said, "I don't know, man. Sounds like you're into conspiracy theories. That's not my thing."

I said, "Tommy and Mikey do that kind of work for him, or are they just security?"

"How should I know?"

"You're his grandson. Are you telling me you don't know shit?"

He sighed at the burden but said, "Tommy, that fat fuck, has been around longer than I have. He once told me he used to bounce me off his knee. I pulled my first gun on him and told him if he ever brought it up again, I'd put three in his forehead."

"Memories," I sang in my most wistful tone.

"Mikey. He's newer, maybe five years now. His father was a loyal soldier. Momo loved him, so he hired his kid."

"You said love in the past tense, did something happen to Mikey senior?"

"Yeah, one night when Mikey was a little baby, the old man he got drunk at Foley's and announced he was fucking Whitey Bulger's girlfriend. No one ever saw him again."

"You serious?" I said with a chuckle. He did not laugh.

His ride came shortly after. I watched Fagle's place for another hour. The sun was starting to set when a Chinese food delivery guy pulled up and rang Josh's bell. Josh answered. About five minutes after that, a slender young woman I didn't recognize drove up in Josh's Porsche, parked and went inside with a bottle of wine. I decided he was settled in for the night and thought it was time I paid a visit to the Boom executive I'd yet to meet.

# 17

Kyan Sharpe lived in Marshfield, a wealthy community on the seacoast south of Boston, which was popular with local rockstars, television personalities, and bankers. His house was in an exclusive community and set well back from the street. The Caprice and I rumbled up a winding drive lined with modern lampposts until we reached an oversized Streamline Moderne home. It was built to look like a 1940s cruise ship with tubular steel railings, rounded corners, glass blocks, and a sprinkling of porthole-style windows.

I parked next to a futuristic electric sports car, walked up a series of flagstone steps, and rang the bell, waited a bit, then reached for it again as the door pivoted open on a perfect arc.

Kyan Sharpe stood with one hand on the door, the other holding a rocks glass filled with something clear over ice and a wedge of lime. He was wearing silk boxer shorts, navy socks, and a loosely tied red silk kimono with a gold dragon on it. Average height and lean, with wavy locks and a several-days-old beard, he peered out at me from tired eyes and said, "Looking for a new place to smash up?"

"Yeah," I said, doing my best impersonation of humble, "I'm sorry about what happened this morning. I left my gorilla at home tonight. I also saved Mona Lisa's hide last night at considerable risk to myself." He acknowledged my point with a nod. "I know it's late, but I'd really like to ask you a few questions."

He stepped aside and waved me into a spacious entry hall with a view straight through the house and out to a glowing rectangular swimming pool. There was music coming from the patio, and I heard female laughter and splashing about. I was reminded that it was Thursday night when people are more apt to let off a little steam ahead of the weekend.

"I'm sorry if I'm keeping you from your guests." He shrugged and led me up two steps into a modern kitchen, full of straight lines. He pointed to the closest of four stools on the near side of a marble island and asked if I was hungry. I wanted to lie and say no, but I was starving and said, "Yeah. I'm famished."

"Good. So am I," he said, tugging on a huge door that blended into the cabinetry. Behind it was a well-stocked refrigerator with nearly everything at eye-height. He reached in, pulled out a platter with an assortment of antipasto, followed by a bowl of fried chicken and a plate of sliced melon. He handed me a dish and a fork and set himself up with the same.

"Jesus, thank you," I said overjoyed at the spread. Then I got greedy. "I don't mean to be a jerk, but you wouldn't have a cold beer in there too?"

"You like Sapporo?"

"If it's beer, I like it."

We dove in, me sitting at the island, him leaning against the counter, and kept the conversation light, though I did have to ask him something.

"Why are you so nice to me after what happened this morning?"

He threw me a mischievous grin and said, "I wish I'd been there to see his face when it exploded—must have been hilarious."

"You and Josh having some difficulty with the partnership?"

"Mmm, you could say that. We have different ideas about the direction of the enterprise, and we haven't been pulling in the same direction lately. Not entirely opposite directions either, so it's not fatal, yet."

"What direction are you pulling in?"

He picked up a spicy pepper and downed it. "I like where we began, managing social media stars. I get a charge out of taking an unknown entity and making them a household name. You know, with a certain demographic."

"Teenage girls."

"Boys too."

"What's Josh want?"

"He'd like to produce more content. He sees content as ..."

I cut him off, "As arms in the platform wars."

"You saw that, huh? That's a good line. That one's a door opener."

"What's Divya want?"

"Divya? She wants to keep her job—she's Switzerland."

"Losing two-fifths of your stable of social media talent has shifted the advantage to Josh, has it not?"

The thought had obviously crossed his mind. He said, "Yes, it has, detective, but that doesn't mean he had anything to do with their deaths."

I was moving fast and became wary of spooking him. I complimented him on the house.

"Thanks, I got it in the divorce."

"Really? You have an ex-wife?"

"No, my parent's divorce. It's a joke, but it's also somewhat true. They had old money and a single child, so as well as I've done in business, I did even better being born."

"That's not something most people would admit to." He shrugged.

"You have great taste," I looked around. "It's beautiful and architecturally true to form."

"You know architecture?"

"A little. I know more about furniture than buildings, but the two go hand in hand. My ex-wife deals in mid-century artifacts."

"Really, what's her name?"

"Roxanne Town, er, it's Palmer now." She kept my name for several years after the dissolution of our marriage but dropped it not long after she began dating Mr. Hedge Fund.

He bit his lip and peered at me. "I bought a Paul Evans credenza from her last year. It's in my office. I'll let you see it if you promise not to destroy it." I promised. "It's olive burl and chrome, a really nice piece. As I recall, your ex was okay too."

"Mmm-hmm," I replied, not wanting to go down that path.

"Isn't she with that private equity guy?"

"Hedge funds."

"Yeah, right. He runs a private equity fund. We talked to him during our Series B phase. He was a prick." The food and beer had worked, I suddenly found myself warming up to the young Kyan Sharpe, who went on. "He's a real aristocrat, put us through the wringer, then turned us down. Said a better investment had come along. Fuck him, I hope he loses his shirt."

"I'll toast to that!" I said, holding up the tasty Japanese lager.

We clinked, and Sharpe said, "You're an ex-cop, right?"

"You did your homework."

He nodded, threw me a sly smile, and asked, "Ever fire an Uzi?"

＊ ＊ ＊

"The original plans called for this place to be built on a slab," explained Sharpe as he cinched up his kimono and started down the first of two sets of stone steps. "It was designed for Los Angeles or Palm Springs, but this is New England, so, I put in a basement and made full use of the house's length. That cost me some money in I-beams, but it was worth it."

We turned the corner at the base of a set of floating steps flanked by a stone wall. I said, "Holy shit, you got eighty feet of range." He beamed like a proud father.

"Here, let's pick out some toys," he said as he flicked a switch. This caused a stir along the wall nearest us as a set of hydraulic doors sparked to life. The doors ran from floor to ceiling on a set of tracks. They slid open to reveal row after row of shelves containing dozens of handguns, shotguns, and rifles from an array of makers. Sharpe had arranged them with care, and each of the shelves was well lit and stocked with more than enough ammunition to have a good time.

Sharpe said, "Take your pick, detective."

"You're gonna think me odd, but I've been thinking about buying a boot gun since I had a near-death experience last fall. Could I try that little Luger? The one with the concealed hammer."

We went through a bevy of rounds in no time at all. The Luger was sweet and the Uzi savory, but I get bored just shooting at hanging targets. Moving targets, that's another story altogether, and a fine time when they're not shooting back. Besides, I had more questions, and we were wearing earplugs under earmuffs to muffle the noise. Conversation was out of the question in the firing range.

I signaled that I was spent and got him to lead us back up to ground level and into his office so he could show me the piece he bought from Roxy. I leaned my back against the door frame nearest the cabinet and admired it for a bit as I imagined the size of the commission she'd jacked him for.

"Tell me about Ray Phillips," I said.

Sharpe pointed to a black leather sofa. I sat, and he sat across from me in a sleek Scandinavian lounge chair.

"Ray was a murderous asshole. Ray Phillips is the reason Josh and I were shooting in the range the night it happened. I was trying to get him comfortable with a weapon because I was afraid Ray was going to try and kill us."

"Really?" I said, "I didn't think his videos were all that bad. He was obviously pissed at you, but I didn't see blood lust in his eyes." Actually, this was Ed's assessment, but he's a good judge of character. It's a family trait.

Sharpe said, "It wasn't the videos that scared me, it was the personal visits. I almost pulled a gun on him about a month ago. I'm leaving work and nearly in my car, and all of a sudden, he comes out of nowhere screaming about how he's gonna show everyone what a bunch of frauds we are. I'm telling you, the man was a bona fide psycho."

"I was told Boom was suing him for what he said on the videos. Is that true?"

"No, our lawyers were preparing a suit, after sending him a series of cease-and-desist letters. That's when he did what he did."

"So, you believe he killed Harlowe and himself?"

"Yes, I do," he said with utter certainty. "Do you know something I don't? I thought the police had closed the case."

"They did. Why do you think he did it?"

"Aside from being a natural born psycho? To spite the wife, like the cops said."

"What do you know about Sharon Phillips?"

"A pious pain in the ass like her husband."

"What about Ginny Angeloni?" I had to ask.

He leaned into his seatback and cleared his lungs of oxygen. "You've met her, huh? She is the exact reason I do not fraternize with the talent. She is unavoidable, but I outlasted Josh on her. He's scared of her father and caved into her demands early on. Now she calls him first, and then Divya if she can't get ahold of Josh. She doesn't bother me too much. But if she's not careful, she'll ruin her daughter's career."

"Career?" I said. "Is this really a career? How long can these girls do this?"

Sharpe stood and walked to a small set of doors built into the shelving unit behind him. He pulled one side open, reached into a small refrigerator, and removed two bottles of cold Italian sparkling water. He tossed one to me as he sat back down.

"I'll tell you what I told them and their parents. It's the foundation of a highly lucrative career. But, to really last, every one of our influencers will need to expand into other areas of entertainment – singing, acting, fashion, whatever it may be. Or, if they have absolutely zero talent, then there's always reality television. Just look at what the Kardashians have done with that."

"I wish someone would come up with a cure for them," I

muttered.

"I know," Kyan said. "Me too. However, that family is a great example of just how valuable a big social media presence can be for establishing other businesses. The youngest one is a billionaire because they parlayed her social media presence into other avenues like fashion and cosmetics. Without the reality show and social media, those business opportunities wouldn't have been there for her to exploit. We have given the Boom Girls a tremendous head start, and now we're helping them build on it. The income they earn now is fabulous, but the potential for success in future endeavors is the true reward."

"Does the talent understand this?"

"Some do, and some think only in the short-term."

"What about Mona Lisa?"

"She's got big plans, but she's secretive about them. She's driven, though."

"What do you think she'll pursue for her next *career*, as you called it?"

He ruminated, then said, "I think it's gotta be acting. She can't sing, and her fashion sense is not at all chic—it's very Revere Beach. Our crew is constantly having to dress her. She does have this crazy idea that she's going to become a political pundit and get a gig on CNN or MSNBC. I don't see how that'll happen, but you never know."

"Tell me about Kenzie Knight's last moments."

"Man, you don't beat around the bush. We were celebrating the launch of the second EP of a Boom client—Fatal Mistake—at Club Karma. We were all there, management, talent, and some VIP fans."

"You were all there, even Josh?"

He thought about it. "No, Josh wasn't able to attend. Divya and I hosted the event."

"What was Kenzie doing?"

"I don't know. I remember her hanging out with the band, but she usually hung around them."

"The band? You mean, Fatal Mistake?"

"Yeah, Trey and those guys."

"I met them last night. They seem more like posers than real rockers, but what do I know."

Sharpe didn't sugarcoat it. "They are posers. That's what pop music is now, maybe always. Fake it 'til you make it. You ever try managing a musical genius? I did once, and the lifestyle nearly killed me. Never do it again."

"But you manage a girl whose grandfather is a mafia don."

"Yeah. Uh, we didn't find that out until she was signed and sealed. Once we signed her, we couldn't back out without upsetting the family. What would the don think of that? Josh was screening the talent then. He screwed up. Though, to be honest, Mona Lisa's talent is worth any trouble it brings with it. And, until that scene with you and the don's ..., what'd you say he was? His grandson?" I nodded. "Until today, when his grandson wasted Josh's office, things were copacetic."

"Anyone else connected to Boom perish recently?"

"Yeah, an intern of Mona Lisa's died today, apparently. Jumped off a roof in the North End after learning the cops were after him for starting the fire last night. I just heard about it before you showed up."

"Really? That's crazy, but I mean Boom staff or talent. Have there been any other deaths or incidents?"

He leaned back in the lounger and looked at me wide-eyed. "Come on, you don't believe these things are connected? We've had some bad luck is all."

"Who else?"

"No one."

"Did the cops ask about Kenzie and the band?"

"No, they didn't ask me about her. Divya also spoke to them, and maybe Josh. They might have asked them, but I think they took it for what it is—a tragic overdose."

"Are Trey and the group into opioids?"

"No way. They're clean. I mean they smoke a *lot* of weed, but if they're doing any hard drugs, they hide it well. They're totally committed to the work and are always where they're supposed to be. They're not like the characters they play."

He was getting antsy, and it was time for me to go. So, I hit him with a haymaker. "So, just how many of the Boom Girls has your business partner impregnated?" He sat up straight, eyes bulging.

"Who told you that?"

"Several people have informed me that Harlowe Phillips was expecting and that Josh was the father. I don't think that's in dispute. I've also been told that a similar situation occurred not long ago and was taken care of, so to speak.

I eyed him and imagined the gears moving in his head, as he deliberated on what I knew and the lies he might still put by me. "I don't know anything about this. I understand there was a situation with one of the girls, but that it has been resolved."

"Which girl?"

"We're done here, detective. I need to get back to my guests."

I stood and thanked him for the food and conversation, but then I said something I'd been thinking since seeing his arsenal. "Excuse me for saying this, but you seem to be at odds with your generation."

"You mean the guns?"

"Mmm hmm."

"Well, most people my age have parents who are still taking care of them emotionally and financially. Both of my folks died when I was a teenager. I don't have a security blanket, so I go with firepower. It helps me sleep at night, as do the women I pull with this place and the fast cars." He chuckled at his glorious lifestyle.

"Speaking of cars. You drive an SUV?"

"Yes. Porsche Cayenne."

"Black?"

"Silver."

We moved to the entry hall, where I pointed out an abstract painting by the door. "You know, I usually hate contemporary art, but I like this composition. The scale and shades of blue and gray work great in this space. Speaking of art, I noticed some gaps on the walls at Boom headquarters."

"Oh, yeah, well, ah, Josh recently sold a few paintings. He handled it directly with some special buyers, not through an auction house. Those guys are thieves."

"I know. My ex-wife works with them all the time."

# 18

The sun had set while I was playing grab-ass with Kyan Sharpe, and I felt as though I was running out of time. The day had been packed with events, not the least of which occurred on a rooftop in the North End, but I was no closer to solving anything. I chewed over my next move and decided to risk pissing off a source to get an answer to a big question before the day was over. So, I made a call and found the party in question to be quite receptive to the idea of old Earl dropping by to ask a couple of questions, even after 10 pm, which it would be by the time I arrived.

When I had finally crossed her threshold and said thanks and hello, she said, "You know how to make an impression, Earl. When I told you to call me by my nickname, you didn't say 'a name so sweet,' or how I 'look as sweet as I sound,' or any of that horseshit. That's worth ten points in my book."

"Hell, it ought to be worth more than that, given how many times you must have heard it, Candy darling," I said to Candace Steinhauer from the clinic. I was back in the city, not far from Fenway Park in the high-net-worth enclave of Brookline Village.

Candy met me at the door with eager eyes and a peck on the cheek and pointed to the corner of a sleek leather sofa. She asked if I wanted a glass of wine. I inquired about scotch. She had Black Label. I said, "Great."

She had wrapped herself in a white form-fitting cocktail

dress and spiked heels. I said, "Are you just getting in?"

"No."

"You always dress to the nines?"

"You always drop in on single women well after dark?"

"No, but I don't know many single women who look like you."

She looked me over and raised an eyebrow as she handed me a tumbler, then she sat close and made a show of her legs as she eased back into the sofa. Candy was lean and built and probably older than I'd realized.

"Are you a runner?" I asked, "Or do you just not eat?"

"That's a nice line, Earl, but business first. What is it that's so urgent?" She arched her back to stretch, and her breasts rose into my eye line. It wasn't accidental.

"I'm working on a couple cases, and there's a chance they may be linked. I believe you will be able to tell me if they are."

"One of them is the disappearance of Kenyatta?"

"Yes."

"And the other?"

"I'd rather show first and tell later. Would you mind looking at a few pictures?"

"Pictures?"

"Yes. Ah, I'm not sure how to broach this, so here goes. There's a code of ethics associated with the clinic, yes?"

"Of course, you know there is, Earl. The decisions our clients make are deeply personnel and private."

"I understand that, but I'd very much appreciate it if you could tell me if you recognize any of these women from the clinic." I held up my phone.

"You mean, tell you if they've had a procedure at the clinic?"

"Yes."

"I can't do that, Earl."

"It's crucial to finding Kenyatta." That was the set-up, this was the knockout blow: "Without it, whoever took her will remain on the street to strike again."

"Jesus." Candace downed her wine and got up to pour another. She kept talking as she opened the fridge and grabbed the bottle. "You sure don't beat around the bush, huh? I mean, when you ask for something, you really go all the way."

She filled her glass three-quarters of the way, leaned her head back and downed half of it, filled it again, and sauntered back to the couch. She said, "Let me see one of them."

I opened my phone and pulled up a headshot of Kenzie Knight. Candy said, "Another." I showed her Madison Pontiforno.

"Wow, she's beautiful too. Next." I showed her Lake Gelson, Harlowe Phillips, and Mona Lisa. She said, "Wait, I know her. I know the prior one too. These girls are well-known! What is this? I know gossip-site bullshit when I see it, Earl. Where are you from, TMZ? The *Herald*?"

"I'm a detective, Candy."

She stood, pulled me off the couch, and shoved me toward the door. "You need to leave!"

I said, "Two of the girls I just showed you are dead. Both died in the last two weeks. I'm trying to save the others and Kenyatta Bell."

She stopped pushing. "Are you serious? Two of them? Dead?"

I Googled a story about Kenzie's death that also mentioned Harlowe's demise and handed her my phone. She wiggled onto a stool by the kitchen counter and read the piece. A look of shock came over her, and she said "Oh my god" several times before handing the phone back. Then she said, "These deaths don't seem to be connected, Earl."

"I know they don't seem to be, but here's the thing. I believe the deaths are related, and Kenyatta is connected to both of them. I need you to confirm it."

She placed the well-manicured fingertips of each hand on her temples and rubbed. "There's still some Riesling in the fridge. Please fill me up. No, scratch that. Just hand me the bottle."

She filled her glass and studied all five of the Boom Girls. She went back and forth over Mona Lisa several times. Then she asked me to hand her a nearby purse from which she extracted a phone and made a call. "It's Candace. Sorry for calling so late. No, no, it's not that. I was just sitting here watching television, and I saw a familiar face. Ah, ha, yes, he'll never live it down. I know! No, look, I was wondering, do you recall the name of that girl who came through last fall? The one who was the big social media star? Remember Locke was over the moon about meeting her? Yes, that's right. Oh, like the artist da Vinci. I get it. Thank you, Penny."

I tugged on her arm until she looked up. I mouthed "Mute," and she did. I said, "Ask her if Kenyatta saw Mona Lisa, or knew about Mona Lisa coming in."

Candy looked flustered like she wouldn't do it, but said into the phone, "Is Kenyatta a fan of hers?" I tried to look into her eyes, but she turned away. "I was wondering. I thought I remember her saying something about it or about her. Oh, you did. She was a fan. That's right, you two talked about it when the second one came in. The one who didn't follow through. Okay, I thought so. Well, you have a good night. Okay, you too. See you tomorrow." She set her phone down and handed mine back. On the screen was Mona Lisa's picture.

"That one," she said.

"Thank you," I said. "You did the right thing, Candy. Though I'm sorry, I guess I've killed the mood, haven't I?"

"She gulped Riesling and squeezed my shoulder. "Oh, I don't know. I'm gonna need something to help me forget this betrayal, Earl."

I scooped up her slender frame and said, "Now, where is the bedroom?"

* * *

I left at about 1 am. The wrestling match was about as good as that kind of thing goes. I don't mean *my* performance. I was a C-minus at best, given the pain I was in from the previous night's exercise, but Candy had all her moves down cold.

It was a nice distraction from the cases, which were only getting more complex and potentially more deadly. The don's grandbaby had been involved in one love triangle with Josh and Harlowe and another with Kenzie and Trey from Fatal Mistake. Funny how both of her rivals were now dead. Momo wasn't going to like this.

The clinic procedure also linked Kenyatta Bell to this mess, further clouding things, and then there was the trailer fire, supposedly set by someone Mona Lisa instructed to do so. Her stink was all over the case. It couldn't have reeked any worse, and I could not envision telling this to Momo. What I could envision was Tommy and Mikey throwing me into a trunk and driving me to a deserted beach, where I'd be dug up forty years later as Generation Next broke ground on a housing development for Millennial seniors.

I was clinging to the hope that Rajeev would be my man. I had no idea how he tied into Boom, or if he did, but his vehicle fit the description of the one seen by Locke from the clinic and Myra on the second floor, and he was evasive when we met. Perhaps I'd get lucky and find that Rajeev was behind all of it, including the Boom deaths. I'd tell Momo and let him take care of it while I walked off with his praise and a wad of cash. Yeah right.

I thought about going home to my bed but looked at the dash clock and knew I could reach The Man Cave before it closed at 2 am. If Rajeev was still working, I'd trail him home and see what developed. If the feds took issue, I'd deal with it. I had to see the case through, and Rajeev was somehow involved.

I made it there in no time and parked in an elevated lot next door that gave me a good view of the club, including the main entrance. The big black Escalade was parked across several spaces as it was the day before. I checked the Caprice for tracking devices but didn't find anything by feel or flashlight. I'd been on the lookout for tails all day, and hadn't seen anything, but somehow Momo had known of my movements that morning. I scanned all around, looking for anything out of place or gangsters or G-men looking back at me. Nothing.

I watched as the clock ran past 2 am, and men began emerging and wobbling to their cars, then exiting onto the desolate strip. Next, a half-dozen tumid women loudly streamed out and into a collection of more upscale automobiles than the ones driven by their customers. About fifteen minutes after this, lights were extinguished, and Rajeev emerged with the security guard who'd given me five seconds to leave the club. They were followed by Missy, the barkeep. She said her goodbyes, climbed into a red Corvette, squealed her tires, and raced up the street. The Coke machine and the scrawny smut purveyor left the lot in a calmer fashion, and I followed at a safe distance.

We drove down Route 1 and onto I-95, then passed a half-dozen exits before getting off in a sleepy suburb. Rajeev's large colonial-style home lay behind a wrought iron gate in a grid of streets not far from the freeway. I stopped about four houses away and watched as he climbed out of the passenger seat, spoke with his security man, and went inside. I ducked as his man passed by while leaving for the night.

I was thinking through my options—stay and observe from the car, get out and get up close, go home and come back in the morning—and was leaning toward the latter when some sneaky mother knocked on my window, and I hit my head on the ceiling. I had my Glock half out of its holster when I recognized the face laughing at me.

Ron Sullivan, FBI special agent, and all-around pain in the ass, but also a decent guy, stood by my window. "Hey, Dingus!"

"Jesus Christ, Sullivan. You're lucky I didn't blow your head off." I rolled the window down, and he squatted so we'd be on the same level.

"So, I'm in town for little thing at the Federal Courthouse today. I go to dinner with a couple of my buddies from 100 Atlantic, you know the Boston office. They start telling me about this guy who showed up and started trouble with this other guy they've been watching. I say that sounds like this asshole who stuck his nose in a case I had last fall. Wouldn't you know it? Turns out, their asshole is my asshole. Maybe you know him too? He looks just like you."

"You're a fucking riot, Sullivan. So, you stayed in Boston to harass me?"

"I have another thing in Boston tomorrow, so the government put me up for the night. All I did was tell them to let me know when you next crossed into their lane, which I knew you would do. Earl Town take instruction from a federal agent? That'll be the day, right? I didn't expect them to call me only hours later, though. Anyway, the look on your face was priceless. It's a good thing for you I didn't think to film it. You'd be a top meme at the Bureau forever."

"Gee, I dodged a real bullet." I could smell the spirits on his breath. "Gin, huh? I thought you Irish cops were all about the whiskey."

"Ah, my old lady wants me to cut a few pounds. I figure clear spirits are probably better for me. The problem is I drink more of them. You hungry? These guys want to go home, and I need a snack."

I hadn't eaten since Kyan's impromptu feast just after sunset. It was now 2:30 am. I said, "I could eat. What's open?"

"You're the Bostonian."

Having only been in Boston for about six years, I never thought of myself as one, but it was nice to be considered a local. I said, "Hell yeah I am. I know a place."

# 19

Sullivan said, "The leather district? You're taking us to the Blue Diner!"

"Yeah, it's open twenty-four hours, and it's great. It's the South Street Diner now."

"Nope, it'll always be Blue to me."

"You know this town better than I do."

"Absolutely, but that ain't saying much, Hampshire boy."

Set 'em up, knock 'em down, that'll forever be Ron Sullivan's jam. He's a lovable asshole. He's my friend, and he'd throw me in jail in a heartbeat if he could. Don't believe me? Here's what he said next.

"You know, there's still no sign of Whitman Endicott."

"We haven't even parked, and you're already giving me shit me about that. We've been through this, Ron. What do you want me to say this time?"

"I just want to know where you buried him. Or scattered the ashes, whatever it was you did."

Whitman Endicott was a man I'd met while on the Greenwich case. The last time I saw him, he was alive and kicking, though I'd have shot him if I could. Actually, I was trying to shoot him at the time. "Maybe I should drop you off. It's been a long day."

"Don't be a wuss, Town. I only mention it because his daughter's trying to have him declared dead, so she'll get the motherload. Strange, a guy worth a couple hundred million just left it all behind instead of doing a short stint for relatively minor offenses."

"As I understand it, he was a sick man. Cancer, I believe. Maybe he threw himself into a volcano. Have you checked any volcanos?"

He snorted and changed the subject, "I talked to Garcia the other day."

I shook my head. "You're just raining haymakers tonight."

"I promised the guys watching the Indian I'd bust your balls. They want to arrest you for obstruction, but I talked them into letting me speak to you first, which is lucky for you. You should take my advice and stay away from the cat you tailed home tonight. You do not want to piss these agents off, Town. They're young and *way* over eager."

I stopped the Caprice, and Sullivan jumped out and announced, "I love this place!" Then he skipped through the door into the blue neon light of the classic diner.

I ordered three eggs over medium, three strips of bacon, and coffee. Sullivan went for a cheeseburger, fries, and a Coke. I said, "Dude, you're only a decade away from a nice pension and the life of leisure. You trying to kill yourself before you get there?"

He frowned. "Maybe I am. Spending my days fishing and fighting with my old lady doesn't hold much appeal."

"An early grave is the better alternative? Jesus, Sullivan."

"Give me a break, I need a little grease to soak up the gin. So, I was saying about Garcia ..." I threw up my hands in surrender, but he didn't stop. "She digs L.A. now and has finally stopped telling me she's moving back."

"You're telling me this, why?"

"You should go visit. She likes you. I don't know why, but she does. She could use some time with a friend from her old life, and you could leave the strip-club boss alone before you get into real trouble."

"Garcia and I haven't talked since before the holidays. I'm pretty sure she's moved on."

"Yeah, well, you never talk to her, so you know jack shit. She's lonely. It's the place she digs, not the people, says they're too plastic."

"Okay," I said. "Consider it considered. Now tell me about Rajeev from The Man Cave."

He put on his thoughtful face and leaned back as the waitress placed our food down. "Tell me you'll leave him alone."

"I'll consider it as well as the trip to Weirdowood."

"Tell me you'll do it, Town." I watched as he lifted the top bun and doused the cheeseburger
in salt before doing the same to the fries.

"I'll drop it," I said, fingers crossed under the table.

He took a big bite and chewed for a bit. It must have been good, as he was humming while he ate. Finally, he swallowed and said, "What can I say without saying too much? Here, he's got an interesting cash flow situation over there. A lot of money moving through that place. Too much money."

"Of course, it's a cash business. We talking Russians? Jihadis?"

"I'm not at liberty to say, but I think his client may be closer to home."

"The mob?" He raised his brows and smiled, and I began to wonder if Rajeev's client was Momo. Just how incestuous were these two cases?

"Now, you talk," said Sullivan, with a fresh mouthful of beef and a tomato seed clinging to his chin.

"I'm looking for a girl who worked at the club. A dancer. She disappeared ten days ago. Rajeev was evasive and lied to me. Technically speaking, he was wildly fucking suspicious. I told this to my friend, Officer Bullpett, who talked to your friends."

I winced as he purposefully licked and sucked burger juice from each finger on his right hand. "I know, they told me. I just want to see if you're consistent. What's her name?"

He sent a text to one of my buddies to inquire about Unique, and I filled in more of the details, while he chowed down on french fries and I flirted with a group of college girls who appeared to be at the last stop of a lengthy bar crawl. They crashed into the diner in a jumble of laughter and shrieks, shoved a couple of tables together, and began barking out orders. One of them kept throwing looks at me while gnawing on a straw, so I smiled and winked at her. This caused a fresh fit of laughter and earned me several smiles back. Sullivan took a call and looked over his shoulder at them as he listened. He disconnected and said, "Into the *really* young stuff, huh? Maybe Garcia isn't your style after all."

I ignored his comment and waited for him to tell me something.

"You said, you think Rajeev might have been seeing your girl romantically?"

"Yeah, her boyfriend supposedly drives an SUV like his."

"You don't have a description of the boyfriend?"

"No, no one has seen him. Don't ask me how."

"My guy says he's never seen Rajeev leave the club with any of the girls. That doesn't mean it's not possible that he's screwing her, but it's unlikely he's your guy, if she's screwing him after her shift as the neighbor claims."

"Is he involved with Momo Ragazzi?"

"Whoa, where's that coming from?"

"You said the client he may be cleaning cash for is close to home. Momo runs the show around here."

"Oh yeah, hmmm. Now cut the shit. Why did you ask about Momo Ragazzi?"

I sipped my water and tried to act nonchalant. It didn't work. "I saved his grandkid in that fire over at the big casino opening, so he's on my mind, that's all."

"You working for him?" The man is part bloodhound.

"This time is different, Sullivan. I'm not a suspect in a case of yours. I don't have to answer your questions."

He changed course again. "I went out to L.A. back in April. Met up with Garcia and went hiking in the Hollywood Hills."

"Yeah?" The drunk girls were looking at me again and giggling. I saluted them with a piece of bacon before shoving it into my mouth. More giggles.

"Amalia's got a studio apartment right off Hollywood Boulevard. Kind of a shitty neighborhood. Well, her place is nice, but walk a half-mile in the wrong direction, and you enter a dystopian nightmare. Anyway, she can walk out her front door and be in Runyon Canyon in under ten minutes."

"Okay. Sounds nice." I then mouthed "what's up?" to one of the girls staring at me. This led to a fresh round of whoops and hoots.

"So, we go for a hike up in the hills, and it's beautiful, man. On my left is the Hollywood sign. To my right is the Griffith Observatory perched up on the hill, like Leo and Kate on the bow of the Titanic."

I had no idea where he was going, but he wasn't asking me about Momo, so I stopped teasing the girls and listened with curiosity.

"You know what you can see when you get up there?"

"I don't know, Sullivan, the L.A. skyline?" I signaled the waitress for more coffee. I needed all the caffeine I could get.

"Well, yeah, of course, the fucking skyline. No, what you can see is right into the backyards of all of these rich fucks who bought these million-dollar houses overlooking the city. Who spends millions of dollars on a place when any old jamoke can come along and watch you swim in your pool?"

"Is there a point to this?"

"Yeah. One, go visit Amalia and go for a hike in the Hollywood Hills. She'd like to see you and the sights are amazing. Two, I can see into your backyard, Town. Tell me something, you spent time around the old-money set in Greenwich last year, and now you're working with mobsters?"

I said, "Any non-comment by me when you say something like that is not an acknowledgment that what you said is true. Understand?"

He laughed, "Oh yeah, sure, Town. So, my question is, who's worse, your friends in Greenwich or your friends in the North End?"

I sipped the thick black java and worked through the many

cons and few pros of the two sides. After a bit, I said, "You know, I guess I just have more issues with America's elites than with mobsters. Pretty sad state of affairs, but my feeling is that at least the gangsters don't sanctimoniously preach values while robbing us blind. Gangsters are far more upfront about their scumbaggery, and I appreciate that."

Sullivan leaned back and patted his belly. He plucked the last french fry from his plate and swirled it in a puddle of ketchup. "Yeah, I can't really disagree with you there. But be careful with these North End guys. I've seen some of their victims. They won't hesitate to cut your throat if it becomes convenient."

I held out my palms. "Me, piss them off? Not my style."

Sully chuckled and said, "Look, send me the photo of the girl, and I'll ask my colleagues to check the video for recent sightings. And, if she turns up, I'll let you know. But here's one more piece of advice. Lay off the Indian. If you keep messing with him, our agents are going to take you down, *hard*."

*      *      *

I went home, showered, and caught about two hours of sleep, then hit the road again. I didn't know what time Josh Fagle left for the office and wanted to be there when he did. I parked a few doors down, with a good view of his front stoop and his sparkling penis, I mean Porsche. I watched his neighbors getting their morning exercise and stumbling out to their cars in suits, hands full of travel mugs, bags, and backpacks, but Josh's place stayed quiet. At 7:30, I called Irving.

"Hello?" he groaned.

"Rise and shine, my Hebrew friend."

"What? Who?" I heard a woman's voice in the background.

"Got company, eh? Unique won't be happy about it, but then again, she was two-timing you."

"Two-timing me? No problem, we weren't serious. You find her?"

"No, but I think I know why she disappeared."

"Really? Do tell."

"First, tell me something. You ever see her with another guy, or see a guy hanging around the club or her apartment in a black SUV with tinted windows?"

"No, I don't recall anyone like that." I could hear his joints cracking as he sat up.

"I know a good chiropractor if you're looking for one."

"Yeah, thanks. It's an old mattress. Gotta get a new one."

"Probably tough finding a round one, huh?"

"What?"

"Nothing, Hef. Did Unique ever tell you about her volunteer work at the clinic?"

"Mmm, I'm not sure, refresh my memory."

I filled him in on the clinic and how I came to find it. Then I gave him some background on the Phillips and Knight deaths and the potential link. He wasn't buying it.

"I don't know, Earl. I trust you because I know you, but just because that girl got a procedure there? You think someone killed those people? I don't get why."

"The *why* is to keep a blackmail scheme from being exposed."

"Who's being blackmailed?"

"I'd rather not say just yet, to protect the innocent, should I be wrong."

"Hmmm," said Irv. "So, when are you going to find out?"

"In about three minutes."

I watched as Josh Fagle emerged and looked all around like a nervous gopher. He decided the coast was clear and jogged to his Porsche, which he promptly revved, threw into reverse, and peeled out in.

✻ ✻ ✻

If I could've reached without my sides aching, I would've

patted myself on the back after I picked Josh's lock and let myself in. It was an airy two-story condo, with marble floors and mahogany trim. The kitchen was over-the-top European styling with Ferrari-red lacquer cabinets and a humongous stainless steel refrigerator and eight-burner grill top. From the kitchen island, I watched waves roll into Marina Bay and saw the sails of distant of boats pass by. It was the kind of place I expected from a guy like Josh.

The décor was not, however, up to snuff. I'd describe it for you, but there was none. There were no sofas, only a couple of chintzy chairs, no dining table, or end or coffee, tables, and no lamps, no electronics, and no shelving, aside from a pair of built-ins on either side of the fireplace. Most importantly, however, was the lack of art on the walls. There were hooks, where it had once been, but the hooks were barren. I wondered why Josh hadn't sold the Porsche until I found the lease agreement in a steel box next to a mattress sitting on the floor in the upstairs master suite.

They'd taken him for everything he had. Whatever it was they had on him, it had to be life and death, at least in his mind. No man would go to this extreme over a small indiscretion. Knocking up the teenage granddaughter of a mafia don seemed to fit the bill pretty well. Now the question was who did the killing? Who was so concerned about Ray Phillips and Kenzie Knight spilling the beans on the blackmail plot to kill them? To whom had Kenyatta "Unique" Bell told her secret? This person or persons had to be the same.

I needed to talk with Josh Fagle. I hopped into the Caprice and headed for the highway and Boom Productions. According to the app, my ETA was 25 minutes. My phone buzzed as I was pulling away from the curb.

"Hey, where are you?"

"I'm on my way to Boom Productions. Where are you this fine morning, Richie?"

"I'm in front of your apartment. Why aren't you here?"

"Uber to Boom and meet me."

"You said you'd meet here at nine."

"Sorry, kid. I never went home last night." I lied. "See you at Boom."

I exited the highway a short while later onto a tree-lined, two-lane road that would take me to a series of office parks, the third of which was the home of Boom Productions. I was doing about sixty in a forty-five zone when an idiot in a garbage truck rolled through a stop sign into my lane. I cut it hard left to avoid a crash. Thankfully, there was nobody coming the other way, or it would've been sayonara Earl. But unfortunately, the hard cut and the speed were a bad combination, and instead of straightening out and moving on with my middle finger extended, I skidded into a ditch, which would've been alright if I hadn't hit an elevated sewage grate that tore up my transmission. The car came to a stop, and I slammed face-first into my airbag, which was good because it muffled the string of four-letter epithets that streamed out of me. I watched the truck amble down the road oblivious as I searched for my Triple-A card.

An hour later, Kamal, Richie's peeved Uber driver and self-appointed spokesman for legal pot, which seems an odd combination for a driver, dropped us off at a Hertz rental agency, where I proceeded to drop a chunk of my fee down on a mid-size Ford something or other. Richie liked it because it didn't look like a cop car. I hated everything about it and begged my mechanic to fix the Caprice by day's end.

We climbed into the new ride, when Richie said, "Okay, onto Boom. Why are we going there, anyway?"

"We're not. My plan was to corner Josh Fagle again, but I watched him drive by as my car was being loaded onto the truck. I called his partner and inquired about his whereabouts ..."

"You on good terms with his partner?"

"Yeah, I went shooting with him last night. You need to keep up."

"So, where is he?"

"Sharpe says he doesn't know. He came in, grabbed a few

things from his office, and left."

"Bullshit, let's go back there and squeeze Sharpe."

"No. For one thing, I just told you he and I were shooting last night. The guy has a license to carry and a small arsenal. Starting fights with guys like him is a good way to get killed. For another thing, I know where Fagle is gonna be in a couple of hours. We'll get him then."

# 20

I had just finished leaving a voicemail for BPD officer De-Shawn Bullpett reminding him of my delicious breakfast and asking why he hadn't gotten back to me regarding the lead cop on the Kenzie Knight case, when my phone buzzed and Pam's number showed up on the screen. I shushed Richie, who was complaining about his cell reception, and answered.

"Don Juan."

"Funny, Town."

"Pam Prentiss, always a pleasure to hear your voice, like a chorus of angels."

"Mmm, hmm. I'm gonna regret this, but where are you?"

"Ninety-three north, about two miles from the tunnel. Why?"

"I have a friend here who would like to talk to you about the Kenzie Knight case."

"Who's that?"

"Get your sweet little ass over here and find out."

"That's harassment, Pam. Not that I mind it," I said with a chuckle. Richie arched his eyebrows.

"No, it's not. Once you have sex with someone, that all goes out the window."

I blinked and thought back to New Year's. Had we really gone that far? I went quiet as I tried to piece together the end of that evening. Pam broke the silence. "You moron. You're wracking your brain trying to remember if we did it. You know, you really are a pathetic drunk. We didn't do it, jackass. Now get your butt over here. I don't have all day."

Pam's unmarked Ford Crown Vic was parked in the lot of an old-timey meeting house in Quincy. I drove past it and parked far enough away for them to not see Richie sitting in my passenger seat, but Pam had a good set of eyes and saw me pass by, which she let me know as I climbed into the back seat.

"Going soft, Town? What's with the family sedan?"

"It's a rental. I had a little accident this morning."

"Who's your friend?"

"Summer intern. He's a criminal justice major at Suffolk."

Pam said, "Yeah, right, and I'm starring in the new Tarantino flick."

"I always pictured you as more of a character actor."

She groaned and introduced her passenger. "This is Lyle Hand of the Boston P.D. He's the lead on the Kenzie Knight case."

Lyle rotated his huge bald melon and stuck a large hand over the seat. We shook and grinned at one another.

"Thanks for setting this up, Pam." I looked at Lyle and asked, "Did DeShawn Bullpett reach out to you?"

He said, "Yeah, he did, but I'll be honest with you. I don't like private eyes. Always getting in the way." Lyle was a large African American man with a neck about as thick as my thigh. He was so tall that his head brushed up against the ceiling liner.

"Did he mention I'm an ex-cop?"

"Yup. Then I asked where from."

"You don't like New Hampshire cops?"

"Nope, small-town guys are almost as big a pain in the ass as private eyes." Pam was getting a real kick out of this.

"So, what changed your mind? I mean other than Pam's powerful persuasion. I'm told she can get men to do things they later regret." Her laughter ceased.

"She mentioned you have a theory about my case, said you may have actually stumbled across something interesting, so here I am."

"So, she's put her reputation on the line, has she? I mean, if I come off as a total idiot, it won't reflect well on her will it?"

Pam said, "If? You're doing a great job already, idiot."

I said, "Okay, here's what I got," and I walked them through the tale of the doomed Fagle/Harlowe union.

Pam cut in. "Come on, I told you yesterday, the blackmail angle is weak if this girl's pregnancy is all you got, Town."

"Ah, but it's not, Prentiss. I've got more now. Just give me a minute. It still needs fleshing out, but it offers a real motive." She raised an eyebrow while Hand cooed a little.

"Harlowe Phillips is not the first Boom Girl that Fagle knocked up. Apparently, the kid's got wandering eyes and super sperm. Before he knocked up Harlowe, he got another of the girls pregnant, and she terminated it." I paused, waiting for Pam to put her foot in her mouth.

"Okay, so he knocked up two girls. So what?"

"Are you familiar with the Boom Girls?"

"Yes," said an annoyed Pam.

I looked at Hand, and he nodded.

I hated to reveal this card, given the identity of my client, but it was going to come out at some point because my hunch sure felt right. I said, "Of the three remaining girls, there's one who has certain family connections."

Hand whistled long and low.

Pam said, "Oh, shit."

"Yeah. If grandpa gangster finds out, little Josh is gonna drop off the face of the earth." I watched as the two cops eyed one another and acknowledged the newly invigorated blackmail motive, and added, "Oh, and Fagle's apartment is empty. His Porsche is leased, so he's still driving it, but his art and furniture are gone. Even the closets are mostly barren."

Hand said, "Maybe the two Phillips were blackmailing him, and he killed them."

"Maybe, but that doesn't explain Kenzie Knight."

Pam chewed on this and said. "Shit, Town, you actually came up with some real cheese here. I'm impressed."

Hand said, "The granddaughter of Momo Ragazzi, unbelievable. So, your assumption is that the blackmailer threatened to tell the don about the pregnancy?"

"You got it, Lyle."

Pam said, "I still don't buy it. So why kill the Phillips girl and her father and Kenzie Knight?"

"I believe Ray Phillips learned of the first pregnancy and threatened to expose this as part of his rage hard-on for Boom Productions. Fagle told the blackmailers hoping they'd kill the two Phillips to protect their scheme, and they did."

Pam said in a skeptical tone, "Would a blackmailer add murder to his resume in order to keep the blackmail plot quiet? That feels like one hell of a stretch, Town." Hand agreed.

"I know. There's still a lot to be fleshed out, but there are too many connections here for it to all be coincidence."

I looked at Hand and asked, "Do you have Kenzie Knight's phone?"

"Yeah, we've been through it looking for a drug dealer, which we doubt exists."

"I've heard that you'll find that Harlowe Phillips called Kenzie in the moments before she died. I have a feeling she also told Kenzie about Mona Lisa's, er, problem."

Pam said, "How do you know this?"

"I'm not getting into sources."

"Wait a minute," said Pam. "What about the kid who set the fire? He worked for the don's grandkid, and he took a dive off a roof in the North End yesterday. Is this some kind of mob war thing?" Lyle's eyes went wide.

"That's a stretch," I said.

"You were there. What did you see?" Lyle asked.

I thought *Oh my God. This is it. They know about the roof and are gonna hit me with manslaughter.* I said, "I was not there!"

Pam said, "What do you mean, meathead? Your forehead is still red."

"Oh yeah, right." I unclinched. "The fire happened so fast I didn't see anything out of the ordinary. I felt a rumble, looked up, and saw a wall of fire backed by screams. A fireman told me it had to be set with accelerant."

Hand said, "Oh yeah, he tried to kill her, but why? Odd thing about that kid taking the header yesterday. Nobody seems to have seen anything. The whole neighborhood just clammed up. Kind of like a mob hit."

Pam slapped the steering wheel. "Exactly! You better not be holding out on us, Town. This is serious shit you're involved in."

"Huh?" I said, meekly. "It's not a mob thing. It's a blackmail thing. Relax."

Pam said, "Fagle lives in Quincy, maybe I should bring him in and sweat him. See what he can tell me about this blackmail business. Not that it changes the fact that Ray Phillips killed himself and his kid. You still got that wrong, Town."

This is exactly what I did not want. I said, "I spoke with him yesterday, and he was really spooked by everything. He might run on you. I recommend surveillance first. See if you can catch him making a drop and catch the blackmailer when he makes the pick-up."

"Thanks for the unsolicited advice. I don't trust you, Town."

Hand said, "So, do you even have a suspect?"

"I did, but I don't anymore." I didn't want to get into Rajeev and the connection to the clinic and Unique.

"Why not?"

"He's being watched by the feds, and they tell me he's not my guy."

"They don't want you getting in their way!" Officer Hand was thrilled to have some support for his opinion of private eyes.

"So, right now, your blackmail story hinges on Fagle being broke," said Pam.

I shrugged. "Maybe he's a gambler instead, but the blackmail angle fits like one of your well-tailored suits, Pam."

"Keep my appearance out of this, or I'll *me too* you. Maybe he has a second home that he's moving his belongings into."

"Maybe he has a unicorn," I said before I changed the subject. "So, Lyle, I've spilled my guts, tell me about the passing of Miss

Knight?"

"This stays between us, cowboy."

"Of course," I said with a little extra verve as though I was offended. I wasn't.

He said, "We're leaning toward homicide. Miss Knight smoked the vape sporadically, not every day. She smoked both tobacco-based and Cannabidiol, or CBD-based, cartridges. She purchased the tobacco cartridges at a shop in Norwood and the CBD ones at a dispensary in Somerville." After a short pause, he elaborated, "The cartridge that killed her was tobacco-based but laced with an extremely high dose of fentanyl. An amount that could be expected to kill the user with one or two tokes. We believe the cartridge was purchased by Kenzie, and previously smoked by her, and that someone removed it from her pen, injected it with fentanyl, and placed it back."

"Got any suspects?" I asked.

"Yeah, we're working a few angles. Social media fans and possible stalkers. Possibly a competing social media influencer."

"You mean, like one of the other Boom girls?"

"Perhaps. What do you know about them?"

I thought of something and asked Pam a question before answering Hand. "Did you look into the landlord?"

"Yup, he reported her missing. His record's clean too." She looked at Hand and said, "A separate case."

"Right," he said, in a Barry White basso.

I wavered on telling her about the connection. I could use their help in identifying Unique's boyfriend, but I also didn't need them getting in my way. I'd already shared too much. I changed the subject back to Lyle's question. "The Boom Girls are an odd lot. I haven't spent enough time with them to really get a good feel. It's a well I plan to tap soon. They're all incredibly successful, and I suspect, also intelligent and deceitful. That is if they're anything like the dead girls."

Pam threw me a curious look. I said, "What I meant is the two dead girls had some big secrets—affairs, pregnancies, drug problems. I suspect the others are keeping secrets too. I'll tell you one thing. For a group of girls whose young co-workers and, to some extent, friends had their lives ended in brutal fashion within the last fortnight, they sure as hell don't seem too upset about it."

Pam and Lyle looked at one another. Pam said, "That's interesting, Town. Why do you think that is?"

"I don't know. Envy probably. You tell me, Prentiss. You know more about what goes on inside the minds of young women. What would you have been capable of if you were competing against a group of girls for fame and fortune at, say, age nineteen?"

"I'm pretty certain I'd have killed at least one of them." Hand and I laughed, but Pam didn't crack a smile.

"You two must have interviewed them. What'd you glean?"

"I didn't *glean* shit," said Pam. "My case was open and shut. I'm willing to listen to what you have to say mainly because Lyle's case is not, and the close proximity to mine intrigues me, but mine was clear cut."

"Duly noted," I said guiltily. "How about you, Lyle? What do you think of the surviving Boom Girls?"

"What do I think about a bunch of spoiled-rotten princesses? Not much. I've seen what you've seen. They don't seem all that upset, and they don't seem to know anything about anything, which is bullshit. They seemed coached to me."

"Ah," I said. "Coached is a good word for it. Have you spoken to Divya Singh?"

"Of course. Didn't get much out of her, though."

"Me either," I said, "but I think she's the one keeping them on message. It's all part of what she does for the brands they promote. Now she's doing it to protect the Boom brand."

"Maybe I need to sweat her, too," said Hand.

"It might be worth a try, but you'll have to find some leverage. Otherwise, I don't think she'll crack. She's smooth." I noticed Pam watching me with a look of disgust as I smiled at the image I'd conjured of Divya.

She said to Hand, "You good?" He nodded. "Okay, see you

later, Town." I climbed out and ducked as she spun her tires and
flung gravel.

# 21

It was time for the host to derive some value from the parasite. I told Richie to call his cousin and arrange a visit. Mona Lisa was home from the hospital, having been released that morning, and was resting. Soon we were on our way to meet with her and her roomie, Lake Gelson.

Boston's queens of social media lived on Columbus Avenue. Their place was only a mile or two away from mine, but worlds apart. They were closer to downtown, the theatre district, Newbury Street, Quincy Market, you name it. Places around there run double or triple what I pay in rent, though I did get an excellent deal for having gotten my landlord's kid out of trouble a while back on a stolen jewelry rap. He was involved, just not to the degree the prosecution alleged, and walked away with a wrist slap. I parked, and we were immediately set upon by an aging, thick-necked mook in a mob uniform—dark jacket, slacks, dark shirt. He stepped out of a Lincoln Navigator and approached my door with intent. "Can I help you?"

Richie leaned across me and said, "Hey, Sonny. You keeping my cousin safe?"

"Hey, kid! I didn't recognize you with the square." We got out of the rental, and he and Richie hugged it out.

Sonny said, "Momo has Tony Two-Face and me on split shift." Then he looked me over and said to Richie, "You hanging around cops now?"

"Nope. Momo asked me to babysit him."

"So, he's on the payroll?"

I said, "I'm a private dick, not a cop. I'm on a brief retainer."

"He used to be a cop, though," Richie chimed in.

"Oh, you don't have to tell me," said Sonny. "It's obvious."

I considered challenging him on what was so obvious, but it was time to fold a bad hand. Instead, I said, "I'm going up." I gave a quick look back at Sonny as if to say *try and stop me*. He didn't, and Richie told me he'd catch up with me.

The section of Columbus on which the girls lived consisted of three- and four-story brownstones, some of which were still owned by wealthy individuals, while others were divided into apartments or condos. The starlets shared a small two-bedroom apartment on the top floor. I knocked, waited, knocked again, then tried the knob. It turned and opened, and I stuck my head in. "Hello."

No answer. "Hello. Anyone home?" I stepped into a small living room and kitchen space at the end of which were three doors. I moved down the hall and heard a shower running from behind door number one. Doors two and three revealed unkempt bedrooms littered with expensive-looking clothing and accessories. Judging by the photographs, the bedroom facing the street was Mona Lisa's. Her window was cracked, and there was loud music wafting in. I peered down at the street to find the source, but the noise seemed to be coming from above. My ears perked as the water shut off, and I decided to investigate the roof before I got mistaken for a peeper. Back in the hallway, I found a narrow set of steps and began my ascension, one that finished with my emergence into the heat of a magnificent sun.

I'd found the apartment's best feature—a rooftop deck, with views of the city skyline and a place for young starlets to sunbath without risk of tan lines, which Lake Gelson was doing when my shadow crossed her eyeline, and she perked up.

"You're the detective."

I slid on my Ray-Ban's, removed my jacket, and perched on the edge of the lounge chair beside hers. I leaned back on my hands, so my shadow wouldn't interfere with her rays and got hit by a pain in my side. She noticed, though I did my best to hide it. "Are you okay?"

"Oh, I'm fine. You're observant, Miss Gelson. That's good. Maybe you can help me."

She shrugged, glanced down, and flicked an insect from her soft, tan flesh into the warm breeze. Ed had actually undersold the view. She wore only suntan lotion and a small towel nestled strategically between her thighs. Her attentive eyes peered at me through over-sized tortoiseshell shades. She ran her tongue over her bottom lip, then sucked it back in and bit said lip.

"You're lucky. There's a lot of men out there who would pay good money to see me like this."

"To see you lounging on a Friday afternoon?"

She giggled and squeezed my arm. She looked down at her breasts and said, "Oh, the wind, it's having an effect."

Her nipples had sprouted, and I wondered if she could conjure that up whenever needed. If so, Boom was missing out on a revenue source. She said, "I made my name teasing men, you know. I'd show 'em just enough to keep them coming back, but I never gave them what they really wanted. It's my motto: *Never give 'em what they want.*"

"What is it that they want?"

She put on her best Scarlet O'Hara and said, "Why, Mr. Town. You all want what's under the towel, of course." She glanced down at her lap and laughed.

Realizing there was no way she could see it with the twins blocking her view, I made an obvious peek at the area down there and said, "Towel?"

She panicked for a second, then threw her head back and laughed like a movie star. I fought to keep my eyes on hers and said, "The night Kenzie overdosed. Sunday was it?"

"No, Saturday."

"Right," I said. I took out my phone, shielded the screen, and pulled up a picture that Nephew Ed had sent me earlier. We'd been exchanging texts to get around the problem of my Italian hemorrhoid. He had found several interesting things on Lake's past and present social media accounts.

I showed the screen to Lake and said, "This photo from your Instagram was taken at the Karma Club about an hour before Kenzie overdosed. She's sitting nearby while you smoke a vape pen. Whose pen is it?"

She had gone back to resting her head on the chairback. She rotated it slightly, peered, and said, "That's mine. I was getting high, but she wouldn't partake. Crowds gave her paranoia. She would've hated the casino show."

"Where do you keep it?"

"It?"

"Your vape pen."

"Uh, usually in my purse or in a pocket, if I feel I'm going to need it in an emergency. You know, like if a photographer or director is being a dick. Why do you ask?"

"Where did Kenzie keep hers?"

"Oh," she said. "It was usually in the console of her car."

"How many people knew it was there?"

"Did you talk to the cops? Cause I already went through all this with them."

"Yes, but Mona Lisa's grandfather needs me to hear it from the source."

"Uh-huh. Well then, anyone who'd driven with her. She kept it in plain sight between the seats. It's cool now, everyone does it."

"Did she do hard drugs?"

"I don't think so. We didn't talk that much. She thought she was better than me. She's not the only one."

"Madison?"

"No, she's sweet. Harlowe, she was religious *and* arrogant. I heard her mother hit the roof when she found my old videos online. She acted *so* shocked, but I'll bet she and her husband had seen worse. You know what they say about holy-rollers."

"Did the Phillips take issue with certain relatives of Mona Lisa's too?"

"You bet they did." She grinned. "You're hanging with the bad girls, detective. Unfortunately, the good girls can't be here, because they're dead." She didn't laugh, or frown or anything, she just said it, like it was nothing.

I nodded and admired the collection of shiny new towers that had sprung up in what had been Boston's rundown waterfront. "The apartment is tiny, but this rooftop deck makes it worthwhile."

"Yes, it certainly does. What are you doing anyway, detective? I mean, you haven't found anything to suggest the deaths are suspicious, have you?"

I shrugged and wiped the moisture from my brow. The breeze had gone, and there was no shade. "Did either of them have enemies?"

She pointed to a bottle of Evian on the ground beside me. I moved to hand it to her, and she sat up and brushed against me.

I said, "No need to get up, I could've reached."

"Now what fun would that be?" she looked into my eyes.

"You didn't answer my question." She threw her head back and took a long sip. I said, "What about enemies?"

She set down the bottle and arched her back. "Enemies?"

"Yeah, as in people who might want either of them dead. Did they have them?"

"No. Of course not."

I said, "Mona Lisa hated her." That startled her. She tensed up, then tried to shrug it off. I added, "She and Josh almost had a family, then Harlowe moves in. That couldn't have gone over well." She lay still, staring at the sun through her big glasses.

"Okay. Here's another one. Why did you lure Ray and Harlowe to their deaths at the old quarry?"

"What the fuck!" She stood and grabbed a robe that had been piled on the ground by her chair. She said, "Who told you that?"

"I got a guy who's really good with computers. He can find anything, even deleted tweets and posts. By the way, I like that you referenced Betty Page in your phony account handle. You do share some qualities." She took a step toward the transom, and I grabbed her wrist. "Who put you up to messaging Ray about the dirty movie shoot?"

"Ow, you're hurting me!"

"That's the idea. You're an accomplice to a double homicide. Who put you up to it? Your roommate?" I squeezed her ulna bone, and she shrieked.

Her shout caught the attention of Sonny and Richie just as they emerged from the bulkhead that led to the rooftop. Mona Lisa was right behind them.

Richie stopped and said, "What's going on, man?"

Sonny approached with menace. I let her go. "She lured the Phillips duo to the murder scene. I want to know who put her up to it."

Mona Lisa said, "Is this true?"

Lake cinched her robe. "No! He's out of his mind! I did nothing of the sort." Eager to avoid further confrontation, she headed for the stairs.

Mona Lisa watched her pass, turned to me, and said, "What are you doing?"

"What your grandfather hired me to do. She's lying. Maybe you can shed some light?"

It was time for Sonny to play tough guy. "I don't like your tone, cop."

"I don't like your line of work, criminal."

Richie stepped between us. "Whoa. It's okay, Sonny. He's not gonna do anything stupid. Momo will make him pay if he does."

I smiled at Sonny and said, "Yeah, maybe he'll send you to do it. You can jump me when my back is turned."

"What does that mean?" said the mobster.

"You think it was him?" Richie asked.

I shrugged. I was just throwing it out there. Sonny's face told me it wasn't him.

Mona Lisa said, "I appreciate what you did for me, but you are rude."

I said, "How about we sit for a minute. I'd like to ask you a few things." I sat on the edge of a lounger and gestured to Mona Lisa and Richie to do the same. I said to Sonny, "Why don't you do your job and keep an eye on the street?"

"Why don't you fuck yourself, cop?"

Mona Lisa said, "Stop it." Sonny gave me hard eyes but did as he was told and walked to the edge of the roof, where he could watch me and the street in front.

"A little birdy told me Kenzie called you the day after Harlowe's death."

Mona Lisa glared at me. "Let me guess, that birdy is obsessed with its Instagram following."

"Is there more you can tell me about this call?"

"Not really."

"I understand you hung up on her, but maybe she told you something first."

Mona Lisa sighed as though she was being wildly put out. "She told me Harlowe called her the night she was killed."

"Is that it?"

"Yes."

"So, she didn't mention Harlowe's emotional state when she called?"

"Yeah! She said Harlowe was upset about something."

"The birdy told me she was frantic."

"Yeah."

"You didn't ask Kenzie why, or what else was said?"

"No, I didn't care what Kenzie had to say. I didn't like Kenzie anymore."

"Todd told us you instructed him to set the fire for publicity."

"I did not! When did you talk to Tard?"

"Shortly before he died."

"I don't believe you."

I threw Richie a look, and he said, "I heard him say it, cuz. But I told this jamoke it was bullshit."

"It's not true," she said.

"Why did he try to kill you?"

"How should I know?"

"Maybe he had enough of being called bitch and tard."

"Maybe," she said with a roll of her eyes.

She said it with such nonchalance, I saw red for a moment and said, "So, did you kill Harlowe and Kenzie?"

Mona Lisa practically shrieked, "What?"

Richie said, "Hold on!"

Sonny left his position along the roofline and started coming my way.

"I know about you and Fagle, and the clinic, and I know that Harlowe knew. Maybe Kenzie knew too. Maybe you wanted to keep it quiet? It's understandable. I mean, the desire to keep it quiet is. Did you do it?"

"You pig," she snarled.

"Did you love Josh?"

"No!" Her body language said maybe.

She whipped out her phone, and I grabbed it away. She had pulled up Mama Ginny's number. I put it in my pocket. Mona Lisa stood and yelled, "Who do you think you are?" Sonny got within inches. Richie moved between us.

"Call him off," I nodded at Sonny.

Mona Lisa said, "Give me back my phone."

I did as she asked, but said, "Leave mommy out of this." She cooled and told Sonny to back off. He moved a few feet away and scowled. Richie joined him.

I said, "Your roommate sent messages to Ray Phillips about Josh filming a dirty movie at the old quarry. She led him and your friend to their deaths. Did you ask her to?"

"I don't believe you, and I haven't killed anyone. You need to leave."

Richie said, "That's a good idea," and tugged on my arm. "You've done a great job pissing everyone off."

As we reached the stairwell, Mona Lisa shouted,

"I didn't tell that retard to set the fire. He tried to kill me."

I looked over my shoulder. "And I saved you. Now you're alive, and he's dead, just like the others. It's funny, isn't it? All three had beefs with you, and now they're dead."

# 22

We were on our way to the first of two wakes for Kenzie Knight, which is where I expected to find Josh Fagle.

"I don't like how you treated my cousin. My grandfather is not going to like it either."

"Momo is paying me to keep your cousin safe. My questioning of her and the manner in which I did it were designed to get her cooperation, which I need to fulfill my mission."

"Cooperation? She hates your guts, as does Lake."

"I'm not here to make friends, Richie."

"Well, you're certainly accomplishing that," he said, as he started tapping his phone. We drove in silence for a while, until he began complaining about our destination.

"I don't wanna look at her, man. It creeps me out, she was so young."

I said, "*You* have a problem with dead bodies? That doesn't really jive with the family business."

"Yeah, well. My grandfather says, if you do the job right, no one has to get hurt."

"You don't really believe that, do you? It's a nice theory, but in the real world, shit happens that you can't control, and the only way to regain control is to eliminate that shit *permanently*."

"Look, man, that's none of your business. Hell, if you'd take care of business and put Momo's mind at ease, I could be doing something more interesting."

"Like what?"

"Like making time with a few girls I got on the line. Like spending time with my mother before I go back to school. She gets crazy when I leave."

"You go to school in Providence. It's an hour away."

"You're not Italian. You couldn't begin to understand."

"Mama's boy, huh?" Richie looked out the window.

"Hey, I think it's cool that you live at school. My nephew, he's a great kid, but he's 31 and still living with his mother. I don't understand what he's afraid of. Life is for living and living requires risk. You gotta climb the rocky slope and hang out over the edge sometimes. You appear to be doing that, so kudos. What are you gonna do after you finish school?"

He watched the scenery and ignored me.

"That sounds great. A man's gotta have a plan. Don't wanna be chasing kids off roofs your whole life."

He held up a fist and slowly raised the middle finger.

I decided to call Ed.

"Where you been, Earl?"

"Oh, just keeping an eye on my client's little grandson." Richie must have had an itch under his chin.

"Find anything?"

"On Kenyatta Bell?"

"Yup."

"No, nothing posted to her social media accounts."

"Any of her friends say anything interesting?"

"No. She manages her social media for business rather than pleasure. Her friends are mostly male customers. If she has personal accounts, I can't find them."

"Did you call Rocky and ask if the cops are on it?"

"Yeah, he said he didn't sense much concern. He said unless her mother calls them, the cops ain't ... uh, let me find the note with his exact words. Ah, here it is, the cops ain't doing jack shit. Your friend Hiney got back to me on Rajeev, though."

"Yeah? Do tell." Despite keeping his eyes on his phone, Richie was obviously listening. If I could've pushed a button and ejected the goofball into the overhanging treetops, I would've.

"He doesn't just let his bodyguards do his dirty work. He did five years in Walpole for manslaughter. Robbed a convenience store with an accomplice who killed a sixty-four-year-old cashier named Floridita DeJesus from Lawrence. He had a couple of B&E busts before that."

"No shit? Anything recent?"

"No, apparently, he's been successfully rehabilitated by the state."

"Oh yeah, he's a model citizen." I looked over at Richie to make him think I was talking about him. He turned, and his eyebrows touched.

"What about the woman in red?" I asked Ed.

"The red Corvette? Your friend Chief Hines said she's clean, aside from a few moving violations. Got a lead foot, apparently. He gave me an address. I sent it to you earlier." I told him to wait for a second and pulled up his text.

"Hey, she lives up the street from where I'm headed. I just might pop in for a visit."

"It's a good thing you finally checked your messages."

"Sorry, Ed. I was on a roof deck with a sunbathing Lake Gelson when you sent it." I heard him knock something over.

"Bullshit."

I turned my phone toward my passenger, and said loudly, "Richie, how did Lake Gelson look naked?"

Richie shook his head and let out a long, loud burst of air, loud enough for Ed to hear. "Pffffffffffffffffffffftttttttttttt," then finished it off with "Mardone!"

I put the phone back to my ear, and Ed said, "Aw, damn."

"Yes, my eyes have never been happier. You know what, Ed?"

"What?"

"You undersold them." I hung up and left him to drown in a deep ocean of envy. Being an uncle is always great, but some days are better than others.

"Who was that?" Richie asked as he cleared his nose by sucking its disgusting contents down his throat.

"Edwina, my assistant. She's my researcher by day and a stripper by night."

"Oh yeah, a peeler? I know lotsa them. Where's she work?"

"Emily's Basement, a private club for nerds."

"Emily's Basement." He thought about it. "That on Mass Ave., by the Brazilian barbecue?"

I nodded.

"Who supplies their liquor?"

"How the hell should I know?" I watched as he took out his phone and made a note to look into it.

* * *

Ten minutes later, I was staring through a screen door at Missy, the bartender from The Man Cave. She was wearing a succinct silk robe and fuzzy slippers. Her brown locks were mussed, and her stance unsteady. I said, "Feeling a little under the weather, are we?"

She said, "What the hell are you doing on my doorstep? And, who the hell is he?"

Richie was wearing sunglasses and gazing over my shoulder at Missy's long, lean frame. I said, "That's my intern, Rico, from Puglia, we heard you make a great Bolognese. Could we come in for a minute? I have a couple of questions about the recipe, and maybe I could make you a cup of a coffee, or pour you a little hair of the dog?"

She blew a loose strand of hair from her eyes. "What do you want?"

"I want to find Kenyatta 'Unique' Bell in one piece, but I'm beginning to fear that's not gonna happen. Your boss seems to be hiding something."

"I don't know anything," she insisted.

"I'm told she had a boyfriend who drives a black SUV. You

know, like the one Rajeev gets chauffeured around in. Maybe it was Rajeev, maybe not. But if it was Rajeev, and he was seeing Unique outside of the club, then you'd probably have some idea of that, wouldn't you?"

She sighed and raised a hand to wave the lock of hair from her eyes this time, and her robe fell open just enough. I wouldn't have noticed except that I sensed Richie was standing on tiptoes behind me, so I instinctively looked down to see what he was looking at. Her eyes followed mine, and she clasped it shut, pursed her lips and raised an eyebrow at me, then him. She said, "You're nothing but trouble," stepped back and started to slam the door.

That's when Richie blurted out, "Joey Smalls."

Missy stopped the door mid-swing, and said, "What the fuck did you say?"

I turned and faced Richie in amazement. He said, "I remember you. He found trouble, didn't he?"

Missy combusted and screamed, "Who the fuck are you?"

Richie looked at me and arched his brow. I said, "You familiar with Momo Ragazzi?"

My words hit her like a jab from Tyson. Her head jerked back, then slowly came forward as she peered through the screen studying his features, which in the light on her porch made him look not a little like Momo himself. I said, "You're looking at his heir."

She stared harder and said, "ID."

I looked at Richie and shrugged. "She's a bartender."

He reached into his pocket and flashed his driver's license. Missy read the name and immediately unlocked the screen door. She stepped aside, and we went in.

She lived in a development of two-story brick townhouse condominiums just off a main street lined with strip malls. Her place had white tile floors, oversized windows, and furnishings by Pottery Barn. She kept it tidy and rather dull for a girl who worked at a strip club and drove a red Corvette. I said, "Geez, the Cleavers would be comfortable here."

They both quizzically said, "The Cleavers?"

"Forget it. When did everybody get so young?"

"Give me a minute to put something on," she said, as she tramped down a short, shadowy hallway.

"Don't do that on our account," I said with a wink at the surprisingly useful nitwit from Brown. He looked bored and took a seat on a stool by the kitchen counter while I scanned photographs on the walls. Being crazy fit, I thought I'd see shots of Missy on the beach or mountain climbing, but it was all family, including a couple of her and what looked to be a husband and a boy toddler. Meet the Smalls.

She fixed herself in a bathroom at the end of the hall. The door was open, and the light threw a shadow of her bare figure on the opposite wall.

"I sidled up next to Richie and whispered, "Was Joey's trouble of the fatal variety?"

He nodded.

"Did Momo have anything to do with it?"

He shrugged, then asked, "What does this have to do with the case?"

"She works with another girl who disappeared and who has a link to Fagle, and I think it's all related." He shook his head and mimicked dialing Momo.

I got indignant, "Hey, dummy, that girl disappeared the same night as the Phillips killings, and she had serious dirt on Fagle. I'm not jerking you around. I'll explain later."

"Better be good." I made a mental note to add the following to Earl's rules to live by: Never allow anyone under twenty-five to get the upper hand.

I raised my voice and announced to the shadow in the hall, "We're on our way to a wake. We don't have much time."

She called out, "I'm almost done."

I watched her twin along the wall as she primped her hair. She said, "What I don't understand is why you're asking me about this girl when you're working with *them*." She held something in her hand. At first, I thought it was a hairdryer.

I shoved Richie with both hands, and he flew off his stool into an aluminum baker's rack. The rack and the plates and pictures that had been arranged on it came down on him as her shot blew a hole the size of a basketball in the drywall.

I let my momentum take me to the floor then scrambled along it until the refrigerator was between Missy and me. I pulled my Glock, pressed my back against the fridge, and watched the shadows for signs that Missy was coming down the hall.

In a flash, Richie had crawled out from under the rack and taken up a similar position against the opposite wall. Back to the wall and in a squat, he held a snub-nose 38 in his hands, which were resting on his knees to stop their trembling.

Over the ringing in my ears, I shouted, "We're both armed! You might get one of us, but try, and you will surely die!"

"I ain't afraid of dying," she announced in an assured tone. "Are you?"

"Come on, Missy. Why don't you let us leave before the cops show up? You can tell 'em you were cleaning the gun and it went it off. Let that robe fall open again, and they'll issue a warning and go home with a smile."

Richie pursed his lips and nodded to show his approval of my offer. Missy was a harder sell.

"Momo destroyed my family. It's worth my life to settle that score." I looked over at Richie, who frowned.

"The kid didn't do it. Maybe his grandfather did, but killing Richie won't settle it!"

"But his grandfather sure would miss him. I can cause that old bastard real pain. Hell, it's better than killing the old man. That kid's got a whole life ahead of him, and I can snuff it out." Richie shook his head and eyed the front door, which was only a few feet from him.

"Not if I kill you first," I said, trying to save a little face after seeing my argument demolished.

Richie shouted, "It wasn't our team! Yeah, he fucked over our family, but we didn't kill him. The Latin Killers did, he fucked them worse. Hell, Joey fucked everyone over!"

I looked over at him and whispered, "That last bit's not help-ful."

"I don't believe you. I'm taking my pound of flesh!" She fired a shot through the corner of the wall about three inches above Richie's right ear. He went flat against the floor, then scrambled across the small living room and right out through the front door. He did not slow, nor look back.

I yelled, "Your son needs you alive!"

"He died six weeks after they killed Joey. Leukemia. So, no, he fucking doesn't!"

I stood and dove across the hallway, banking on her not being fast enough to get a shot off. She didn't fire. I raced out the door, stopped, and pressed my back against the wall, afraid she'd shoot me as I booked it to the car, but she didn't bother to come to the door. I heard her sobbing inside and hoped she'd be alright as I holstered my Glock and sprinted off.

# 23

We passed the first police responder as she turned into the complex, and I made haste for the funeral home. I turned to Richie when the coast was clear. "I'm surprised you can sit so comfortably with your tail between your legs."

"You led me into a trap. Momo wants to see us. *Now*."

"A trap? Maybe you should've realized that acknowledging her murdered husband might piss her off. And, speaking of traps. You left me in there with a maniac! You sure do fit your stereotype, you know that?"

He roared, "Stereotype! What does that mean, old man? You got a problem with Sicilians?"

"No, I got a problem with nepotism. You ran from conflict, then called your granddaddy. That's why you left me there. You're a coward." My eyes had barely been on the road. I turned away from sneering at him to see where I was steering us. That's when the little bastard punched me in the side of the mouth. Given the confines of the medium-size sedan, he wasn't able to put much on it, but I still swerved halfway into the other lane, which, fortunately, was empty. If we'd been in the Caprice, he would've had more room to wind up, and I would've been sucking meals through a straw for a while. I braked hard and cut the wheel, and we slid into the soft shoulder. I hopped out and stormed around to his side. He stayed seated and seemingly relaxed and looked up through the window at me.

I wiggled my index and middle fingers and danced. "Let's go, boy!"

The wannabe gangster calmly opened his door and stepped out. He squared up.

I said, "It's on," and waited for him to put his hands up. He reluctantly did, and I threw a right to make sure he was paying attention. He blocked it. Then I hit him with two quick left jabs. The second one opened up a small cut under his right eye, which would match nicely with the shiner he was also going to have. He didn't punch back or try to duck. He dropped his hands and said, "Are you done? Are we even now, cop?"

I hadn't been this unsatisfied since a seventh-grade game of spin the bottle led to an underwhelming closet encounter with a budding feminist. I said, "Come on, Goddammit, fight back!" but he shook his head, disinterested.

We got back in the car and rode in silence. We were on the highway for a bit, then moved onto back roads and block after block of indistinguishable middle-class homes, past a couple of meadows, to a narrow, wooded road and finally to an expansive iron gate behind which was a cobblestone driveway. It was then I realized the high stone wall I'd been driving alongside for several blocks encased Momo's compound. I pulled up to the gatehouse, out of which popped the head of an olive-skinned 30ish man. He looked past me to Richie and said, "One moment Mr. Ragazzi. Someone will be right here to escort you."

"What's on the tube?" I asked him.

He looked over his shoulder at the tablet on his desk. "Steve Harvey."

"He wearing pinstripes today?"

"When isn't he? The man dresses like a *boss*."

"It's nice stuff. I'll bet he pays three-grand a suit," I said.

"Probably more like five."

"What do you think, Richie?" He didn't feel like answering. I started fantasizing about shoving him from the vehicle and tearing out of there, but then Skinny Mikey and Fat Tommy pulled up on the other side of the gate in a black Escalade.

Tommy waved to the guard, and the ornate wrought-iron barrier began to roll back behind the wall. Mikey stepped around it and barked at me, "Get out and spread 'em against the hood, Columbo."

"You really that desperate, Mikey?" I did as asked, and he responded with a hard shove to the center of my back. I was expecting him to pull something like this, and without making it obvious, I had braced myself on all four points. He threw his weight into me, but I barely flinched. He groaned at his failure, then coughed to cover it up. Then he patted down my right side, moving from top to bottom. He finished at the ankle, stood up straight, and moved behind me to get at my left shoulder. As he did, he slammed a fist into my right kidney. This, I was not prepared for. I dropped to one knee and grabbed my side.

Skinny said, "Oops, sorry, detective." He laughed and turned to look at his airship of a partner, who was busy laughing too. I bit my lip and slowly climbed to my feet, steadied myself, and slipped a leg between Mikey's cheap footwear. Then, when he turned back to face me, I wrapped my calf around his right foot and drove my shoulder into his chest. He went down hard on his back, and I went down on top of him, making sure to throw all of my 200 pounds into it, hoping to crack a few ribs. Then I grabbed him by the lapels, but that's when Richie pulled me off him.

Mikey stood up fast and said in escalating volume, "You mother ..." That's when I planted my right leg, pivoted, and whipped a roundhouse kick across his chin.

He jumped back and did a double-take in stunned silence as a trickle of blood ran from his lower lip.

Fat Tommy looked at him and said, "Jesus Christ, he gave you a rug burn."

Mikey went for his gun, and I did the same. We stood not ten feet apart, guns drawn like in the Old West, and I remember thinking my odds for survival were no better than fifty-fifty. The guard was watching the scene through his window, shouting into a phone. Richie was dancing nearby, trying to calm things down. "Come on, you morons. Put 'em down. Jesus, Town, what is wrong with you?"

Tommy said, "Mikey, not here. No violence in the don's home."

Without taking my eyes off Skinny, I said, "Your concern for my safety is duly noted, Tommy."

The big man said, "You're right. I'll shoot you myself," and reached for his piece, as my odds dropped to about one in a million.

I said, "Richie?"

I didn't have time to see what he was gonna do before an ominous voice entered the fray.

"What's going on?"

The guard held his cell phone out the window. Momo was speaking.

"Put the weapons away, now. This is my home."

I waited for the goons to go first. They did. So, I did. I said to Mikey, "Next time, finish the frisk before you launch an assault."

He said, "Oh, we're gonna finish this, Town."

I grinned and watched as he wiped his bloodied chin. "Oh, I'm counting on it."

At the end of the drive sat an English cottage frosted with red brick and pumped up with a massive steroid regime. Cottage style it was, with all the peaks, arched doorways, and wide brick chimneys ornamented with grey stone trim. Cozy? Absolutely not. Momo's manse was three or four oversized red brick English cottages linked together to form a vast U-shaped mansion.

Sweaty Tommy and fuming Mikey led us around to a side section and through a wide arched doorway into a corridor that led straight through the house and onto a red brick patio surrounding an oval swimming pool. We were in the center of the U. Momo and a long-legged woman in a white one-piece swimsuit, dark hair, glasses, and a big floppy hat were catching rays side-by-side in a pair of cedar lounge chairs.

The don pointed to a wrought-iron table and four chairs by

the far end of the patio. He excused himself from the senorita and met us. He sat and asked if I wanted a cigar. I hadn't smoked in months and didn't want one, but I said, "Sure," and beamed at his humiliated lackey as Momo snapped his fingers and said, "Bring the small humidor." I smirked at Mikey, *Fetch the stick, little doggie. Fetch the stick.*

Momo studied me across the table. Richie sat to my right. Tommy sat on a cushioned bench under a large maple tree well within earshot. Momo said, "I called you here to find out why you led my grandson into the home of a crazy woman, but then Ginny called hysterical, saying you made accusations against my granddaughter."

I started to speak, and he held up his hand. I clammed up. "Furthermore, my grandson has a shiner, and Michael has a fat lip, and you pulled a weapon on my property. Now, leave the Missy Smalls situation be for a moment and explain the other. And make it good, because you are on my last nerve."

I sat up straight, looked the old man in the eye, and said, "Your granddaughter's roommate lured Mr. and Ms. Phillips to the murder scene. I want to know why, and Mona Lisa wasn't very helpful. I pressed some buttons to see if she's hiding something, and the result is ... I don't think she knows anything. Look, my methods aren't always pleasant, but I get results."

"Okay, and ..."

"Your grandson sucker-punched me while I was driving, and Michael punched me in the kidney without provocation while searching me for a weapon. Their wounds are a small payback, and more importantly, a means to set some boundaries."

He turned his ancient eyes to Richie, who lowered his gaze and said, "That's what happened. Only, I just slapped him, and I didn't fight back when he hit me. I didn't want to hurt him until you told me it was okay."

Momo leaned back from the table and watched as Skinny Mikey returned with a black lacquer box and large marble ashtray. I kept my eye on the ashtray, which, in the right hands, could kill a man.

Momo directed Mikey to offer the box to me, and I helped myself to one of twenty or so dark-leafed beauties. Mikey extended the offer to Richie, but he waved him off. Then he placed the box in front of Momo and took a seat next to Fat Tommy.

The stogies were long and thick as a thumb. My host applied a golden punch to the tip of his and handed it to me. He said, "This is a special Cohiba. The tobacco comes from a field once prized by that shit bird Fidel. He was a prick, as is his brother, but he knew good tobacco."

"You still hold the revolution against him. Whatever happened to forgive and forget?" I said with a wink.

"I forgive nothing, and I forget nothing. Now tell me why you almost got my grandson shot by Joey Smalls' psycho wife." He snapped his fingers and Mikey handed him an oversized gold lighter. Momo fired up his cigar and stared into my soul. He took a long puff and slowly released a cloud from one side of his trap. The breeze blew it across the pool toward the woman in white.

I rested an elbow on the table and said, "Some of what I'm going to tell you, you'll wish had only reached your ears and that of your grandson, of course."

"Why is that, Town?"

"It pertains to your granddaughter and her social life."

Momo eyed Tommy until the fat man lifted himself from his perch and mumbled in Mikey's ear. Then they both moved to the other end of the pool. Mikey would have to throw his daggers from a distance.

I put flame to Cohiba, pressed leaf to lips, and pulled in a mouthful of dense bitter smoke, which I knew would mellow slightly with each successful toke. "There's another girl, one who disappeared the night the Phillips father and daughter were killed," I said, smoke filling the space between us. "She volunteered at a family-planning clinic and had access to patient records."

"Clinic?"

"Yeah, an abortion clinic."

"Jesus Christ, I don't like where this is going," said Momo. Richie listened quietly, respectful in the presence of the don.

I glanced at Momo's trusted henchmen. I'd counted three others on the property and suspected there were more lurking about. Fat Tommy appeared to be trying to calm Skinny Mikey as he examined his chin in his phone screen and spat invective at me.

"The girl's name is Kenyatta Bell; also goes by Unique when she strips at a club on Route 1. I have it on good authority that Mona Lisa had a procedure at her clinic last year."

Momo growled.

"I believe Ms. Bell told someone this information. And they used the threat of you discovering it to blackmail Josh Fagle, who, I'm told, was the father. Fagle's apartment has been cleaned out. I think he's damn near broke."

Momo stood and brought a hand down hard on the metal tabletop. He shouted, "Bring that son of a bitch here!"

The fat man and his skinny associate leapt from their bench. I said, "Wait!"

Momo turned my way and said, "Watch your mouth."

"Look, we don't know who the blackmailer, and likely murderer, is. I need Fagle to find out."

I shifted my eyes toward Skinny Mikey, who came running at Momo's outburst with Tommy waddling up behind him. The liver-spotted patriarch weighed what I'd said. He ignored Mikey and waited for Fat Tommy to arrive, then said, "Go back."

The don deliberated for a bit while I enjoyed the cigar and the view of Skinny Mikey stewing from across the water. Finally, Momo said, "Mikey will extract the name of the blackmailer from Fagle. He's good at that."

I felt a tremor in my spine at the thought, then said, "If the blackmailer is doing it right, Fagle doesn't know who he is. I need more time to catch him in the act or track him down."

Momo considered this and said, "You still haven't explained Missy Smalls."

"Missy works at The Man Cave with this girl, Ms. Bell. I wanted to ask her a few questions, see if she could identify a man Ms. Bell was seeing, and who may be the blackmailer. She was going to shut the door in my face when Richie brought up Joey, which got us inside. I had no idea you and she had a past."

Momo said, "Riccardo?"

Richie said, "Yeah, that's what happened."

Momo said, "How long?"

"It's only been three days since you hired me. You paid me for five. Give me two more."

"No," he said as he stood and threw off his robe. "You have one, and I mean twenty-four ticks. After that, we do it my way, and Fagle rues the day he laid his hands on my angel."

# 24

Nephew Ed was following Boom Productions and its talent stable on social media. He sent me an Instagram photo of Josh Fagle and Madison Pontiforno smiling with a couple of people in suits I didn't recognize. They were meeting at Boom's studios at that very moment, so I headed south. We weren't on the road for more than a minute when Richie started in on me.

"You're keeping secrets. You didn't tell me about Mona Lisa's procedure."

"You're not paying me. Your grandfather is. It's my responsibility to tell him."

"Yeah, well, I'm his surrogate when we're together. You tell me whatever you tell him."

"Nah," I said as I moved to pass a slow driver. "Some information is for the boss's ears only. Some information is for the peons. You become the boss someday, I'll give you all the information."

He snorted. "I become the boss, you're gonna regret this."

"You had your chance to fight me."

He inspected his fingernails and said, "If I had, you'd be in the hospital, and my grandfather would be pissed. That's the only reason you're still standing."

"You punched me, and it was as though a butterfly landed on my cheek."

"As I told the old man, I only gave you a little slap. You don't want me to punch you."

I laughed. "Okay, in any case, it won't be worth your time to settle old scores with me, if and when you become boss. Believe me, you'll have much bigger priorities."

"No. I'm like my grandfather. Never forgive, never forget."

"Kid, that's a business motto for people who get in the way of his making money. Settling scores doesn't pay the bills. It only causes problems. You'll need to learn that if you want to be godfather."

He turned and studied me as he licked his lips like he was preparing to eat a lamb chop. I had begun to believe a sociopath was riding shotgun.

The rest of the ride was quiet, and it wasn't long before we arrived at Boom. Richie broke the ice when he said, "Why look at that. A nice fresh pane of glass. Maybe I'll throw Fagle through it this time."

"Only after I finish with my questions. And watch out for ancient weapons. He may come at you with a mace." Should I have tried to talk him out of going inside, considering what he'd done the day before? Of course, but it would've been a waste of time. Plus, my attention was diverted by a late-model black Range Rover parked three spaces from Fagle's Porsche.

The look on the face of the receptionist when he saw us coming was one of genuine terror. He stood and waved his arms like one of those inflatable tube men that car dealers use to annoy me. "No trouble. Please, no trouble." It was the same kid that we'd seen during our prior visit, but he'd ditched the blouse and dress pants for a more pure statement. He had on a long denim dress with large square pockets on the hips, and a single red rose embroidered on the left breast. On his head, he wore a hot pink page-boy wig, which matched his fingernails. He wore dark lip liner, but no lipstick, and blue eye shadow.

I was amazed at the transformation and asked, "What's your name?"

"What do you want?" His eyes boomeranged between my

nutcase and me.

"Josh Fagle."

"He's not here."

"His car's out front. Look, ah, *Valerie*?"

I'd spotted a nameplate for Valerie Swanson on the desk. I expected him to tell me he was filling in for Val, but he said, "Yes."

"Who owns this car?" I held up a snap of the Range Rover on my phone.

"Trey, from Fatal Mistake."

I smiled at the thought of seeing my friend Trey again. I said, "The one with the spikey hair."

Valerie returned the smile and said, "They all have spikey hair."

"Right. The one with the spikey hair and the attitude."

"Trey's the worst," Valerie sighed.

I said, "Valerie, I love what you got going on here. I really do." I turned and prodded Richie, and he nodded his approval. "And, I very much liked the pearl earrings yesterday too." Val smiled nervously. "We have to see Josh, and his car is parked out front, so we know he's here. If you really can't bring him, then please get Divya or Kyan. And get them now." I then leaned in to whisper, while rolling my eyes in Richie's direction, "I didn't want to bring him with me, but I had no choice. And, I have no control over what he does. The only way I know to restrain his violent streak is to do what he wants, which is what I've just asked you to do."

Val walked to his desk and picked up the phone, and it wasn't long before I was gazing into the brilliant, amber eyes of Divya Singh.

"Mr. Town and, friend?" She asked as we shook hands. She was in a burnt orange skirt that stopped just above the knees. I glanced down at the lucky tiger restrained by the straps of her high heel shoe. She'd wrapped her upper half in a white silk blouse and capped the look with an engrossing smile.

Richie, ever the young bull, took notice and stood at attention. I introduced them and watched with irrational concern as they smiled and shook hands. Richie gave her his full-on hundred-thousand-kilowatt smile with dimples, but to my relief, she returned the opposite. Divya squinted, frowned, then flashed anger. Richie stepped back.

She said, "Are you the jerk who destroyed Josh's office? Because that cost us fifteen hundred bucks."

Richie took another step back, and she took two toward him. I stepped in between and said, "Divya, Richie was defending himself. Josh was swinging a Samurai sword at his head."

As I figured, Josh hadn't told her the full story. Of course, neither had I, having failed to mention that Richie was threatening to wipe the smug from Josh's face. It worked, as Divya's stance shifted. She said, "That figures. Look, Josh is in a meeting, and will be for a while. What can I do for you?"

"I'm sorry," I said. "I didn't make myself clear. It's imperative that I speak with him. I'm not sure just how much you know about the intertwining of Josh's personal and business lives, but the cops are going to be paying Josh a visit very soon. I have information that could help him, and Boom, avoid trouble, but I'm concerned he's going to flee before I get a chance to do this, and if he does, this company will really be screwed. I'd like to physically see him, so I know he's not sneaking out through the back door. I can wait to speak to him."

"What is going on?"

"I suggest you let me talk to him first. Then you two can have a conversation. Get the news directly from the source, or, in this case, the culprit."

She frowned and contemplated my request. "Follow me," she said, as she turned and walked from reception into a wide hallway at the end of which was a set of doors; across them was stenciled "PRODUCTION." Divya looked back over her shoulder at us. She said, "Welcome to the heart and soul of Boom, gentlemen—our state-of-the-art production facility, where we produce content that has already generated over one billion minutes of viewing on YouTube this year." She pushed open one of the two massive steel doors and stood back arm outstretched against it. I went in first.

It looked more like a warehouse than the home of a burgeoning social media empire. It was a square room with high ceilings and concrete floors. At the back were a couple of loading docks, in front of which was stacked an array of video and audio equipment and lighting. There were a couple of vans parked along a side wall, as well as a wide stretch of green fabric that served as a backdrop for filming talent in front of computer-generated backgrounds. Lining the opposite wall was a series of glass-walled offices and a glass-fronted conference room. Inside this room, engaged in conversation, were Josh Fagle, Madison Pontiforno, and several other casually dressed young executives, some of whom I recognized from Boom's website or backstage at the casino opening.

In the middle of the room were a ping pong table, a pool table, and a collection of chairs and small tables for informal conversation, all of which were situated on a long stretch of blue Astroturf. Making use of the ping pong table were the three members of Fatal Mistake, whom I'd already had the pleasure of meeting. They looked about as they had back then, with ripped jeans and t-shirts with studded belts and bracelets, and wild hair streaked in neon colors, but this time they didn't appear to be wearing eye shadow. Divya eyed someone setting up equipment by the green screen and announced, "You two can wait here if you like. I need to get a few things straight with a production assistant. As you can see, Josh, Madison, and our creative team are meeting with Rankhouse Games about promotions for their fall releases. They should be done soon. Please don't get any ideas and interrupt them. In other words, *behave*."

I said, "Yes, ma'am," and took note of Divya's smile for me and glare for Richie. Then we made our way over to the pseudo boy band. They weren't happy to see me.

Trey was serving to Felix, the guitar player.

"Gentlemen. Hard at work, are we?" They played the point without looking our way.

"Trey, Felix. I never got your name." I stared at the bass

player. He looked away.

I turned to Trey. "What's his name?"

He served, and I whipped out a hand and caught the ball.

"Hey, what's your problem?" said Trey.

I looked at Richie, who said, "He asked you a question."

"What's with you telling those girls I was sick the other night?" Trey whined.

"Hell, Trey. You looked a little blue around the gills. I was concerned about you. Didn't want you spreading disease to those nice young ladies."

"Blue around the what?" asked Felix.

"You told them I shit up the trailer," said Trey.

"Well, you had previously shit up the stage, Trey, so it was a safe assumption."

"Screw you," said the bass player.

I looked at Trey and said, "What's his name?" He looked like he was going to tell me to go to hell, so I added, "Don't forget, I know about you and Kenzie."

"Shssssh!" Trey said, spinning around looking for anyone in earshot.

I said, "What are you so afraid of, Trey? What's Mona Lisa gonna do to you?"

Trey took a while formulating his answer, so Richie answered for him. "If she's anything like her mother, she'll cut his dick off and choke him with it."

I smiled and nodded at Trey, *there you go, how about that*? Then I thought about what he said, and I turned to Richie and asked, "Wait, are you saying Ginny actually did that?"

Richie arched his brow, and I wondered if Ron Shields knew this. Then I said, "Oh, by the way, this is Mona Lisa's first cousin, Richie Ragazzi." Richie flared his nostrils and stood up straight. He was a good half a foot taller than any of them.

Trey said, "Look, the Kenzie thing is history, obviously. There's no need to ever speak of it again, right?"

I said, "I asked you something."

Felix said, "Calvin. His name is Calvin."

I looked at Calvin. "Calvin, Felix, and Trey. Where's the drummer?"

"Teddy has other commitments," said Trey.

Felix said, "Yeah, he has a family." He looked at Trey, and he and the bass player cracked up.

I said, "Maybe he knows that what you're doing won't last, because you can't play or sing a note, can you?"

Trey showed me something I didn't think he had in him. He got defiant and said, "Why does it matter, man? Who are you to tell our fans what they should like? You think they get off any less over us than your generation did over Led Zeppelin or Van Halen?"

I looked at Richie and said, "You're young, you don't like their shit, do you?"

"I like whatever gets my date in the mood, and some of their shit does that."

Trey leaped up, hand in the air, and shouted, "Boom! Take that!"

I shrugged it off and placed my phone in the center of the table facing Trey. Felix and Calvin came over to have a look. On the screen was a photo of Unique. "Friend of yours?" I studied their faces. No one recognized her.

"No," said Trey, then Calvin, then Felix. I noticed Josh and Madison standing. The meeting was adjourning.

I said, "Richie, what do you think? You believe 'em?"

He smiled and looked each one over. "Yeah. I don't think they're stupid enough to lie to us." He eyed Trey and added, "Besides, I owe my cousin a call."

"You know anyone else with a black SUV?" I asked.

"Yeah, everyone, practically," said Trey, who had a point.

I said, "Guys, get yourself some music lessons, and be nice to Mona Lisa."

Richie added, "Or else." I watched Trey choke on a little spit.

We caught up with Josh as he was leaving the fishbowl-like room.

He stopped in his tracks halfway out the door and said,

"You're lucky I haven't already called the cops. What do you want now?"

"A little of your time. Can we just talk in here for a couple of minutes?"

"No, absolutely not. You threatened me yesterday and damaged this office."

I leaned in, so the two stragglers who were still lingering wouldn't hear and said, "I know you're being blackmailed. I want to know who is doing it." His look told me I was right, and he quickly turned and asked the others for privacy. Then he sat down at one end of the long conference table. Richie and I sat to his left, me acting as a buffer between him and the mafioso with training wheels.

Fagle looked me in the eye. "You're wrong. I am not being blackmailed." Richie chuckled at my error.

"Then where's all your shit? I've been to your place, Josh. You've been cleaned out, and it wasn't a robbery."

"I *was* being blackmailed, but it's over. I'm free now." I looked at Richie. He looked away.

"When did they stop?"

"Two weeks ago."

"So right after Ray and Harlowe Phillips died?"

"When I ran out of money."

"Why were they blackmailing you?"

"I'd rather ..."

I held up a palm. "I know why. But I want to hear it from you. Don't lie to me, Josh."

He grimaced and pinched the flesh between his eyes. "I was indiscrete with one of the girls."

I slapped his hand away from his face and said, "Stop obfuscating. Name the girl and what you did."

He looked over at Richie, unable to mask his fear. I said, "I'll shoot him if he attacks you."

Richie went, "Pffft."

Fagle sighed and said, "Mona Lisa. She got pregnant. It was taken care of. I paid for everything."

Richie said, "You're lucky you're still breathing."

"Where was it taken care of?" I asked.

"At a clinic, where else?"

"Which clinic?"

"Why?"

"Which clinic?"

He confirmed it was the *one*.

I said, "That's how the blackmailers found out."

He said, "No shit? Maybe I should sue them."

"The girl who leaked the information is missing. Most likely murdered by your blackmailer."

The blood drained from his face. "You're kidding?"

I showed Fagle a picture of Unique. He didn't recognize her.

"Who was blackmailing you?"

"I don't know. I never saw him."

"Him?"

"Yeah, we spoke before each drop."

"He called your phone?"

"No, one of those prepaid ones. He gave it to me for use with him only."

I nearly jumped from my seat. "Where is it?"

"It's gone. He made me put it in with the last drop."

"How did you get it?"

"One night, I'm leaving here, and I hear a weird ring tone coming from my console. I open it and find one of these prepaid phones. I'd never seen it before. So, I answer it, and it's him."

"When was this?"

"Two months ago. I thought it was a prank. Then he says he knows about Mona Lisa and who her grandfather is. Says he'll tell the grandfather if I don't give him fifty grand."

"Fifty? That's it?" said Richie.

"Yeah, that was only the first time. It was fifty each time after that too. In cash. You have no idea what a fucking nightmare it is coming up with fifty grand in cash. You can't just take it out of the bank. Not without the feds coming at you for money laundering or some other B.S."

"How many times were there?"

"Six in all. That's all I had. He bled me dry. People think I'm rich, and I want them to, but this is a start-up, man. I'm cash poor. All my money is in this company."

"Now it is," I said. Richie giggled.

"Tell me about the drops," I said.

"He'd call, always on a weeknight, but the days differed. He would tell me to have the money ready the next morning when he would call again with the location. I always had to put it in one of those reusable shopping bags from the supermarket. It had to be blue, so I bought a bunch of them at Market Basket."

"Where did you make them?"

"I just said I bought them."

"The drops, hipster doofus. Where did you make the drops?"

"In dumpsters. Always a smelly dumpster full of trash. I would put it on top and scram. He said there were people watching, and if I didn't follow his instructions, he'd tell the godfather, and I'd be dead." He looked at Richie. "I'm dead now anyway, aren't I?" Richie grinned from ear to ear.

I said, "I already told Momo."

Josh wailed like a wounded animal, then said, "Wait a minute. Is that why those guys worked me over? I thought it would be much worse."

I turned to Richie. "You want to tell him?"

Richie said, "Yes, I do. That beating was because the don found out you were screwing Harlowe Phillips. He didn't know about Mona Lisa." Richie looked around the room. "You got a good health plan here?"

"Oh shit," said Fagle.

I had him tell me the location of each dumpster and made notes. Then I drew an area map, on a yellow legal pad that had been left on the table and marked the location of each one.

"These are all in Boston, but man are they spread out," I said.

"Yeah, tell me about it. It was miserable. He'd call and only give me just enough time to just make it there. Like, I had to literally run from my condo and drive like a maniac to get there in time. One day I ran into a road crew and almost lost my shit."

"Tell me about the last time."

"He called and told me the location like every other time, but he also said to put the phone in the bag. He said this was the last one, and that I was lucky to get off easy, but if I ever told anyone about this, I would be dead."

"He would kill you, or he would tell Momo, and he would kill you?"

"He didn't say, and I didn't ask. I was glad to be free."

"When was this?"

"Last Monday."

"The night Harlowe and her father died?"

"Yes, that's right," he said.

"You know why it was the last one, don't you?"

"Because I'm broke, I guess."

I turned to Richie, "He's lying."

Richie started to get up, and Josh said, "No, wait. I don't know what you want me to say."

"The last call with the blackmailer wasn't like the other ones, was it?"

"Jesus. How do you know this?"

"Tell me what you told him."

Josh closed his eyes. "I didn't know what he was going to do. I just didn't want Momo to find out. If I had known, I never would have told him. I swear to God!" Tears began to roll down his cheeks. They weren't for Harlowe and their baby. They were for him and his predicament. This made me angry, and I had to take a few breathes and remind myself of the mission.

"Tell me what you said to him."

"I told him Ray Phillips knew I was being blackmailed, and why, and was threatening to expose me. I didn't know what he would do. Why would my blackmailer kill him and Harlowe?"

"How did Ray find out?"

"Harlowe told him. We had a big fight and she spilled the beans.

"When was this?"

"A couple of weeks ago. She came by my place uninvited, saw how empty it was and thought I was moving out without telling her. She freaked out. I had no choice but to tell her about Mona Lisa and the blackmailer. She knew I had dated Mona Lisa, but not about Mona Lisa's pregnancy. It really upset her."

"Shocking," I said.

"I know, right?" said the guy with no sarcasm detector.

"Have you had any contact with the blackmailer since the last call?"

"No, I made that last drop, and that was it."

"What did he sound like?"

"Deep voice, muffled like he was disguising it."

"Any ambient noise?"

"No, not that I noticed. The phone wasn't great, though."

"There must have been something. You spoke to him at least a half-dozen times."

"One time, I heard pop music. Oh, and a couple of times, I heard trucks in the background."

"Trucks?"

"Yeah, the engine noise, and beeping too. You know, when they're backing up."

"Any other voices?" He shook his head.

Divya Singh poked her pretty face into the doorway and surveyed the room with a stern eye. "The crew is concerned. Everything okay in here?"

I said, "Did you know he's been knocking up the talent?"

She backed out and shut the door behind her, as Josh turned pink. I asked him, "Was that news to her?"

"No, probably not."

"Take out your wallet."

"What? Why?" I looked over at Richie, and Josh said, "Okay."

"Give me your license and all of your credit and debit cards. I already took your passport when I searched your apartment yesterday."

"You're stealing my identity? I don't get it."

"I'm taking your identification and credit cards so you can't flee. I know you're going into hiding, but I want you to stay close by, and I want you to give me your cell phone number and answer my calls. This thing is coming to a head. In a few days, I'll give you your shit back. That is if you stay close and answer when I call or text. And, of course, if you manage to stay alive."

# 25

Richie and I were trudging across the parking lot when I noticed Madison watching from a nearby convertible sports car. She got out, waved, and asked if she could speak with me. I tossed junior the key fob and followed the starlet to a sleek oak-slatted bench outside the main entrance. He followed me and stood nearby. Madison looked up at him. "Who are you?"

"I'm working with the detective."

Dressed in a clean white business suit, the young entrepreneur had the blue eyes, high cheekbones, and broad smile of a model, with the brains and tenacity of a corporate CEO. She said, "I'd like to speak with him in private," and glared at him. He glared back for a bit, averted his eyes, then shuffled off to wait in the car.

"Impressive," I said.

She looked about as if looking for spies, turned to me and leaned in close, "Am I in danger?"

"I don't think so, Ms. Pontiforno, but your question is a wise one."

"Did someone murder Harlowe and Kenzie? I mean someone other than Mr. Phillips?"

"I'm not sure yet, but signs are pointing that way."

"Is it true that you're working for Mona Lisa's family and not Boom?"

"Maybe. Does that matter?"

"Yes."

"What part of it matters?"

"That you're not working for Boom."

"Why is that?"

"I don't trust Boom. They don't want the truth to come out. They'd rather let things stand as a murder-suicide and drug overdose. That way, nothing can be blamed on them, and everyone moves on."

"What do you think happened?"

"I don't know. Did Todd really set the fire?"

"Yes, he did. I've seen the evidence. The only question is why."

"Evidence?"

"Photos of Todd spraying the trailer with an accelerant and lighting it on fire."

"Oh, I didn't realize. So, could he have killed the others too?"

"I don't believe so. The fire doesn't appear to be connected to the other events."

She dug around in her purse, removed some gum, and popped a piece in her mouth, then offered me some. I declined. She said, "I don't think Mr. Phillips killed his daughter, and Kenzie didn't smoke that stuff on purpose. She was going to expose Josh for the heel he is. I thought Mona Lisa ..." She stopped mid-sentence.

"You thought the same forces tried to kill Mona Lisa." She nodded. "Why was Kenzie going to expose Josh?"

"She and Harlowe had grown close. Harlowe told her about the pregnancy and what Josh was pushing her to do. Kenzie was simmering over the situation. Then Kenzie found out about Mona Lisa's procedure, and Josh's role in it."

"How'd she find that out?"

"I told her. I hate Josh."

"I just watched you sitting alongside him in a meeting as though all was fine."

"That was business. He's a creep."

"How was Kenzie going to expose this?"

"Through a troll account. She was going to pose as an anonymous insider and post his secrets online."

"When did she tell you this?"

"At Harlowe's funeral. That really set her off."

"Did you know your friend Lake Gelson had a troll account?" I had never heard of a troll account before. Ed told me that's what it was called.

"No. Lake? Why?"

"She used it to communicate with Ray Phillips."

"No!" she gasped.

"Is she seeing anyone new?"

"Lake?"

"Yes, is Lake seeing any new guys? You know, in the last month or two."

"Lake sees a lot of guys."

"No one special, then?"

"There is this Italian guy."

"*Really*?" She nodded.

"Have you met him? Know what he looks like?"

"No."

"Know what he drives?"

She shook her head.

"Do you own a gun?"

"No, of course not."

"Have a big burly boyfriend who owns a gun, perhaps?"

"You do think I'm in danger!"

"I don't think anything, but it's not out of the realm of possibility. What about that boyfriend, someone you can stay with for a few days?"

"No. I'm in between relationships, and I'm into nerdy momma's boys anyway."

"Okay. Look, I'm glad you came to me, and I'm sorry about this, but I think you should go someplace where no one will find you and stay there for a couple of days. It won't take any longer than that. I'm getting close." She stared, mouth agape, head slowly tilting.

"Don't tell anyone what we discussed, or where you are. And don't put any pictures on the Internet that will give away your location, like the one you posted earlier."

\* \* \*

Richie was on the phone when I climbed into the driver's seat. "Here he is now. You wanna ...? Okay." He handed the phone to me.

"My grandson says he thinks you've figured it out. So, who did it?"

"I can't say just yet. Give me an hour, maybe two. Then I'll either have it, or I won't."

"And if you don't have it?"

"I'll move onto the next suspect. I have others."

"I want to know who your number one is. I'm paying you to tell me."

"Right, and I will, once I have enough facts to back it up. Until then, I'm not incriminating anyone. Capiche?"

There was a lengthy silence. Then the don actually chuckled a little. He said, "Okay. Your ass is hanging out here, Town. Do not disappoint me." He hung up.

I tossed the phone to Richie, and said, "Thanks, that was pleasant."

"You're walking the line, man. Walking the line."

"What does that mean?"

"You're being disrespectful to the godfather."

"No. You're wrong. I'm not being a patsy. If I don't hold up my end, the don will lose respect for me, and then I'll be in real trouble."

He shot me a dubious gaze.

"Here's the thing, Richie. Fagle may not be the only one motivated by the abject fear of your grandfather finding out what they've done. And don't ask who else. I'll say no more until we get confirmation, which I intend to do next."

∗ ∗ ∗

"You still got that sweet espresso machine?"

"*Yeah.* Who's he?"

"Richie Ragazzi, vice president at New England Waste Management."

"*Ah*, right," said Irving Wechsler as he cinched the knot around his terry-cloth robe with the Ritz Carlton emblem on the left breast. "Why are you here, and why didn't you call first?"

"You gonna let us in?" We were standing on the threshold of Irv's century-old Victorian, a short walk from Inman Square in Cambridge.

"Yeah, I guess. Hold on." Irv kept his hand on the door and shouted up the staircase, "Make yourself decent, a pain-in-the-ass client just showed up." Then he stood back and made a big show of opening the door and bowing with arm extended. I winked at Richie and went in first.

The kitchen was on the immediate right. I suggested Richie pull up one of two stools while I went for the coffee maker. "I'm sorry, man, I did call you. Your phone is off, which is the only reason I didn't call you a liar when you acted like you had a woman here."

"Dink," he muttered.

"Look," I said, "I need a few shots of liquid cocaine. I didn't get much sleep last night."

Irv looked at Richie and said, "Tell me he's not just here to make espresso?" Then he turned to me. "Come on, leave. I got a thing happening here. I was just warming the oils."

"Oils, eh?" I walked toward the stairs. I said, "You know, I gotta use the bathroom. I think I'll go upstairs where it's more private."

Irv blocked my path. "No, you don't. Now, why are you here?"

I placed a hand on his shoulder and looked into his better eye. "I'm about an hour from solving at least two of the killings, but I need your help to do it. Put your libido on pause, get dressed, and let's go."

Irv looked at Richie, who shrugged and said, "I think he means it. I can smell the gears turning."

I grabbed the day's *Herald* from his countertop, rolled it up, and smacked Irv hard on the ass. "Vamoose!" He took off up the stairs.

* * *

The plan was for Irv to go into The Man Cave alone and talk to Missy. The last time I'd seen her, she tried to murder me, and Richie was the one who'd set her off. I didn't want Irv to ask the question, though. I needed to see her eyes and know if she was telling the truth.

I instructed him as we stood in the parking lot. Before I could get to the plan, he wanted to talk money. "Give me twenty bucks for the cover," he looked at me and nudged the bridge of his glasses.

"You want me to give you twenty bucks when you're my client? You know I'm going to bill you for this."

"Yes. But until then, I get to use your money instead of mine. Time value of money, my friend. So, give me twenty."

As I forked it over, I said, "Listen, this woman is wound a little tight." When Richie chuckled at the understatement, Irv grew suspicious. "Tell her Earl Town is sorry for bringing that jerk to her place today. He didn't know about her husband. He wants to ask her one question, that's all. Then he'll leave. If she balks, tell her Unique's life is at stake."

"You really think she's still alive?"

"Yes, Irv. I do." I lied. There's no sense delivering lousy news based on speculation. "Now, repeat the key beats of that back to me."

"Earl Town is very sorry about bringing that jerk today. What happened exactly?" He gave me the stink eye.

"Just a little misunderstanding with Richie and me. No big deal, right junior?" I looked at Richie.

"Right, Gramps. Just a little shooting."

"Shooting!" Irv took off his glasses and began to polish the lenses, which he does when he's nervous.

I threw a glare at Richie. "He's kidding. It was nothing. She just got a little upset because we'd woken her up. She'll be fine now."

Irv pursed his lips. "I don't know about this."

"Do you want to save Unique or not?"

"Okay, so I ask if you can ask a question, then what?"

"Then you text me that it's cool that I come in and ask her. It's easy. You got this, Irv."

"Okay, the sooner I get this done, the sooner I get back to my evening of ecstasy." Irv applied a fresh coat of Chapstick to the edges of his maw, marched across the lot to the bouncer, showed ID, and went on in.

Richie and I leaned back against the hood of the rental. The warm night air was not doing much to take the chill off our association. He said in a nasal tone, "So, what are you gonna do when Plan A goes to shit, and he comes back with his tail between his legs?"

"Uh, wait until she leaves and corner her, I guess. The problem is getting her to answer without getting shot." I sighed, "But, I don't think we'll need a second plan. She's a good egg at heart, just not a fan of yours. This is a common thing with you? You know, running into people who want to revenge-murder you?"

"Comes with the job."

"The job? I thought you were going to Brown. Isn't there something else you'd rather do than the family business?"

"Old man, with what I'm learning, I'm gonna take the business to another level."

"Business major?"

"Hell, yeah."

"What's the point? You guys don't do business like they do on

Wall Street."

He turned to me and laughed. "You think the guys who run Wall Street aren't gangsters?"

"Alright, I'll give you that, but what's Momo's plan? Cause I haven't gotten the vibe that you're a lock for the job. There must be a few other cousins around, no?"

"Pffft, there are others, but I'm the clear favorite. As long as you don't fuck it up."

I was about to say something wise about him being the root of my problems when I was saved by a buzz from my phone. It was Irv telling me the coast was clear.

I said to Richie, "I told you it'd work. Wait here. She sees you again, there's no telling what kind of hell she'll rain down on us."

This is where the task got hairier. I didn't want to run into Rajeev or the mountainous bouncer who'd chased me out. The guy at the door was different. Similar size, but white, with blonde dreadlocks and letters tattooed on his knuckles. He looked over my ID and handed it back. He looked away and didn't say anything, and I went on in.

The sounds of heavy metal and money being extracted from horny dudes—"Hi, I'm Chantal, buy me a drink?"—filled the atmosphere. The place was carved up like a continent of small nations. By the mouth of the main stage were the frat guys in oxford shirts with short haircuts and rubber charity bracelets on their wrists. The someone-just-turned-21 gang was east of the stage, throwing dollar bills at the dancer, who more than made up for her small stature in other areas. The business guys in suits were in the back, or south of the stage. Each one had a girl on his lap and a glint in his eye. A group of cool brothers whooped it up in the west, where a sister with a colossal caboose was pretending to run her tongue along a chrome pole. Around the bar sat a collection of working men, many in uniform, and a lawyer in a plaid jacket, thick square frames, and an unruly mop.

Missy watched as I made my way over. She leaned against the bar back, arms folded, sucking her gums. I held out my hands to show I came in peace and said, "Thank you for doing this. I'm sorry about earlier today."

"Give me a hundred," she said, right hand extended, but sans firearm this time.

I looked at Irv, who said, "Sorry, I didn't bring my wallet."

"You lie!" I reached into his plaid jacket and extracted it.

"Give me that!" I handed it back to him and removed mine.

"Here's fifty. Look at this and be straight with me, and you'll get the rest." I held out my phone. On it was a picture of a man I'd stealthily snapped earlier in the day, before I added some character to his face.

Missy eyed it. "Oh yeah. I've seen him in here. Real strong silent type. Is he connected too?" Her eyes flashed anger.

"No. Just an asshole. Do any of the other girls know him? I trust you, but I'd love a second opinion."

She waved a waitress over. A dancer wearing a Kleenex came along with her.

The waitress said, "That's Unique's man. How's she doing? Weird she hasn't been around."

The dancer, who had a colorful horn of plenty inked over her c-section scar, said in a high-pitched squeal, "Hey, that's Rajeev's friend, Mikey."

I thanked Missy for the assist and was handing over the other fifty, when Irv tugged my sleeve, "Earl, we got a problem. A couple of them."

I turned and looked down into the black eyes of the impresario of smut. Behind him was the bouncer who'd threatened me during my first visit, flanked by the one I'd just met out front.

I said, "Rajeev! You know, I think I've been overserved. My friend and *lawyer* here," I squeezed Irv's puny arm, "is going to take me home now."

Irv and I watched as Rajeev weighed his options with tilted head. Then he stood up tall and said, with as much menace as a guy in the fruit-fly weight class could muster, "I told you not to come back. You think I'm gonna let you leave?" He stood on his tiptoes, chin up, and said, "I should've told those guys to kill you."

I looked over at jaw-dropped Irv and said, "Didn't I tell you it was this bitch that paid those guys to kick my ass?"

I turned back to Rajeev and smiled, "I knew it was you!"

He returned my smile, obviously savoring his next move. Too bad, I wasn't about to let him make it. Instead, I stepped into a textbook right hook and crushed his jaw. A look of shock flashed in his eyes at impact. Then his head flew back as his feet left the ground, and he collapsed into a heap a few steps away. The big goons came at me as I directed my follow through at the handle of my gun.

But *damn* was Dreadlock even faster than he looked, as he clamped a big hand on my right wrist and forced me to drop the weapon. I looked up at him as he showed me his teeth and lifted me off the ground like I was a Styrofoam Santa Claus. With both arms, he reeled back and slammed my old bones onto an oak table around which a nude blonde and two rednecks had been negotiating the rules of engagement in the champagne room. The legs gave way and absorbed some of the energy, and I scrambled onto my feet and tried to avoid his grasp, but he caught me by the scruff of the neck and lifted me up again.

While I was in the air, I noticed the other bouncer carrying Irv like a duffle bag and heading for the exit. Dreadlocks stood me up by the bar and reared back to strike me. But the music stopped abruptly, and my captor and I paused and looked down at the source of the loud moaning that now filled the air. Rajeev looked up at me through teary eyes and said, "You bo my fuffin yaw!"

I said, "Shut up, or I'll break your arms too." That's when the blonde goon threw a roundhouse at me. I ducked and tried driving my knee into his groin but got mostly thigh. He grabbed my shirt and slammed my back against the bar rail. Then I saw the other ogre grinning wide and coming toward me. He'd dispatched Irv to the parking lot, and now the pair were going to team-up.

That's when Missy yelled, "Behind you!" and I watched as the ogre dropped to his knees, then sidestepped his huge frame as he fell face-first onto the disgusting carpet. I grinned at Richie, who stood holding the back of a broken chair. He'd snapped it over the ogre's head.

Dreadlocks looked down at his partner, released me, and reached for his gun, but it was too late. Richie raised his 38, and the bouncer raised his hands.

Richie kept his eyes on the man and spoke to me. "Bring that whore who tried to kill us over here into my line of sight."

I said, "What? Why? We got what came for. Let's get out of here before the cops arrive."

"Do it now, Town, or I'll splatter this clown's brains all over your loafers."

"You like these?" I said. "They're Italian."

Missy, who hadn't moved from behind the bar, then did what any woman with a hair across her ass would do in such a situation. She made things worse. "Fuck you, Ragazzi," she said. "You think you can take anything more from me? Go ahead and try. Send me to heaven and spend the rest of your life behind bars."

Richie stepped back from the goon, keeping his gun hand steady. I looked around. The bar had cleared out, except for a couple of the dancers, one of whom was loudly complaining that Rajeev had better make this up to her, because, "Y'all scared away my *Goddamn business!*"

Richie told the muscle head to stand behind the bar with Missy.

I said, "Richie, come on, man. You're gonna shoot these people? This is no time for revenge, son. Let's go."

He pointed his barrel at Missy's cleavage and was just about to speak when he felt the barrel of my gun pressing against his spine, and I spoke instead, "I will shoot you to save her. My life isn't worth much. I'm old and tired, and heart disease runs in my family. Your grandfather will be doing me a favor. Now hand the gun to me."

"No. What's your game, Town? Why do you wanna help a bitch who tried to kill you?"

I increased the pressure. "Because, apparently, your family killed her husband."

"You better watch your mouth."

"You asked the question. I answered. You prefer I lie? Look, why can't we call it even and go home? Give me the gun."

"No."

"Then, I'm going to shoot you in the back, in three, two, one. Aw, come on, Richie! I swear I'll do it."

He stood perfectly still and spoke calmly, "No, you won't. But I'm feeling magnanimous. I'll holster it, and we'll leave, but you're not taking my gun."

"Give me the bullets."

"Fuck your mother."

"Fine, let's go."

Rajeev was sitting on the floor, back against the bar while clutching his face and moaning. I leaned in close and squeezed his shoulder on a particularly painful pressure point. My breath was fouled with caffeine and an empty stomach, and I let him have it, as I said, loud enough for Missy to overhear, "Mr. Ragazzi and his clan have strong feelings for your bartender. If anyone is going to fuck with her, it'll be him or his family. If you, or your goons, ever lay a hand on her or mess with her livelihood, it'll be the last thing you do. Capiche?" The damn word was growing on me.

He didn't answer, and I recalled what his goons had done to me two nights prior. So, I kicked the little puke over onto his side and rested the heel of my loafer on the fingers of his right hand. I said, "Answer me," and pressed down until he squealed.

"Gapeek!"

We found Irv pacing outside with a crowd of stragglers wondering if their night was really over. A couple ducked behind cars when we emerged.

Irv said, "Let's go! I called the cops five minutes ago."

We passed two sets of blues about an eighth of a mile down Route 1. No one said much of anything after that. My thoughts were on the punk kid sitting next to me, wondering just what he was going to do next. Pulling a gun on a guy like Richie was surely going to generate a response. I glanced over at him. He was staring at me and grinning like a kid anticipating Christmas morning.

# 26

Streetlights illuminated Irv's boney shoulders and cast his shadow all the way to his doorstep. I turned to face Richie. "I was hired to solve a mystery, which, with your help, I'm about to do. I won't take part in any grudge settling. I don't care that she shot at us. We lived and got what we wanted. Now we need some actual tangible evidence or an admission of guilt. This is all still conjecture."

He didn't respond, and I felt a trickle of sweat run down my side. I decided to head back toward I-93 and Boston.

"I'm sorry, but I had no choice, Richie. Your grandfather would be even more pissed at me if I'd let you murder the bartender." Silence.

"Thank you for bailing me out. I was wrong about you being a coward. That took balls to come in and save me." Still nothing.

"You on Thorazine, by chance?" Crickets.

"Aren't you gonna call the old man and tell him what's up?"

He looked up and sighed. "I'm going to be civil with you until this case is over. Then I'm going to make you wish you'd never been born. If I tell him now, my grandfather will send in his guys to take care of it. I want a chance at Mikey first. Killing a traitor will be good payback for the stress I feel at delaying your inevitable demise."

"Well, it's certainly comforting to know that my slaying will bring you peace of mind, Richie."

"Where are we going?" he asked.

"I'm not sure. We could go to Mikey's, and if he's not home, break in and look for evidence."

"Okay. And, if he is there, we can kick the door down and slit his throat."

"No! I told you, we're still at the point of conjecture. Let's not do something we'll regret. Like murdering a guy who looked suspicious but turned out not to be guilty."

"You don't believe that," he said.

"No. I mean, yes. I don't believe he's innocent of the murders, but I don't know for sure that he's not. That's my problem. I need to remove the doubt."

He shook his head and looked back down at his phone.

"Well," I said, "there is another place we can go. We could try to corner ourselves a rat."

"You think he knows?"

"Does a mafia hood shit in an Italian social club. The question is, is he in on it, or just a casual observer?"

"Either way, Momo's not going to like it." I nodded. "Do you think he'll spill on him?"

"No, probably not," I said. "But, with your brains and my brawn, maybe we can trip him up." Richie didn't get the joke.

* * *

A breeze from the extra-large CPAP mask strapped over Fat Tommy's oversized snout and piehole tickled the hairs on the back on my hand as I placed the barrel of my well-oiled Glock G-20 just above his eyes. I pressed my other hand on his massive shoulder, squeezed the flab, and gave it a good jiggle. I sang him a little lullaby, "*Wakey, wakey, Mr. Snakey.*"

The big man lay on his back, enjoying the restorative benefits of deep sleep. I shook some more, and his eyes snapped open. I smiled down at him like a loving Italian mother and said, "Hi there, sleepyhead. My gun is resting against your temple. Do you feel it?" He tried to sit up. I stuck my free hand on his chest and forced him back down. He made a guttural sound that was magnified by the mask and tubing.

I said, "Move again and die, fatso. There's another gun three inches from your balls. Is that right, Richie? Three inches?"

"Nah. I'd say it's more like two," said the kid. Tommy lay still, chins squished against his chest, belly heaving, sweat beading above my barrel.

I pulled back the sheets, thankful to find he was wearing boxers the size of a sail. I said, "Roll over on your belly and put your hands behind your back. Try anything, and I'll turn you off like flipping a light switch." Tommy strained as he turned over, sweat ran from his temples, bringing traces of his jet-black hair dye with it.

He finally managed to roll all the way over. I removed a zip tie from my pocket and handed it to Richie. I eyed Tommy's fat, yet powerful wrists, and gave him another.

After considerable effort, we managed to get him seated in a sturdy ladder back side chair in a small dining room with bare white walls, except for a bronze cross and portrait of the Virgin Mary. We moved the table and placed the porker directly under a pendant lamp. I sat in the shadows while Richie rummaged in the refrigerator.

He said, "Oh, yeah. Now we're talking. There's mortadella, capicola, prosciutto. You know how to stock a refrigerator, traitor."

Tommy said, "You got things wrong. I would never be disloyal to the godfather."

I did my best to act unimpressed, which was natural given Tommy's shape, yellowed boxer shorts, and not insignificant case of eczema on his big bulky legs. I said, "There's a shiny new Cadillac in the driveway, and that recliner with the magic fingers still has some of the packing material stuck to it. You come into some money recently?"

Tommy Palermo must have been a comic because he went straight into a Dangerfield routine. "What money? My ex-wife, she took everything. The car is a lease job. I'll show you the papers. The recliner is a gift from Mikey." Richie caught my eye, but I shook him off. I would've said the same thing if I was in Fat Tommy's position. He was trying to deflect our suspicion back to Skinny Mikey.

He went on. "I don't know what you're after, but you're wrong. Now, let me go, and we'll forget about this. What? Am I gonna complain about the boss's grandkid? Nah. Now that you know the truth let's pretend this never happened."

I said, "Oh, and I forgot to mention something. We found the stash in your closet. You're a heavy sleeper. What do you estimate that at, Richie?"

Richie had peeled off a near-transparent slice of carefully cured ham from the wax paper. Like a seal eating a fish, he threw his head back and dropped the aged ham into his mouth one curl at a time. He savored it, then said, "Two-hundred. It's two-hundred thousand."

Tommy eyed him or the meat, or both, and said, "Come on, kid. You know how it is. That's just a little spending money." He looked at me. "What, you think I bring all my earnings to the bank? The IRS would love that."

I said, "We also found a gold Rolex with a poignant engraving to someone named Joshua. Who might that be, Tommy?"

That rat played one of the only cards he had left. "Richie. Come on, kid. I have been nothin but loyal to the old man. I would never ..."

Richie cut him off and held up a fresh slice. "Where'd you get this? It's delicious."

"At Salvatore's just off Salem by ..."

Richie strode across the room with intent and drove the heel of his boot into Tommy's face. The fat man crashed onto his back and skidded a few feet on the big grey tiles that tied the dining room and kitchen together.

I said, "Sounded like the chair gave way."

We were both huffing by the time we managed to haul him back up. That's when the begging started. With all the blood in his maw, it was a particularly pathetic sight. The round man's nose was most certainly broken, and his smile was now more rustic, but he kept on talking.

"Come on, Richie. I'd give my life for you and your kin. What did this cop cocksucker tell you? Never trust a cop, Richie. Let's go talk to Momo. He'll straighten this out."

"He'll put you in the ground," said Richie. "You betrayed him."

"No!" The big mug employed a new gambit. He looked at me and said, "You took it too far, Town! The kid passed the test. He passed! The old man will be thrilled. Now come on, let me go!"

He looked at Richie and said, "This is all your grandfather's idea. It was all a test to see if you could hack it. You passed, kid. You passed!"

Richie began to stomp around Fat Tommy, sneering and spitting his words at the condemned man. I watched and wondered if I could get him under control. He said, "How dare you disrespect my family, you dirty rat motherfah ..." He stopped, and we looked at one another.

I said, "Car door?"

He nodded.

Far away from the light switch, I picked up a chair and swung it into the pendant lamp, causing it to explode onto Tommy and the tiles. Richie kicked the refrigerator door shut, and we were in the shadows. It wasn't quite dark, given the streetlight coming in through the picture window, but we'd made ourselves harder targets. The hum of the air conditioner and ticking of a clock on the mantel were the only sounds.

I took a couple of careful steps toward a front-facing window, and the big man started to shout, "Help! They got me tied ...!" Richie flew across the room and slammed the side of Tommy's enormous head with a toaster oven, and I watched as the big man slowly tipped over onto his side.

"Nice swing. You play ball?" I whispered.

"Fat traitor," he said under his breath. "Where are they?"

I said, "Keep an eye on the back door. I'll watch the front."

"You ain't the boss."

"Jesus, Richie. Staying alive is a team sport."

"Who is it?"

I peered around the curtains. "It's not the cops. Ours is the only car out front. There's a truck across the street that wasn't there before."

"What kind of truck?"

"Shh," I said. "You hear that?"

"Hear what?"

We held our breath and listened. The sound of breaking glass broke the silence, and we watched as an object the size and shape of a lemon came through a pane in the picture window, bounced off a coffee table, and rolled into the fireplace. A near half-century of watching war movies triggered something in me, and I screamed, "Grenade!" The only move I had was to dive behind the big hood lying on his side in front of me. I plunged down to my belly and pressed in against him. Eyes closed tight, ears covered, I waited ... for about two seconds, then there was a succinct and thunderous blast, followed by a deafening whoosh. I felt Tommy's body rock, then lift off the ground, as a warm concussive wave washed over us. The debris-laden air ricocheted off the walls and blew dust and broken bits of glass, furniture, and shrapnel over us.

I gasped for air, which tasted of iron and smelled of sulfur. It took a few seconds to recognize that it was the stench of the explosive load combined with burning flesh and hair. I opened my eyes and examined my life-saving barrier. From my side, Fat Tommy looked as he had—peaceful like he was in a deep sleep. Then I stood and saw what had become of his other side. For a gangster, the man sure had a big heart and a big brain. I know, because I saw them or what was left of them. His face and chest had been torn open and ripped to shreds.

From behind me, I heard Richie say, "Madone! I can't believe you're not dead."

"Yeah, you either."

He was examining the refrigerator door, which had two deep

baseball-size tears in it. One was about two feet up, and the other about four.

"Good thinking hiding behind that," I said.

"How's he doing?" He pointed to Tommy.

"You guys got a gangster Valhalla?"

"Val what?"

"You know, like the Vikings." He didn't know. I said, "Think they're still out there?" That drew raised eyebrows and a crouch. We both drew a weapon, and he followed me in stepping around a smoking hole in the formerly sparkling maple floor to cautiously observe the street from one of the blown-out windows. The blast had destroyed all of them.

The truck I'd seen earlier was gone and the sound of distant sirens began to filter through the ringing in our ears, so we left quickly via the front door. Head low, I jogged to the rental car and began to slide into the driver's seat. Richie, who had moved to the other side, said, "What's that?"

I stopped, looked up, and saw another lemon bounce off of a sewer grate at the foot of the driveway. It bounced twice more off the pavement and then rolled under our car.

I took a couple of strides and threw myself flat on the ground, covering my head and ears. The initial blast was muffled by the Ford, but then the gas tank ignited, and that explosion lifted the compact sedan into the air and threw it against an old elm tree where it rocked back and forth for a while before coming to rest on the driver's side. Rims that had been stripped of rubber spun and caught the light of the flames rising from the passenger compartment.

I moved into a crouch, eyes and weapon trained on the street. Richie rose up from behind a small brick planter box and dusted himself off. He said, "You okay?"

I examined myself. "Yeah, somehow, I am. Get low, man, before they shoot you."

"Nah, Darryl doesn't like guns. Besides, he's leaving." He pointed at the end of the road, where a large, noisy garbage truck was pulling away with its lights off."

I said, "A friend of yours who likes to play with military ordinance?"

He sniffed the pungent air. "More of an acquaintance."

"Does he have tattoos all over him?"

His eyes narrowed. "Yeah. How do you ..."

"I saw him at your grandfather's place on Commercial Street. He was working on the trucks."

"That's him. Momo calls him the Mad Bomber."

The sirens were closing in. Blue lights lit up the distant sky, and porch lights were coming on all around us. I said, "Let's take cover in the trees over there and see if we can keep from getting picked up."

"Really? The ex-cop wants to run from the cops? I'm impressed," he said as we jogged toward the woods behind Fat Tommy's heir's new home, through which we could see the lights of another neighborhood in the distance.

"There's no time for cops. Mikey needs to pay for this and everything else he's done."

# 27

We cut through a patch of trees and scrub grass. Richie went charging off like a bull, while I did my best to stay upright. He was about fifteen feet ahead when he disappeared for a few seconds, then reappeared and shouted, "Hole!" I changed course to avoid it and met him at the tree line behind a small Cape Cod-style house at the top of a cul-de-sac.

Richie said, "You see what I see." Below us, in the distance, was a gleaming beacon in the dark night.

"Store 24?"

"Yeah, my mouth tastes like a scouring pad." He smacked his lips. "I need a pop."

A short while later, I was staring at the boundless array of energy drinks making up my mind when a squeaky yet determined voice arose from behind me. "I just knew I'd find you here. Damn, I am one hell of a cop."

I turned slowly, palms out. "Why, Pam! What a coincidence? You on duty tonight, are you?"

"That's funny, Town. But a coincidence would be you and I just happening to come into this place at the same time. What this *is*, is me getting called to investigate explosions and a charred body. Your exploded rental car being at the crime scene, and me knowing what a dipshit you are, I figured I'd find you stupidly hanging out at the Store 24 that I'd passed by on my way there."

I grinned at her like this was all good fun, and I wasn't screwed. "You're right, Pam. You're always right. I was incredibly lucky to survive an attack on my life. And, now, I'm on the trail of the man who killed Harlowe and Ray Phillips."

"I told you, Ray Phillips did that."

"Yeah, and I get military-grade weapons hurled at me every day. Why do you think someone tried to kill me?"

"Tried to kill *you*? And, pray tell, what is up with the dead mobster tied to a chair in the living room?"

"I never got a chance to find out. I'd just arrived when a freaking grenade rolled under my car and I got the hell out of there."

She leaned back on her heels, arms folded, knowing smile. "Alright, let's go for a ride, Town. You can ride in the back and pretend I'm your driver instead of the arresting officer."

"Come on, Pam. The fat mobster was killed by another mobster named Michael Colaposa and his henchman, whose name is Darryl something. Colaposa is the guy who blackmailed Josh Fagle and killed the two Phillips, Kenyatta Bell, and probably Kenzie Knight, whom I suspect knew about the blackmail plot. Colaposa is leaving town as we speak. Please help me stop him. Otherwise, he's gonna get away, and when this comes out, and it *will*, you are going to take the fall for it."

She began to chuckle. "That was a mouthful. You can explain it all, *slowly*, at the station."

"Colaposa works for Momo Ragazzi. He should've told Momo about his granddaughter getting knocked up by her boss, but he ran the blackmail scheme behind Momo's back instead. Momo would've killed him when he found out. Colaposa's desire to stay alive is the motive. I solved the case, Pam!"

"So, who's the dead guy again?"

"Colaposa's partner, Tommy Palermo. Colaposa must have decided it was too risky to leave him alive. Just give me a couple of hours to catch this guy. Go back to the scene, do your thing, and I'll meet you at the station first thing in the morning. We'll work it out so that you get credit for it. I swear to God."

"Jesus, Town. How stupid do you think I am? We'll do this the hard way. Turn around and put your hands behind your back. Come on, move it."

I stepped closer and looked down into her eyes. "I know some guys are put off by your aggressive nature, Pam. But I'm not one of them. I like it. I like it a little too much. That's my problem. I've been pushing you away because I have strong feelings for you. I fear what will happen if I let you in. I'm not sure I'm ready for that."

"I told you to turn around."

"Really, Pam. I mean it. You think this is gonna drive me away, but it's only making my attraction even stronger."

She undid the snap on her holster and enunciated each syllable as she said, "Turn around now."

Richie appeared over Pam's slim shoulder. He was standing near the exit and shouted, "Ride's here Town! Let's go!"

Pam turned her head in confusion. I took advantage of the brief reprieve and placed my hands on the small of her back and pulled her into me. I leaned down and kissed her neck, then her lips, which, to my surprise, were exquisite.

I had been right about her feelings for me. She didn't fight me, not right away. Her instinctual response was to moan and kiss me back. Then she came to, and her eyes flashed anger. She tried to wriggle from my grasp. "Let me go!"

As she did, I grabbed the handle of the ice cream freezer against which her behind was pressed. I slid the door open, placed a hand in the center of her chest and pushed her small frame down into the icebox so that only her hands, feet, and head were sticking out. I said, "Sorry, Pam, I gotta see this through. I'll see you at the station. I promise."

I blew her a kiss and followed Richie out the door as she tried to reach her gun and screamed, "Come back here, Town! You're under arrest, bastard!"

* * *

The ride was courtesy of a young woman named Petra and her friend Gabby. They went into the store for some late-night snacks and scored a Mafioso in training and an aging detective. Shoulda bought a lottery ticket instead.

They'd been clubbing and didn't appear to be particularly sober. Richie, who was riding shotgun, turned to me, "Gimme your phone. I lost mine in that ditch, and I've gotta wake the old man up and tell him about Tommy."

Petra said, "You guys wanna party? Gabby's got some more Molly."

"More?" I said. "Are you on Molly, now?"

"Maybe," Petra, the driver, answered with a giggle.

Gabby, who was leaning into me, and reeked of booze and cigarettes, said, "It's okay, she just had a coffee. Caffeine levels her out."

"Oh, perfect," I said as I dug my phone out of my jacket. "Oh, no." The screen had a chunk of steel about the size of a thumbnail embedded in it.

Petra cut a corner, and Gabby fell into my lap with a squeal. "Your phone's broken," she announced.

"I know." I held it up for Richie, and said, "I must have caught a ricochet. Ah, shit, my jacket's got a hole in it."

"You're lucky you don't have one too, old man."

"Old man?" said Gabby. "How old are you? You're cute."

Petra cut in. "Where are you going? Do you wanna party or not?"

I said, "Take the next right. We're gonna pick up my car. It's not far."

"You wanna follow us to my place? The night's still young."

Richie said, "We can't tonight, gotta catch a traitor."

"Aw. You're a bummer."

Richie said, "Which one of you is gonna loan me your phone?"

Gabby handed him hers, and he made the call while I watched the road and made sure Petra managed to stay between the lines. Soon after Richie got Momo on the phone, he reached between the seats and handed it to me. I tried to wave him off, but he wouldn't have it. I took the device, which had a rubber case with cat ears and whiskers, and prepared myself to take heat from the godfather.

"Earl Town."

"My grandson says he was nearly killed by a grenade. What the fuck is going on, detective?"

"Actually, it was two grenades. Your grandson is fine, and so am I, thanks for asking. Your man, Mikey Colaposa, is behind all of this, and he and Darryl killed Tommy, and I believe Harlowe Phillips and her father and Kenzie Knight as well."

There was a lengthy silence. "That dirty rat, mother; where is he now?"

"My belief is he's gone home to pack a few things before going on the run. We're on our way to his place, but we're delayed as Darryl blew up our ride."

"I'll get some men over there. You take care of my grandson. Put him back on." I gladly handed the phone back to Richie.

Eventually, Petra got us to my mechanic's garage in one piece, though she nearly took out a sign tearing out of there after we rebuffed her offer of a few tokes to commemorate our brief union.

"What'd the don say to you?"

"He wants me to go to his place until this blows over. The grenade thing freaked him out. He doesn't want to have to tell my old man he got his son got killed."

"Reasonable. What about Mikey?"

"He wants him alive, so he can get medieval on him."

"I can't be a party to torture," I said.

"Yeah, I know. He said for *us* to go to his place. I think you're done. You figured it out, now he'll take care of it."

"Oh, good. That means you can murder me now." He nodded in agreement.

We were standing outside the gate that allowed entry into the yard at Tim's Towing and Auto Repair. Tim, who everyone called Cookie, probably because he looked like he ate a lot of them, lived in a small farmhouse next door.

Richie changed the subject. "Nice move with that cop. I don't think she's gonna wanna be your bae anymore after that stunt."

"Yeah, great. Don't tell me what a bae is. I don't wanna know."

"It means ..." His expression turned fearful, and I spun around to see what was up. Maxey and Daisey, Cookie's Doberman Pinschers, were running at us full speed. Fortunately, they were stopped by the barbed-wire-topped chain-link fence that separated us, but they made an infernal racket. "Come on, Maxey. It's me, baby!" I said to the smaller of the pair. He wasn't buying it.

We covered our ears and watched as the porch light came on, and the dogs quieted down and awaited their boss, who soon emerged in a loose flannel bathrobe, XXXL briefs, and ancient moccasins. In one hand was a flashlight, in the other a chrome-plated Colt Python 357.

"Who's there?" he shouted from the porch.

"It's Earl Town! I got your voicemail about the Caprice being ready for pick up!"

"It's 3:30 in the am, Chief," he shouted as he began the long walk to the gate.

"I'm sorry, Cookie. The thing is, my rental car just blew up, and I really need the car, man."

"Blown engine?"

"No, grenade under the gas tank." He laughed. I'm a real cut-up.

He stepped up to the fence. Cookie made the recently departed Fat Tommy look like a decathlete. "Who is that?" he said with a glance at Richie.

"My intern." I slumped down and whispered, "I'm kind of his hero. He thinks I'm a modern-day Jim Rockford. I'd hate to let him down and come off looking like a jerk."

Cookie looked at Richie, then me, and said, "Might as well get it over with. Otherwise, I'll have to put up with your shit tomorrow." He hit the button that started the gate rolling back.

We were on the road toward Momo's when Richie brought

Pam back up. "You know, that was impressive. I didn't think you had any game. Hell, I heard you couldn't take your eyes off Lake's tits."

I glanced over at him. "Did she really say that?" His serious expression didn't change. "Damn. I tried not to look. Wait a minute, I saw you staring too. What'd she say about you?"

"She don't care about me. I'm a young, virile man. You're a dirty old man. There's a difference."

He stared at me. I said, "What?"

"You did good. You figured it out. I didn't see it, but you did."

"Thanks. Where do you think he's going?"

He eyed the double and triple deckers lining the street, broken only by the occasional bar or convenience store. Few lights were on. Daybreak was still more than an hour away. He said, "I don't know. South, I guess. If it were me, I'd head south and stay on the coast, get a boat in Jersey or Delaware, and head for the Caribbean."

"Is your grandfather waiting up for us?"

"Waiting up? He probably finished breakfast. He don't sleep much."

"I have a hunch about another place Mikey might head to before he really starts running. He may need to pick something up."

Richie raised an eyebrow. "Where would that be?"

❊ ❊ ❊

"How did you know?" Richie said as we pulled up across the street from one of Momo's black Cadillac Escalades, which was parked a block from the apartment shared by Mona Lisa and Lake Gelson.

"I told you earlier, Lake lured Harlowe and her father to the quarry by convincing Ray that Fagle was shooting a dirty movie up there. Ray went up there to catch him in the act and show his daughter what a scumbag Fagle was. A woman at the clinic where Kenyatta Bell volunteered said she had been upset that her guy was seeing someone behind her back. She was sure of it, she said. Today, Madison told me Lake had an Italian boyfriend. Plus, Kenyatta and Lake share a couple of prominent attributes. It all makes sense that Mikey and Lake were an item."

"You figured it out from just that?"

"Mmm, that's not the only thing. Lake gave me a big tell this afternoon when she asked me if I was okay. At the time, I thought maybe she saw me wince, but I'm good at hiding pain, and she's not particularly bright. If she was, she wouldn't be banging a mass murderer. I think someone told her about the beating I got the other night."

"Pretty good, Town."

"Yeah, I wasn't certain until I saw the SUV just now. Let's move before he comes out. He can't be planning on staying long."

"Wait a minute," said Richie. "Where's Sonny?"

"There's his Lincoln. Maybe he's asleep?"

"I'll call him," said Richie. He held phone to ear, "Straight to voicemail."

We split up, each staying low and using parked cars to conceal our approach. Richie moved south, away from the apartment, crossed the street a block down near Sonny's wheels, then made his way back in shadows on the same side of the street as the apartment. I went north, past the target, crossed the street and worked back to it in the same shadows. I kept my eye on the windows in their pad and saw no movement. My other concern was the roof deck. The skinny prick could be up there watching our every move.

Richie stayed in the shadows as I bolted up the steps and began working on the lock. Normally I'd buzz the owner, but nothing about this was normal.

Richie said, "Car's empty. Sonny's gotta be inside."

"Keep your eyes on the stairs, I'm a sitting duck." I made fast work of the lock, swung the door wide, and pressed fingertip to lip. He went in first and stepped aside. I led us up the stairs, guns at the ready, eyes wide, hearts pounding. Neither of us took a breath until we reached the third-floor stoop. We stood on the landing just outside the apartment, listening. Something moved inside.

Through the door came a voice, frantic and garbled. Richie said, "Who's there?" It became hysterical. The kid grabbed the knob and walked in. Mona Lisa lay on her side, not five feet from the door. She was hogtied and gagged. I worked the gag, while Richie found a knife for the knots. I got it loose and said, "What happened, and where is he now?

"Mike C. jumped us when we walked in," she said breathlessly. "He tied me up, took her prisoner, and left. He didn't say where to."

"He took Lake?"

"Yes."

"By force?"

"Yes!"

"In what? His ride's out front."

"He took her keys. She's got a BMW."

Richie said, "Where's Sonny?"

"Up on the roof, I think," said Mona Lisa as Richie severed the last of the twine, and she twisted and stumbled to her feet.

"How long ago?" I asked.

"Fifteen minutes? I thought I'd be there all night."

She ran to the powder room, and Richie took off for the roof deck. He came back in under a minute, his stare intense and moist. He was out of breath, but not from the stairs. "He killed Sonny."

Mona Lisa returned, looked at Richie, and said, "Is he?"

Richie asked for her phone and dialed Momo.

"How long has Lake been seeing him?"

"Not long, a month, six weeks." Mona Lisa wore a sparkling cocktail dress and stiletto heels. She stood with hands on the countertop, fingertips that matched her dress, tapping nervously. I realized that instead of calling the cops like any other young woman who'd just been the victim of a felony, she was waiting for Richie to get orders from Momo. Momo was law with these people. Everything else was a distraction.

I said, "Look, Lake is with a mass murderer. He also killed Harlowe and her dad, and probably Kenzie."

"What? *He* did it?"

"Are they in love?" I asked.

"No. Lake would never fall in love with him. She has a thing for bad boys. He came by with a gift from grandfather one day, and they started hooking up. It isn't serious."

"Why did he come for her tonight?"

"I don't know."

Still on the phone, but also tracking our conversation, Richie covered the speaker with a palm and said, "Come on, cuz, think."

"Is he running away from grandfather?"

In unison, Richie and I said, "Yes!"

"Well, Lake has her pilot's license and a plane."

"Where?" we demanded.

"Ah," she looked up at the ceiling, "North, somewhere. Um, what's it called?"

I said, "Beverly, Lawrence? Manchester?"

She shook her head.

"Pease? Laconia, Plum Island?"

"Plum Island. Yeah, that's it. Plum Island."

"Are you sure?" I asked her. "That's not much of a track. It's for very small planes only."

She looked at her cousin incredulous at my questioning her. "Yes! She has a Cessna."

Richie grabbed my shoulder and shouted, "Let's go!" I stepped toward the door, and Mona Lisa stepped in front of me.

She said, "You clowns aren't leaving me behind. Hold on while I grab my 45 and some sensible shoes."

# 28

We were leaving Boston on I-95 for Plum Island, only about forty minutes away, when the light bulb went off. "This is a micro airport. It's not going to take more than fifteen minutes for them to get airborne once they arrive. It's also located on a narrow stretch of road across from a salt marsh." I eyed Mona Lisa in the rearview, and said, "It sure would be helpful if they ran into a little traffic."

I watched it click in her head, then she went at her phone, thumbs ablaze.

Richie asked, "What's she doing?"

"Slowing them down."

Mona Lisa reached a hand through the seats and showed us a message she'd sent to her minions. It read: *Urgent! Arriving 5:30 am, Plum Island Airport, need crowd for music video. All who come will be featured. Be a star!* I gave her a thumbs up. She went back to typing.

Richie looked at it and asked what platforms it went out on, and she rattled off a dozen of them. Then she said, "Ooh! My Trey is coming! He's a little confused and possibly jealous that I'm keeping secrets from him. Yay!" Her thumbs hit high gear.

I said, "You're texting him? Why don't you just call and talk to him? Be a lot faster."

"Shush," she said.

Richie said, "Old man, nobody talks on the phone anymore."

"You talk to your grandfather all the time on yours."

"Yeah, well, that's his choice."

Mona Lisa stopped typing, "Phone calls are abrasive. Texts are more respectful. He is jealous!"

"You guys are crazy," I said. "You need to get information to him quickly. For Christ's sake, be a little abrasive."

I turned to Richie. "What's the deal on Momo's guys again?"

"A pair of guys left Stoneham about the same time we did, so they should be a few miles ahead of us, and there's a couple more trailing us."

"Excellent." I looked at the beauty behind me and said, "Please tell Trey to leave the tough-guy act at home. There's a real tough guy involved in this. You wouldn't want to see your boy's pretty face messed up."

Mona Lisa smirked, and said, "Trey can handle himself." I looked at Richie, who just shook his head.

We were getting closer to our exit in Newburyport when we passed a Lincoln Navigator in the breakdown lane with its hood open. Richie spun and eyed the pair standing in front of it, gazing at the radiator, which was blowing steam.

"Are those your guys?" I asked.

"Pffft," he let some air out in disgust. "Yup, can't count on anybody."

"Geez, save the cynicism until you hit your thirties, at least."

I gazed in the rearview at Mona Lisa, who was still tapping aggressively on her phone. "We really need help now. Are troops on their way?" She didn't hear me. I cleared my throat and asked again.

She said, "Yeah, we passed several. Didn't you see them?"

"No. Please tell them to pick up the pace. Tell them the plane is arriving early. We need them there in ten minutes."

Richie said, "What's this?"

We pulled up alongside two young girls in a Mini Cooper. The driver had the same hair color and cut as Mona Lisa. "Is this more of them?"

Mona Lisa slouched down in her seat. "I'm supposed to be

in the plane, dummy." She kicked the back of my seat, and said "Speed up before they see me."

Richie smiled and made eyes at the passenger. "That my bae, right there. She's alright."

"She looks like your cousin," I said. He clammed up.

Mona Lisa's phone kept buzzing, and she kept ignoring it. Richie turned and looked at the screen. "It's your mother. Why don't you answer it?"

"Because I'm ignoring her calls."

"Why? She's worried about you."

"No," said Mona Lisa. "She's loco."

"Yeah, runs on that side of the family," said Richie.

"You mean, Momo's side? That's also your side," I pointed out.

"No," he said. "I mean the *women*." I extended my fist, and we bumped.

Mona Lisa shouted, "My fans are arriving. They're asking where to go!"

"Tell them the video is about Lake being kidnapped. Their role is to make sure her plane doesn't take off before you arrive and save the day. Tell them to block the runway if necessary."

"What if he shoots them?"

"He won't. There'll be too many to shoot. Look, there's more ahead." We were approaching the off-ramp, and there were a good ten cars lined up at the lights that separated the exit from Route 133, which would take us into Newburyport. "Just look at those SUVs. There's Boom stickers on at least three."

"My fans are the best in the world," she said.

I said, "Aren't you worried about them getting pissed at you when there's no film crew there?"

"Oh, I'll film them."

"With what?"

"With my phone!"

"With your *phone*?"

She and Richie shared a look. Then he said, "Yeah, Gramps, the camera on a new iPhone is state of the art."

"Oh yeah?" I said. "The sound isn't."

Mona Lisa said, "I'll give the video to Boom, and they'll put some music under it. And, just as I promised, my fans will be in a music video for Fatal Mistake. And they will be thrilled to be forever immortalized as members of MonaNation."

"Damn," I said. What more was there to say?

Mona Lisa said, "Oh shit. They're there, look!"

"Where?" I stared through the windshield and scanned the edges of the road.

She leaned against my seat and waved her phone between us. One of her fanatics was streaming live video of Lake Gelson and Mikey arriving at the airport. Lake was driving and looking stressed. Mikey looked evil. The caption read: *Lake is here to welcome home Mona Lisa! This is going to be huge!*

I said, "Can you talk to her?"

"Not with this app, but I saw someone in the crowd I can Skype."

"Skype?" I had to ask.

"Video chat," said Richie.

From behind me, Mona Lisa said, "Yes, it's really me, Sonja."

A girl on the other end squealed loud enough to make me wince, then said, "Mona Lisa is Skyping me from the plane!"

I turned and looked at the screen, a girl with a round face, braces, and acne was surrounded by others with a similar look. Mona Lisa turned the phone back to her and said, "Where's Lake? Show me Lake, please."

A chorus of "There's Lake" and "Lake's over there" went up. Mona Lisa sat back and held the phone out. She said, "Look in the rearview. Can you see it?"

"Richie, move your head. Yes, I can see it. Good idea. Oh shit."

I watched as Skinny Mikey stomped up to the phone and tore it from Sonja's stubby fingers. He stared wild-eyed into the screen and said, "Son of a bitch! Is that you, Town? I got business to finish with you."

"Yeah, you do!" I said. "I'm gonna give you some more bruises to go with that fat lip. Don't you go flying away on me."

Mikey walked as he spoke. He approached a small plane parked alongside the airstrip. Someone, Lake, I think, was preparing the plane for flight. I almost drove into the back of a Subaru with a "Yoga is Life" bumper sticker as I struggled to follow the action behind Mikey along with the road in front of us. I would've hit it too if it hadn't moved aside for me. It was the third car to do so. Field Marshall Angeloni had directed her troops to clear the way for us.

Mikey stuck his mug in front of the camera again. "Cop scumbag! You better hope you don't catch up to me. Cause, I promise you Town, I'll kill you if you do."

"Yeah, yeah," I said.

Richie grabbed the phone, stared into the lens, and said, "You went behind the godfather's back. You're as good as dead, Mike." Then he handed it back.

I said, "Thanks, Richie."

"Are we ready?" said Mikey to someone nearby. "Come on, let's go!"

Out of the blue, a woman, not Mona Lisa, said, "You leave the ground, your ass is grass, Colaposa."

"Who the fuck is this?" said Mikey.

I took my eyes off the road and leaned closer to the screen. "Pam, is that you? How'd you get into our video thingy?"

"Butt out, Town," she said. "Listen scumbag, we caught Darryl Leavens, and he had a lot to say. I'm arresting you for conspiracy in the death of Thomas Palermo, at a minimum. This is just the first of many charges."

Mikey held the phone up to his nose. Spittle hit the screen as he shouted, "Fuck off, cop! You ain't catching me!"

I had passed through the old-timey center of Newburyport. The mouth of the Merrimack River was on our left. We were no more than a half-mile from the airstrip. I shouted, "What'd you do with Unique after you murdered her?"

Mikey said, "You don't know shit, Town."

Pam said, "Turn yourself in, Colaposa."

I said, "Pam, I'm trying to get answers."

"And I told you to shut up. I got a set of handcuffs here with your name on them too."

Mikey took one last look at the camera and said, "Both of you go to hell." Then he looked into the distance and shouted, "Here crybaby!" The phone spun through the air, landed on the grass, and rolled onto an edge. I watched as Mikey climbed into a two-seater and listened as the little bird fired up its engines and rolled onto the runway. Then a chubby-faced teen picked up the phone and said, "Who is this?"

I said, "Pam, where are the cops?"

"On our way, jerk. Where are you?"

Sonja said, "Cops?"

I could see the runway off to our right. There was a line of thirty cars stopped between us and the small building that served as offices and storage. I said, "Hold on tight everybody, it's gonna get a little bumpy!" Between the airstrip and road, there is marshland, but near the entrance, the marsh turns to solid earth lined with logs that provide a barrier between airstrip and roadway. There is no fence. I'd passed the marsh, and now I cut the wheel and launched off a log through the air before slamming back down on a strip of dewy grass. The moisture sent us into a sideways slide that ceased when the tires on the passenger side caught the edge of the runway, and the car lurched so far to the right that I thought for sure we were going to tip over.

We rocked to a stop. Mona Lisa poked her head between the seats, and the three of us stared straight ahead at the Cessna, which was taxiing directly at us.

"What are you gonna do?" asked Richie.

"I'm going to step on the gas and stop them before they take off. Get out now if you don't want to crash." Nobody moved. I gunned it. In a few seconds, the plane would either lift off or smash into the Caprice. I'd hate to see my baby come to its end this way, I thought before I realized my ass was on the line too. Death by propeller was like being fed through a deli slicer. Mikey leaned out of the plane with his gun extended. Mona Lisa shouted, "Duck!" and I swerved. He fired and missed. The passenger-side wheels hit the gravel on the edge of the runway, and we nearly skidded off into the marsh. I cut the wheel and made it back onto the airstrip in time to see him raise the revolver again. This would be his last shot. There was no more time. Impact was coming.

This time Richie shouted, "Duck!" as I swerved again. I heard the bullet glance off the rear quarter panel. We'd avoided being shot, but we were only seconds away from crashing. I could see the terror in Lake's eyes as she fought to get the plane off the ground. "Hold on tight!" I shouted as I chickened out and cut the wheel. We veered right as the plane finally began to lift off. As its wings caught the first updraft, the plane jerked from side to side, and this caused one of the wheels to drop right in front of us.

Mona Lisa screamed, and we all ducked as the wheel hit the windshield dead center. The glass shattered into the gap between Richie and me, as the tire left a deep crease in the middle of the roof and shattered the back window.

The downward force of the plane's wheel, and its sudden release, caused the Caprice to corkscrew, and we flew into a series of spins, which culminated in a skid. We finally stopped in the center of the runway, facing the Cessna. Lake had been forced into a rough landing, and the plane sat unsteadily in the grass a short distance away. The prop still turned, but a wheel was missing, and the plane slumped to one side. From behind it emerged Mikey and Lake. He had an arm wrapped around her neck and his gun to her head.

The crowd was closing in on a hundred, almost all of them young women. A few were in tears and shouting in fear for Lake, but most had gotten Mona Lisa's message and thought it was all part of the video shoot. They watched in awe, most filming the action with their phones.

I said, "Take cover!" and opened my door to use as a barrier, and Richie did the same. Mona Lisa climbed over the front seat and told me to move over, which I did.

Mikey stepped toward us, using Lake as a shield. The screaming sirens of a half-dozen approaching police cars filled the air. He shouted over them and the plane's engine, "I'm taking the car, Town! Drop your weapons, all of you!"

Richie shouted, "No! You're gonna die, traitor!"

I said, "Let me handle this," then shouted, "The car is dead!"

He stopped and looked around. Seeing no better alternative, Mikey said, "I don't believe you! I'm taking it!" But he didn't advance.

I said, "There's no hope, Mikey! That way is an island. The only way out is past all the cops. Unless you got a boat!"

"I got a hostage, so I think I'll be alright!"

"A hostage or an accomplice?"

Lake said, "What? He kidnapped me!"

"Why'd you lure Ray and Harlowe to their murders?" I asked her.

"He made me! And, I didn't know he was going to kill them!" Mikey reared back and smacked her in the side of the head with his weapon, then tightened his grip around her throat and lifted her off the ground.

I started to shout something, but Mona Lisa cut me off. "You bastard, I'm gonna make you pay for that!"

I said, "Be careful. Do not kill your roommate by accident." Then I yelled, "Where's Unique?"

He played it like a rat, as I knew he would. After he said, "Screw you, princess!" to Mona Lisa, he turned his eyes to me and said, "I don't know her!"

I said, "Half the staff at The Man Cave IDed you. They miss your tips, big spender!"

The first police cars were arriving and trying to get through the crowd, which was also still arriving. Skinny Mikey looked around and appeared to become resigned to his fate. He began to speak some truth. "I liked Unique. She became a problem."

"I asked what you did with her."

Mikey chuckled and said, "You know, we were just about done with that kid. That Fagle. Then the girl's father sticks his nose in."

"How did he know it was you?"

"He was watching Fagle, saw him make a drop and followed Darryl after the pick-up. That guy was a good snoop, put you to shame, Town."

"You didn't have to kill him and his kid, Mike. That was stupid."

"That was business."

"What you did to Kenzie Knight, was that business too?"

He said, "I don't know anything about ..." Lake Gelson slipped from his grasp, drove her knee into his groin, and ran toward salvation. She had almost reached us when Mikey regained his composure and pointed his weapon at her back. I aimed for his chest and was just beginning to clinch my trigger when a thunderous boom set off a thousand alarm clocks in my right ear.

Mona Lisa had fired a round from her 45 straight into his groin. The creep dropped his weapon, clutched his crotch, stumbled backward, and stepped into the Cessna's whirring propeller. The spectacle turned out to be more woodchipper than deli slicer, I thought to myself, as specks of blood, tissue, and bone splattered the door behind which Mona Lisa and I had taken cover.

"Ew, disgusting!" she said, while brushing a piece of Mikey from her shoulder.

Pam Prentiss and a small squad from her department, along with about three dozen state police officers, descended on us within seconds, and despite the protestations of a social media star and mafia heir, Pam slapped on the cuffs and hauled me off to jail. She hit me with resisting arrest—a felony charge at that, as she said I had created a substantial risk of serious physical injury or death to several persons, which I guess was true. She also hit me with a second felony for incitement of a riot, as well as a number of misdemeanors. I didn't blame her. I had it coming. Anyway, Irv owed me, and I was too tired to care. I couldn't wait to get into a nice calm jail cell, and when I finally did, I curled up on a bunk and slipped into a deep, restful sleep.

# 29

I awoke to the steady tapping of a baton on the sole of my loafer. A gruff cop stood over me. "Come on, get up, buddy. This ain't the Holiday Inn."

I shook out the cobwebs and stumbled down a dim hall into an interrogation room. In the room sat Lyle Hand. The big man smiled. I smiled back and took note of his finely tailored plaid jacket and silk pocket square. Across from Lyle sat Irving Wechsler in something made of petroleum byproducts and probably constructed before the advent of the microwave oven. He glared at me and pushed his glasses up his rather lengthy honker. I turned and found Pam Prentiss leaning against the wall by the doorway. I'm not sure if the look she threw me was mostly disgust or hate, but it contained more than a pinch of each. I decided to play against what she'd expect and scowled at her as I sat where Lyle was pointing.

She took the bait. "Are you fucking kidding me, Town. You're giving me attitude?" She took two strides and glowered down at me. Without averting her eyes from mine, she said to Irv, "Lyle and I are going to step out and get us a coffee. When we return, your client better adopt a new attitude or the deal's off. You hear me, counselor?"

Irv practically jumped out of his seat. "Yes! Absolutely. He will have a new attitude when you return, or he'll have to make do with a public defender because I'll quit."

Pam held her stare on me as she turned to leave, the big man trailing right behind her. He looked my way too and said, "You are either dumb or crazy."

I gave him wild eyes and said, "Why can't it be both?"

My counsel shushed me and glared. I sat back and waited for the tsunami that was about to breach the cove.

"Jesus Christ, Earl. I have been working on a deal all Goddamn day, and you walk in here, and without saying a word, you take a dump all over it. You are not worth my trouble and certainly not at a reduced fee."

I said, "I'm sorry about Unique. You did hear what he said?"

"Yeah, I got a copy of what you told them during the arrest." He held up a Manila folder. "Look, you delivered a serial killer to Pam. The guy killed four people that we know of, including Unique and the gangster on the roof. Now, Detective Prentiss is not happy that you worked it out that he killed Harlowe and Ray Phillips after she publicly stated Ray did it. Of course, she didn't know about Unique before, because nobody gave two shits about her."

"You did, Irv. That's why this whole thing came together, because you cared about her."

"Yeah, well, thanks, Chief. Look, Detective Prentiss may be willing to drop some of the charges, which, as you know, are incredibly serious, but you need to apologize, and you better walk on eggshells because she is itching to destroy you. In twenty-five years, I've never seen a cop with a hair across his ass the size of hers. Just what did you do to her?"

I stared at the table, unable to look him in the eye. "If I tell you, you're liable to quit on me, so I'm not telling you, not while we're both sober. It was about as bad as it can get, though."

He was staring wide-eyed at me while working through the potential horrors when Pam and Lyle returned.

They both held coffees. Pam had two actually, one of which she handed to Irv. He thanked her, then offered me the first sip. Pam sneered and said, "Don't you fucking dare, counselor."

Irv apologized and moved the cup out of my reach.

I said, "Pam, I'd like to apologize to you for the horrible things I've done. I'm not going to insult you by trying to excuse my actions. I just hope you'll permit me to assist you and Detective Hand in any way I can."

Lyle said, "Why, how about that? He's a new man."

I folded my hands on the table and smiled at him.

Pam took a seat to my left while Irv was across the table. I had an overwhelming urge to make a crack along the lines of, "So who's dealing?" But I fought it off like a champ. You know I really think it's true that men mature later than women, and I fully expect to reach maturity somewhere in my early sixties.

Pam leaned back, arms folded, and said, "You got some seriously fucked up friends, Town. I got a call about you from Momo Ragazzi today. He sang your praises, then called me honey, and told me not to let my sexual frustration impact my decision-making—whatever the fuck that means. Just what are you involved in?"

I looked at Irv. I could tell he wanted to object to the question but didn't dare. I figured it was rhetorical and kept silent until Pam said, "Well, say something, you hairy ape."

"Momo called? That's nice."

"Shut the fuck up."

I pressed my lips together and admired the wall clock.

Pam went on. "Speaking of your underworld friends, I told your pal Momo's grandson that your ass was in a sling, but he didn't so much as make a peep to help you out."

"Ah," I said. "I'm not surprised. He was bred to hate cops. He's a good kid, though. At least I think he is. He goes to Brown. On the fencing team, too, so they say."

"He's got a record, and he's done time in maximum security," she said.

I grimaced while Lyle showed everyone his immense skill at making the precise sound of a World War II bomb falling from a B-17 and exploding.

"Well," I said. "He was helpful in rooting out Mikey Colaposa. Richie's not entirely stupid, kind of devious." *And likely a danger-*

*ous sociopath*, I added only to myself. Though the look Irv shot me suggested he was reading my mind.

"Let me ask you this, mister big-shot detective," Pam said as she leaned in close, and I caught a whiff of her breath, which was minty. She'd brushed her teeth just for little 'ol me. She smelled nice too. "You have anything on Colaposa other than circumstantial evidence and that supposed airport confession that not one of more than fifty video recordings picked up over the sirens and plane engine? Aside from the confession of a twice-convicted felon with a grenade fetish, I've got nothing else, and I got people crawling up my ass with questions about a closed case. Now, I'll admit to a mistake if I made one, but I kind of need some evidence to do so. You got any evidence, Town?"

"What about the mobster on the roof?"

"Stabbed, the knife wiped clean. The mafia princess and her friend, Ms. Hindenburg tits, will testify to the kidnapping, but neither one saw him kill the gangster."

I looked at Irv, and Pam took my chin between her thumb and forefinger and turned it to her.

Irv said, "Officer, that's ..."

Pam cut him off, "You got a problem with what I'm doing, Town?"

"No," I said as best I could with limited jaw mobility.

She released me and waited for my answer. I said, "I'm afraid I don't have any physical evidence. It's not ideal."

"Not ideal," she parroted me. "Lyle, what do you think about committing several felonies and a string of misdemeanors in the process of collecting zero fucking evidence that a crime was committed by a man who is then blasted into a moving airplane propeller by one of your associates? Is that ideal, or not ideal, in your book, Lyle?"

Lyle looked at Irv then me, chuckled a little, then realized Pam wasn't laughing and got serious. He said, "Detective Prentiss, in my professional opinion, that is *not* ideal."

She bit her bottom lip and raised her brow, like a school principal about to mete out punishment. "What about Kenyatta

Bell? You and your friends say he admitted to killing her? So, how and where, and where is she now?"

"Ah, I, I can't answer that," I muttered.

"What's that? You said what?" She leaned in close again. I think the scent was sandalwood.

I said, "I have witnesses that can attest that she was dating him and that she had access to the information Colaposa used to blackmail Fagle."

Pam slammed a palm on the table, and Irv spilled coffee on his polyester tie. She said, "And where the *fuck* is Fagle?"

"Ah, well, I don't know where, specifically, but I can reach him. I made him a deal that he couldn't refuse on that front."

That made her chuckle. "You hear that, Lyle? A deal he couldn't refuse. He sounds a bit like a gangster. Figures, since that's who he's been palling around with."

Lyle said, "It's a shame to see a man ruin his reputation with behavior like that. I'm sorry, Pam, but I got a dinner to get to. Can we get to my case?"

Pam got a wild look in her eyes. She said, "You want him to tell you he has nothing for you too? You go right ahead, Lyle." She folded her arms and leaned back.

"Thank you, Detective Prentiss. Town, you got anything for me on the Knight case?"

I sighed, knowing what I was about to say. "You heard what Colaposa said when I asked him, Detective Hand?"

"You mean what he started to say before your associate shot him in the dick and his top-half was whisked into chum?"

"Yes," I said. "And, yes, that's all I've got."

Surprisingly, Pam did not spike the ball but stayed reclining and looking dejected.

I said, "Look, I know I haven't made this neat and tidy."

Pam practically choked at the understatement.

"But we'll find the evidence. What's up with forensics? Surely, they can tie him to one of the murder scenes. A print, a hair, a fiber of clothing?"

"We're working on it," said Pam.

I looked at Lyle and said, "Is there anything you can share that might help me make a connection?"

"There you go!" Irv interjected. "Let's work together." Pam rolled her eyes and sighed.

Lyle thought about it and said, "She had her vape cartridges delivered to her by this guy. His name's Matthew Black, also goes by Blackie. You come across him anywhere?"

"No. I'm sorry, I didn't," I said.

"Of course not," said Pam. "You know, I got two FBI agents telling me to throw the book at you. You couldn't stop yourself from beating the shit out of that strip-club owner, could you?"

"He was going to kill me. Irv was there, he'll tell you."

She turned to Irv and smiled, "You were there, while he was assaulting this man."

"He was defending himself. The guy has these big bouncers. If Richie hadn't been there, I don't know what would've happened."

"Yeah," Pam agreed as she smirked at me, "It's a good thing Town's mafia buddy bailed him out."

I began to plead my case, then remembered what I had meant to ask earlier: "Hey, how did you find out about the chase to the airport, and since when can you bust into a private call like that?"

"Mona Lisa Angeloni's downstairs neighbor told us she overheard you shouting about the dead guy on the roof and driving to Plum Island Airport. And, if it's on the Internet, it ain't private, Sherlock."

A silence fell over the room until Irv broke the ice. "What about Lake Gelson? Has she shed any light on Colaposa, Bell, or Knight?"

Pam said, "We have evidence, as well as a confession, to Gelson's role in establishing an online persona through which she communicated with Ray Phillips in the days preceding his and his daughter's deaths. She said Colaposa forced her to do it, and she was too afraid to tell anyone. She says she had no idea he may have killed the others."

"Do you believe her?" I asked.

"Yes, and, believe me, I don't want to." She sniffed the air as though it were foul. Perhaps it was, as I'd been quite a few hours without a shower or a change of clothes.

I looked at Lyle. He said, "Same. She's either a damn good actress or telling the truth."

"How would you know? You couldn't take your eyes off her rack," said Pam. Lyle stared into his coffee cup after that.

I said, "Set me free and give me a little time. I might be able to find Miss Bell. I know some people."

Irv perked up. Pam looked disgusted. "Sure, I'll bet your friends know where all the bodies are buried."

"I don't know about all of them, but I'm only looking for one."

❊ ❊ ❊

Irv dropped me off at my place. It was nearly 11 pm, and the lights were on.

"Ow," said nephew Ed rubbing the back of his head where he had whacked it on the refrigerator after snapping up when I walked up behind him while he was reaching for one of my beers.

"There better be two in there, or you're out of luck, Ed. Cause I sure as hell am drinking one."

"I figured as much and picked up a fresh rack of Modelo on the way over," he said, as he tossed a can my way. I popped the top and downed most of it in one long draft.

"You had a chance to see the news?"

"No," I said as I sat back into my sofa and lifted a tired foot onto the coffee table. "I've been in a cell and interrogation room for about the last sixteen hours."

"Yeah, I can smell."

"Uh-huh. What you smell is the smell of failure, Ed. I caught a mass murderer but have no evidence to prove it."

"Don't the cops have anything?"

"Nope. They're praying forensics comes up with something. What's up with the news?"

"There were a lot of people filming the showdown, and it's all over the place."

"Yeah?"

"The coverage doesn't really mention you. It's all been focused on Mona Lisa. The video of her blasting that dude into the propeller has gone beyond viral. She and her boyfriend are blowing up social media—the top story on every platform. She's a huge star now. Thanks to you."

"Her boyfriend?"

"Yeah, the punk rocker with the pink hair. He's taking credit for your work."

Ed walked over and showed me the back page of the *Boston Herald*. The headline read: "Crimefighter in a Cocktail Dress." Underneath was a picture that must have been taken after I'd been locked in the back of a cop car. Mona Lisa and Trey were embracing next to a puddle of Mikey's insides. The mafia princess had one hand on her 45 and the other on Trey's boney ass.

I downed the last of my beer and said, "Oh nice, he finally showed up."

# 30

Three days later, I found Irving leaning into the bar at Bob Loo's slurping a vodka martini. It was his second, and it was 10:30 am. His terminally unruly brown mop looked as though it'd been quaffed by Frank Gehry. I slid onto the red leather stool next to him. The little old proprietor looked at me expectantly, but I shook him off.

I said, "You don't have to do this, Irv. It's been nearly two weeks since he did it. It won't look or smell pretty. You're better off remembering her as she was. Stay here, slow down, and let me take care of it."

"No, Chief. I want to be there. I want to find an empty basement, so I can believe she's moved on. If she's there, I want to see her and get closure. She was a good kid, Earl. What kind of guy murders a kid like her?"

I decided it wasn't too early, signaled old Bob, and pointed to the tequila. He held up the bottle, and I responded with two fingers. It took the edge off as I listened to Irv moaning on about life's inequities.

"You seemed okay a couple of days ago. It hit you hard, huh?"

"I was repressing it. Then the dam broke."

"What I don't get, Irv, is what was so special about this one?"

"Aside from her likely being murdered by a mobbed-up psychopath?" he raised his voice.

I smiled, "I'm on your side, Irv."

"Sorry, I'm having trouble squaring the fact that you were working with this guy."

"No, I thought we went over this. I stopped the scumbag from destroying more lives."

"I know, but how many do you think he killed for Momo?"

Bob went wide-eyed and turned away from a replay of the last Michigan-Notre Dame tussle. I shook Irv's shoulder and said, "Keep your voice down, Irv. And leave names out of it. Can't take you anywhere."

I sipped the golden agave. "You are the last person on earth I would expect to start giving me shit over my client list. You know how this works, Wechsler. In fact, I caught flack the other day for working with a certain defender of scumbags."

"From who?"

"From a cop who heard about you and your middle school tugger."

He went wild-eyed and said, "You're right, fuck me! I am an *asshole!*" He raised his arm for another round, so I grabbed it and pinned the wing to his side. Then I talked Bob into slowly stepping away from the Boston shaker. "No way, Irv. I'm not carrying you out of here. No more booze for you." I stood and paid the check, then pulled him off his stool and out into a pristine June morning.

"Here's what you need. Vitamin D. What the hell did you do last night, anyway?" I asked as we climbed into another damn rental. The latest repairs to the Caprice were gonna take a week.

"Fuck if I remember. Bob woke me up as he was opening." I shook my head.

"Hey, man, I'm a sensitive guy. So what?"

"You really love an underdog, don't you? That's what this is about. It's not her, so much as the idea of her." We drove on city streets dappled by the late spring sun. Fresh green leaves burst from the trees. People were out in short sleeves and shorts, relishing the warm air and dreaming about even hotter days in the weeks to come.

After a long while, Irv said, "Yeah, there's truth to what you said. I dug her, man. She was a good kid, but I used to tell her, 'You know, you got talent, you got looks, youth, great skin, hair, everything. You can do big things.' And I think she got it, and she was going to do big things. And I think we're all worse off for her not getting her shot."

*  *  *

The rotting, gray-paint-flecked Cape sat on a side street in Dorchester, two blocks from the sea. It was an upscale neighborhood of old triple-deckers that had been turned from rooming houses and apartments into large single-family homes for Boston's executive class. The owners of two of these mini-mansions had installed tall hedges on one side to block the view of the small dilapidated eyesore stuck between them. The little shack was turned so that one of the gable ends faced the street. It ran back about 30 feet into a micro yard, which backed up to, of all things, a Boston Patrolman's Association building.

We sat for bit while I looked for prying eyes. When I felt it was clear, we made our way around to the back of the shack, as I had been instructed. I made quick work of the padlock on a rusty bulkhead door and gradually swung one door up and open, making as little noise as possible. I turned on my Maglite and signaled Irv to lift and tighten the bandana I'd affixed around his neck.

As we made our way down the four or five steps, Irv said, "You are way too proficient with that set of picks, Earl. You want to tell me something?"

"I'll take that as a compliment and hold onto my secrets, thank you, Irv."

The first thing in the ancient cellar that turned my stomach wasn't the smell, though it was foul. It was the beam of light coming in through the small window in the southwest corner. It was what it revealed about the air. That it was filled with a flotilla of animal and plant matter, shit and insects, and dirt, dust, and flesh that been trapped in this room for years. That was the air we were breathing.

It wasn't more than a few seconds later that I registered the source of the fetid aroma. It emanated from a dark form along the back wall.

Kenyatta Bell had been buried for nearly two weeks, dug up and brought here. Wherever she had been was a secret because she probably had some neighbors. My latest client had done me a solid and arranged this, and it depressed the hell out of me. I now owed him something. Guys like Momo always collect on favors. But Irv needed to know what happened to her, and the cops needed clues to tie her to Mikey. So, now I was beholden to the guy I thought I was done with.

The body was wrapped in clear plastic. Irv peeled back the folds as I reminded him, "Careful, don't go leaving any DNA or prints behind."

We heard a squeak and watched as a rat sprang from inside the plastic and scuttled past Irv, who, to his credit, did not scream. In a loud whisper, he said, "I think I just died." He picked himself up and stared at the youthful beauty for a good while before finally pulling the folds together. "Goddamn shame, just a Goddamn shame."

We stopped at a nearby Cumberland Farms with one of the few remaining payphones in New England. Irv called Pam and told her where to find Unique. I told him to disguise his voice, thinking he'd go deeper. Instead, he went higher and topped it off with a lisp.

As I was driving him home, I said, "Sometimes a guy like me gets lonely at night. If I were to call and offer to pay you to say sweet things to me in that voice, would you do it?"

He didn't move, and I thought he was mad that I made a joke. Then he said, "Five bucks for the first minute, three for each additional."

"It's a deal, I'll work fast," I said.

❊ ❊ ❊

That evening was the world premiere and closing performance of *Brains, Brawn, and B\*lls: A Life in Three Acts*—the school
administrators had insisted on the asterisk. I'd received an in-
vite from the work's creative genius and subject matter expert
via a visit from his new right-hand thug. He was standing by
a double-parked SUV in front of my stoop just like Fat Tommy
and Skinny Mikey had been. He said, "You Earl Town?"

"I am."

He held out an envelope. "Mr. Ragazzi instructed me to give
you these tickets and to express his great desire that you attend
this exclusive one-night-only performance of his life story in
words and music."

Ed was my date for the show. I know it's a weird choice, but
I was still in between women, and I had an ulterior motive. Of
course, rather than be pleased that I'd extended the invitation,
he was giving me grief.

"Why not? I'm not a kid. I can handle meeting him."

"Really? Then why are you still living with your mommy?"

"Screw you."

"You're my sister's kid. I'm not introducing you to the godfather. I will never hear the end of it if I do. You know that's the
truth!"

He sighed and buried his nose in his phone.

A while later, I was complaining to another theater maven
about the lack of alcohol at the refreshment stand. He was ex-
plaining to me that we were in a high school auditorium, and
there was no booze allowed. I said to the guy, "I'll bet half the
teachers' desks in this place have a bottle stashed." He wouldn't
take the bet, even after I offered to go two to one. That's when I
saw her and waved. She came over as I was telling Ed to stand up
straight.

The radiant Madison Pontiforno said, "Hi, Mr. Town! Thank
you for what you did!" She threw her arms around me. I almost
told Ed to get lost, but I introduced him instead.

"Madison, it is wonderful to see you. Ed, this is Madison
Pontiforno, easily the most beautiful and talented of the Boom

girls."

"Aw, you shouldn't, Mr. Town," she squealed with irresistible, youthful delight.

"Oh, yes, I should, Madison, I'm so happy you were able to come tonight because I would like to introduce you to my nephew Edward Chase, a computer whiz who was instrumental in helping me solve the case. He's also unattached at the moment."

Ed's expression transformed from nervous to confused. Madison beamed and said, "He's cute. Can I borrow him?"

"That is precisely why I brought him, ma'am." I made a big show of stepping aside as she locked arms and led Ed away. There was no point in warning the boy. He would've chickened out if I'd told him in advance that I was going to introduce him to a ten with a thing for geeks.

It was time to find the patriarch. I asked a kid I recognized from rehearsal where I could find him. He was already in costume and wore a shark-skin suit over a black turtleneck. Apparently, he was from the Stanislavski School of Acting, as he looked me over and said in a surly tone, "Who's asking?"

I leaned in and whispered conspiratorially, "He told me any kid who screws up gets a pair of cement shoes, so I went home and got his valium. It's best for everyone that he's sedated."

The kid dropped character and pointed to a door with BAND on it. I knocked. "Come in," sang Ginny Angeloni.

I entered what was a band room, alright. There were two rows of music stands, the back row elevated. Momo and Shirley Munson were seated on their canvas director's chairs in front, while Ginny had a cheek-and-a-half on the teacher's desk, and Ron Shields leaned against a wall observing from a safe distance. I nodded to him as I made my way to the popular clique.

Momo was saying something along the lines of, "He's gotta be in the spotlight when the shot goes off. If he's not in the spotlight, it loses all dramatic effect. He's got to be there."

She said, "And I keep telling you, he will be, Giacomo."

Momo looked up at me and said, "There he is, it's about time you showed your face. I appreciate what you did, you know." He stood and shook my hand between both of his.

"I did what you paid me for, Mr. Ragazzi. Nothing more."

"Yeah, well, you made my granddaughter a movie star; that's what you did."

"What do you mean?"

Momo looked at Ginny, who was about to speak and said, "Where's Richie? Get Richie, let him tell Earl the news." This was the first time he'd used my first name. It didn't feel good. I prefer murderers stick to calling me Town.

Ginny went to look for Richie. Momo nudged Shirley and said, "Ms. Munson has done an amazing job preparing her students. You are in for a real treat tonight. You are staying?"

"Oh yeah. I can't wait for the curtain to fall."

"Good, good. Shirley, how are we looking for time?"

Shirley, who had outdone herself in a red velvet suit, said it was time for a final check and excused herself. I watched Momo watch her leave. "She has a way with exits."

"Entrances too." He grunted his agreement.

I heard Richie approaching before he burst through the door saying, "Where is he?" He spotted us and marched over. "You're looking good, old man. Staying out of fights?"

"Physical ones, yes," I said.

Ginny said, "Tell him about the call today before I do."

Richie said, "When the video of Mona Lisa went viral, everything went into hyperdrive. She's getting offers from everywhere. She's getting movie deals, music deals, fashion. Today, she cut a deal for a comic book based on her crime-fighting adventures for sale in China. A billion four people they got over there. Did you know that? A billion four!"

Ginny cut him off. "And, she sold the movie rights! I want her to play herself, but they're talking about an established star for the lead and my baby in a smaller role like that dancer girl." She leaned in and whispered, "They're talking to J-Law."

"And the Harry Potter chick," said Richie. Momo smiled at me, seemingly crediting me for some of the good fortune befalling his clan.

Richie said, "Guess who's playing me?"

"I don't know, Redford?" I said.

"Man, are you old," he said. "I don't actually know, but I want Harry Styles to play me. Can you imagine that? They're telling me maybe Nick Jonas, though. I guess that'd be okay."

I said, "Who's playing me? They talking to Pitt, DiCaprio, Craig?"

"Ah, sorry, Town. They're going younger with that part."

"Okay, so Pattinson, Pine, Hemsworth?"

"Not exactly." He looked at his shoes.

I looked at Ginny, and she broke the news. "They think the story will sell better if the protagonist is another young Boom act."

I said, "Oh no, please don't tell me they're replacing me with Trey Savage."

She clammed up and averted my eyes, as Momo broke into a fit of laughter, and slapped me on the back. He said, "Hollywood is a tough town, Town. You'll get over it. Tell him what I told you, Richie."

Richie smiled at me. "Mona Lisa is going to get you hired onto the film as a special consultant. Ten thousand, minimum, maybe more."

I thought about breaking the mood by turning it down and getting out of there, but then I asked what Trey was gonna get for the right to base a character on him. After all, apparently, it was he and Mona Lisa who'd solved the case. When Richie told me the figure, I told him I wanted twenty thousand or no deal. He looked at Momo, who said, "I think they'll be amenable. By the way, I'm an investor."

"No kidding," I said. "So, here we are at your first opening night on the stage, and you're already getting into the movie business. You don't waste time, Mr. Ragazzi."

"I've no time to waste, detective."

I thought about sharing a few case notes with him and soliciting his professional opinion on Mikey's position that he had nothing to do with Kenzie Knight, but he wasn't there to talk about that. It was his big night. So, I told him to break a leg and asked Richie if I could speak with him in private. We moved into the corridor.

"I'm glad this worked out for you, kid. Are we good, or am I gonna have to watch my back as you look to settle scores?"

He looked me in the eye and seemed to age about a decade. "When you were pressing the barrel of your gun into my back and counting down, you said you had nothing to live for."

"That's not exactly what I said."

"Shush." He held up his finger, and the hairs on the back of my neck stood at attention. "The thing is you were right about everything. You uncovered a traitor in the organization. So, no, I'm not gonna kill you, Town. I may need you someday. You are an asset."

"Aw, geez, Richie, do me a favor and lose my number, okay?"

"Nope. Stay safe, Town. Don't do anything I wouldn't do."

"That doesn't exclude much, Richie, but okay."

We shook hands, and I had turned to go when he grabbed my arm, moved in close, and whispered, "It's sad what happened to Rajeev. Cut down in his prime."

I started to ask what exactly had happened, realized my error, and said, "Aw, yeah, it's too bad," as we shared a smile.

Ed was nowhere in sight when I got to our seats shortly before the curtain went up. He didn't show until the second act, and I'm pretty sure he had lipstick on his collar. Anyway, I leaned back and settled in for the show, which was wildly entertaining in a let's-see-what'll-happen-next fashion. It was well-produced by Ms. Munson and the kids, who really made chicken soup of you-know-what. It was also eye-opening. I nearly fell out of my seat in *Brawn*—the second act about the ways in which Momo went from being just another hood to Boss. If I had to sum it up in a few words, I might call it *The Night of Decapitations*. The soliloquy on the finer points of extracting information from unwilling informants, via a metaphor on the way a bee extracts nectar from a flower, was simply breathtaking.

And, I almost forgot, for the opening number, they kept *hunt* and went with *muffs*.

In the hours after the show, I kept thinking about a scene in Act One: *Brains*. Something about young Momo taking care of his dying mother stuck with me. It took me a couple of days, and Ed's help to work out why.

# 31

I rapped a couple knuckles on the door of 83 Belmont Lane, a red clapboard Colonial with a history. True to its brag about being built all the way back in 1749 (the numbers were displayed nearby), the door had black strap hinges that stretched three-quarters of the way across. It was a nice touch. So was the step down into the first floor. I had a vision of a Redcoat visiting the very doorstep to harass an early widow of the American Revolution and shuddered at the thought.

I was in my usual costume. Smug superiority and a finely crafted secondhand sport coat. Sharon Phillips wore a fuzzy pink sweater, tan slacks, and a look of confusion.

"Mr. Town. What brings you here?"

"Mrs. Phillips. I have some news on the Kenzie Knight case, and I thought I might share with you if you have a moment."

She shrugged and stepped aside, then pointed to a pair of wingback chairs sitting on either side of a huge, well-broken-in, open-hearth fireplace that anchored an exterior wall. She said, "I was just reading a good mystery and enjoying some sweets. Would you like a chocolate, Mr. Town?"

I rubbed my hands together, a nervous tell that I've tried and failed to stop numerous times over the years. I jammed my hands into my pockets. "No, thank you, Mrs. Phillips. I'm taking a break from that particular vice at the moment, as I'm juggling several others."

She looked me over and said, "Do not get drunk on wine, which leads to debauchery. Instead, be filled with the Spirit, Ephesians 5:18."

"That's a good one, Mrs. Phillips. The spirit is just what I need."

"We could all use a little more of that, Mr. Town." She sat down across from me. Her thin frame was overwhelmed by the wide leather wingback. The room was classic New England colonial—exposed beams, low ceiling height, wide plank floors, and eerily calm and quiet.

I looked about. "Kudos to you for really committing to the aesthetic."

She set the box of chocolate aside. "Don't dawdle at the pulpit, Mr. Town. What do you have to tell me?"

I smiled as I began, "Well, you've spoken with Detective Prentiss?"

"Yes."

"And she told you that she has compelling forensic evidence that a member of organized crime was responsible for the deaths of your ex-husband and daughter?"

"Yes. She told me, but it doesn't matter."

"May I ask why not?"

"I have been comforted in my time of mourning." She pointed to the ceiling and said, "He heals the brokenhearted and binds up their wounds, Mr. Town."

I checked my watch and strode over to the picture window that provided most of the light in that half of the house. "Your neighbor, across the street there, Ted. He's a real character."

She leaned forward and rested chin in hand. "You know Ted?"

"Know him? I wouldn't say we were friends. If he was my neighbor, I'd probably hurt him. No, we talked business one afternoon a while back, but nothing came of it. I noticed at the time that he is very protective of this neighborhood and you, Mrs. Phillips."

"You were talking business with Ted?"

"Yes, you wouldn't know to look at him, in his knee-high

socks and all, but he's pretty well-versed in the latest home-security technology, and that's of interest to a man in my business."

"What does this have to do with poor Kenzie Knight?"

I sat down in the wingback and crossed one leg over the other. I like to be comfortable when I drop the hammer. "Here's the thing, Mrs. Phillips. If someone were to commit a crime in front of your house, Ted can tell you who did it and when. And he can produce evidence that even the best lawyers probably can't beat in a court trial."

I gotta give it to her. She didn't blink, and I wondered if she was busy conjuring just the right bible verse to talk her way out of it. She said, "Why would Ted be able to tell me all of that?"

"Why, indeed? Mrs. Phillips. Before I tell you that. You gotta tell me something. Kenzie Knight didn't just tell you about Mona Lisa's terminated pregnancy, did she?"

Sharon's phony smile ran screaming from the room. It was replaced by a look of deep concern. "I think you should leave."

"Kenzie told you about her plan, didn't she?"

"You're not making sense. What plan?"

"Her plan to expose Josh Fagle for what he had done, not only to Mona Lisa but to Harlowe as well. Kenzie didn't like having a predator as a boss. I'll bet he came onto her too. Did she tell you that, Mrs. Phillips?"

"This has nothing to do with anything, detective. Let me say it again, I think you should go, now." I didn't budge. "You're harassing a widow and the mother of a murdered child, Mr. Town."

"Let me refresh your memory, Mrs. Phillips. When you called me that day. Remember when Ginny Angeloni threatened your trash pick-up? Yeah, that day, you said Harlowe's pregnancy had come on the heels of the death of her grandmother. I did some investigating, Mrs. Phillips. Your mother, God rest her soul, was a very ill woman, and in a lot of pain. So much pain that when you took it upon yourself to provide for her in her last weeks, you learned to medicate her intravenously with oxycodone and when that wasn't available, fentanyl. Your daughter Harlowe shared this with her fans on a Facebook Live stream, just eight weeks ago. She said the opioids were the only thing that freed your mother from spending her final days in agony. Would you like to see a recording of this?" I held up my phone. Sharon glared at me but said nothing.

I played with the screen and said, "Here are some photos I'd like you to look at, and which I sent to Officer Lyle Hand, the lead investigator on the Kenzie Knight case, before I exited my vehicle in front of your house not fifteen minutes ago." I held the phone in front of her and flipped through several shots. She didn't look away.

"These were taken from video recorded by your neighbor Ted's security cameras on the afternoon of the mercy meal following Harlowe's funeral. They show someone who looks exactly like you, in the same clothes you wore that day, which, by the way, was also documented on social media. This individual is taking something from Kenzie Knight's car, which was parked in front of your house, and then returning to the car eleven minutes and thirty-four seconds later."

Sharon stared, resigned, and mum.

"You spiked her vaporizer because you didn't want Harlowe's secret exposed."

She didn't say anything for a while, then she uncorked this pile: "The heart of man plans his way, but the *Lord* establishes his steps."

I leaped to my feet. "Oh no, you don't, Mrs. Phillips. You do not get to excuse this as the work of a higher being. You must be suffering. Why in hell did you inflict the same pain on the Knights?"

There was a knock at the door. I said, "I'm sorry, Mrs. Phillips, but you need to get that. It's your ride to jail."

*　*　*

A scorching early summer evening, a couple of weeks after

Sharon Phillips was hauled out of her house in hysterics, I was on the phone with my cop friend Ron Hines while watching the sun set between the buildings across the street. "Vicky says Pam isn't angry anymore. She was livid at first, but she calmed down when you got her some credit for the Knight case. That was shrewd."

"That's why they call me Shrewd Earl."

"Uh, huh. Well, Vicky says she's apathetic now. I think you're rid of her for good, Chief."

"That's great."

"Really? Cause you sound unhappy."

"Nope, I'm happy as a clam in nice buttery broth, my friend." The bell rang, and I made my way downstairs, thinking, perhaps hoping, I'd find the vulgar pipsqueak in a pantsuit had finally shown up to set things right. I'd been thinking about that kiss, and her moan, too much since Irv had convinced her and the DA that it was in everyone's best interest, especially hers, that no charges be filed against me.

Instead, I found a certain Boom executive who had dropped by to discuss my role as a script consultant on the big Mona Lisa and Trey adventure/murder mystery, and if that went well, set consultant too. I threw open the door and mimed "come in" via an exaggerated wave of my free hand.

As she approached, the young go-getter held up a bottle.

I muffled the phone with my palm, "Is that Bollinger?"

My guest nodded and threw me one of the most spellbinding smiles ever directed my way.

"Who's that?" asked Hiney.

"Sorry, Ron, I gotta go," I said as I disconnected and said a proper hello to my guest. Then I savored the spectacle as Divya Singh led the way up to my apartment, my eyes trained on the tiger standing guard on her lean brown calf. I was beginning to see the good in social media after all.

## A NOTE ABOUT THE AUTHOR

The son of a policeman, who has spent a quarter-century working with the world's largest asset managers, C. James Brown has lived a fish out of water story. His goal is to make writing fiction his final career and for Earl Town to become a regular part of the reader's life. Killing Influence is his second novel.

Please visit him at **www.cjamesbrown.com**, on Twitter @C_James_Brown, and Facebook @CJamesBrownAuthor

If you enjoyed the story, please rate Killing Influence, and perhaps even leave a review, on Amazon, Goodreads, etc. Thank you!

Made in the USA
Las Vegas, NV
28 July 2021